Modern Crimes

A WPC LOTTIE ARMSTRONG MYSTERY

CHRIS NICKSON

MODERN CRIMES

For Mrs Florence E. Parrish, Miss Anne Carnegie Brown, and Mrs Florence G. Strickland, who paved the way as the first women police constables in Leeds.
And for all the people who had to live in the shadows until we saw the light.

First published 2016

The Mystery Press is an imprint of The History Press
The Mill, Brimscombe Port
Stroud, Gloucestershire, GL5 2QG
www.thehistorypress.co.uk

British Library Cataloguing in Publication Data.
A catalogue record for this book is available from the British Library.

ISBN 978 0 7509 6983 3

Typesetting and origination by The History Press
Printed and bound by CPI Group (UK) Ltd

CHAPTER ONE

Leeds, 1924

As she walked into Millgarth Police Station, Charlotte Armstrong nodded to the desk sergeant then strode back along the corridor to the matron's office. The day shift of bobbies had already gone on patrol and the building was quiet. She rested her hand on the doorknob, took a deep breath and straightened her back.

'Good morning, ma'am. WPC Armstrong reporting.'

Mrs Maitland looked up, giving her a quick inspection. She was a pinch-faced woman in her late forties, dark hair going grey and pulled back into a tight bun. She'd never mentioned Mr Maitland, but in two years the woman had never revealed anything personal; the job seemed to be her life. She was here first thing in the morning and long into the evening, as if she had no better place to be.

'There's a hair on your jacket, Armstrong.'

Lottie looked down. One hair, dark blonde, hers. She plucked it away, annoyed at herself and at the matron.

'Sorry, ma'am.' She stayed at attention.

Maitland returned to the letters on her desk. This was her way. Keeping someone waiting was how she enforced discipline.

The door opened and Cathy Taylor marched in. She was late and she knew it. Lottie could see it in her eyes. But she just winked, stood to attention and said, 'WPC Taylor reporting, ma'am.'

'You were supposed to be here at eight, Taylor,' Mrs Maitland said.

'Sorry, ma'am, my watch must be running slow.'

The matron sniffed. There were only two women constables in Leeds and she had to keep them in order.

'Well, since you're finally here, I have a job for the pair of you.' She scribbled an address on a piece of paper. 'Go and see her. She runs a home for unmarried mothers. One of her girls has been acting strangely and causing a fuss.' She stared at the pair of them. 'What are you waiting for? Off you go.'

'It's in Woodhouse, we might as well walk,' Cathy said as they set out up the Headrow. She folded the note and put it in her uniform pocket. Early September but it was already feeling like autumn, enough of a nip in the morning air for their breath to steam. 'Bet you the girl's just gone off to find some fun. It's always old cows who run those places.'

'At least it makes a change from talking to prozzies or chasing lads playing truant.' Lottie sighed. She loved the job, but she wished the force would let them do more, rather than treat them like delicate flowers with tender sensibilities.

Still, it was better than labouring in a mill or being a housewife. Like so many others, she'd developed a taste for freedom when she worked. Earning her own money, that was important. Stuff the vote. The government had only given it to women over thirty; she still had five years to go.

Lottie had been a clerk at the Barnbow munitions factory in Cross Gates during the war. 1916, she was just seventeen, fresh in the job with everything to learn, newly promoted from the factory. But she'd managed, even finding time to flirt with the procurement officers who came to check things.

Geoff had been one of them. Shy, diffident, still limping badly from a wound he'd suffered the year before at Gallipoli. He had a modest charm about him, like he had nothing to prove. In his uniform he looked quite dashing.

Lottie was the one who made the running. Someone had to and he wasn't the type to put himself forward. On his third visit to the factory she'd suggested an outing to the pictures, watching him blush as she spoke. From there it had taken two years until they reached the altar. By then the fighting was over and he'd returned to his job in the Dunlop area office.

She tried to become a housewife, but life chafed around her. Other women were having babies but Geoff's injuries meant she never would. Lottie needed something, but there was nothing that appealed, until the Leeds Police advertised for policewomen. They particularly wanted married women. And suddenly life excited her again.

'You'll be getting yourself shot if you keep coming in late,' Lottie warned.

Cathy pouted. 'It was only a couple of minutes. Anyway, Mrs Prissy wouldn't know what to do if she didn't have something to complain about.' She stifled a yawn with the back of her hand.

'Late night?'

'I went to the pictures with my friends, then they wanted to go on dancing so I couldn't say no.'

Cathy was twenty-four, a year younger than Lottie, with a husband who was gone most of the time in the merchant marine. No children. Hardly a wonder she liked to be out a few nights a week, dancing and flirting and enjoying herself. Married but single, she called it with a small laugh.

Lottie had gone with her a couple of times after work, changing into civvies at the station then on to a see a film at the Majestic. It had been fun, but not something she'd want to do often. Cathy had wanted to carry on, to have a cocktail. God only knew where she found the energy. By the end of a shift all Lottie wanted was to be at home and off her feet. When the working week was over, she was exhausted. She was lucky to stay up until ten, never mind the wee hours.

But Cathy wanted to embrace life. She was pretty enough for a portrait, always getting looks from men. She wore her hair in a modern bob, and had a pair of shapely legs and that bony, modern figure that always made Lottie feel huge in comparison.

'What are you going to do when your Jimmy comes home?' Lottie had asked her. 'You can't go gadding about then.'

'We'll enjoy our time together. After a month he'll ship out again. Don't get me wrong: I love him and I'd never, you know… but I can't sit at home every evening, can I? He wouldn't want me to, anyway.'

They matched each other step for step along Woodhouse Lane and out past the university, going towards the Moor, with its library and police sub-station on the corner.

'Down here,' Cathy said, turning briskly along Raglan Road, followed by the first right and second left. She scratched at her calf through the skirt. 'God, I wish they'd do something about this uniform. It's not bad enough that it itches, it's so heavy, too. Like wearing a battleship. This is it. Thirty-six.'

On a street of imposing terraced houses, this one loomed on the corner, detached, standing apart at the back of a long, neat garden and looking out over the Meanwood valley, with all the factories and chimneys spewing smoke into the air. Hardly an inspiring view, Lottie thought.

She knocked and waited. Some lovely stained glass in the window; she wouldn't mind that at home. She was miles away when the knob turned and a small woman in an apron stared up at her.

'I was wondering how long it would take the police to get here.' There was no welcome in the voice. The woman raised an eyebrow and stood aside. 'Well, are you coming in or do we do it all on the street?'

Lottie led the way, following an open door into a neat parlour. A Sunday room, still smelling of wax, the wood on the furniture gleaming.

'Go on, sit yourselves down.' The woman bustled around, flicking off some non-existent dust.

'You run a home for unwed mothers here, Mrs…' Lottie said.

'Allen,' she answered briskly. 'Yes, I do. It's a Christian thing, and I try to put them on the right path.' She sat very primly, back straight, her stare direct.

'One of your girls has been causing problems, is that right?' She took her notebook and pencil from her pocket.

'She has. She went out and didn't come back last night. No word this morning, either.'

That was bad; a missing girl. Lottie's eyes flickered towards Cathy, and she felt a prickle of fear.

'Could you tell us a little bit about her, Mrs Allen? Her name, what she looks like, where she's from.' Lottie smiled. She kept her voice calm and even. There was usually a simple explanation.

'She's called Jocelyn Hill. Seventeen, but she could easily pass for younger. You know the type, looks like butter wouldn't melt, but she's a sly little thing. Always out for a chance. A bit of extra food, this and that.' She shook her head in disgust. 'Half of me wishes I'd never taken her in.'

'What does she look like?' Cathy asked. She liked facts, something solid.

'Only about five feet tall, I suppose. Dark hair in one of those bobs they all seem to wear. Like yours,' she added. 'Thin as you like, no figure on her at all. Apart from the baby, of course.'

'How far along is she?' Lottie wondered.

'Eight months,' Mrs Allen replied, 'so it's not like she can hide it.'

'Has she gone missing before?'

'Of course not.' She snorted. 'They all know the rules when they arrive. No going out, only family to visit, in bed by ten. Break a rule once and they're gone. I won't stand for it otherwise. I give them a warm, clean place to have their children and I help find good homes for the little ones. I'm not about to let them take advantage of me.'

'Have you had others disappear, Mrs Allen?' Cathy asked quietly.

'Only the one,' the woman said after a while. 'Three years ago. But she was wild, wouldn't ever settle down here. Jocelyn liked to push things, but she was nothing like that.'

'Where did Jocelyn come from?' Lottie had her pencil poised, ready to take down the address. Mrs Allen took a ledger from one of the empty bookshelves, found a pair of glasses in her pocket and began to search.

'Here we are.' She read out an address in Cross Green. Lottie glanced towards Cathy and saw a tiny shake of the head.

'Thank you,' she said, standing. 'Is it possible to take a look in her room? Perhaps we could talk to some of the other girls who knew her?'

'Nothing to see in the room,' the woman told them. 'I've already packed her case. If she shows up at the door she's out on her ear. And she never really got along with the others. Kept herself to herself.'

'Maybe a look in her case, then…' Lottie suggested.

'Two dresses and some underwear that's as flimsy as nothing. Not hard to see how she ended up this way, is it?'

The door closed quickly behind them. As they walked back along the street Cathy looked over her shoulder.

'She's watching us from the front window.' She shivered a little. 'Blimey, I think I'd run off from that place, too. She's…'

'Strange?' Lottie suggested.

'Worse than that. Did you smell it in the hall?'

'You mean the mothballs?' She crinkled her nose. 'She must have them everywhere.'

'I could feel the joy being sucked out of me as soon as I walked through the door.'

They didn't even need to talk about where they were going next. Over to Cross Green to see if Jocelyn Hill had gone home. A tram back into the city centre, then a walk through the market and up the hill towards St Hilda's and Cross Green.

Wherever they went, people stopped to look at them. Policewomen were still a novelty in Leeds. By now Lottie was used to it. If she had sixpence for every time someone had asked if she was a real rozzer, she'd be a rich woman. She was every bit as real as the beat bobbies out there. Probably better at her job than half of them, too.

Even Lottie's mother had been doubtful about her taking the job. It wasn't *becoming*, she said. Not like marrying a grocer three months after being widowed and upping sticks to Northallerton. *That* was perfectly acceptable.

There was nothing inspiring about Cross Green. Not even much that was green. Street after street of tired-looking people and back-to-back houses. Small groups of men hung around on the street corners and outside the pubs. Far more than there should have been, Lottie thought. But what were they supposed to do when there weren't any jobs?

The men who fought had been promised a home fit for heroes. Fine words, but if they'd built any homes it hadn't been in Leeds. There had been jobs when the women were sacked, but not much of that work had lasted. According to the newspapers it was the same all over the country.

There was nothing she could do about that. Lottie was just glad Geoff's position was secure. And that she had work of her own.

'You're miles away,' Cathy said.

'Sorry.'

They passed another group of men and she was aware of them watching her backside as she walked. Someone said something in a low voice and there was a flurry of laughter.

'Ten to one that was a mucky remark.'

'More like two to one.' Cathy smiled. 'Look on the bright side. At least they noticed.'

Lottie wasn't too certain. Just because that was part of life didn't mean she had to like it.

'Charlton Street,' she said. 'Down here.'

It was close to the railway embankment. Number nine stood towards the far end, exactly like its neighbours on either side. She assessed it quickly: dirty windows, mud on the doorstep. No pride in the place.

'Ready?' she asked.

'As I'll ever be,' Cathy said.

The woman who opened the door stared at them with folded arms and a glare on her face.

'He can't have done too much wrong if they're sending the lasses out,' she said. 'What is it this time?'

'Jocelyn,' Lottie said. 'Is she here?'

'Here?' The woman's expression moved from surprise to panic. 'Why would she be here? Oh God, something's happened, hasn't it?'

'Why don't we talk inside?' It was a gentle question, and Mrs Hill gave a short nod, leading them back to the scullery. A scarred wooden table, battered chairs. Stone sink and a blackleaded range. How many of these had she seen in the job?

'Right.' The woman had gathered herself. 'You'd better tell me what's going on. What's happened to our Jocelyn?'

'She left the home last night and hasn't come back.'

'Stupid little bitch.' She spat out the words like venom. 'I told her it were for her own good.'

'Why don't you tell me about it?' Lottie suggested. 'Then we can find her.' She gave Cathy a look: make some tea. As she started to bustle around, Mrs Hill was looking down and biting her lip.

'Why did you send Jocelyn over there?' Lottie asked softly but the answer was obvious. Woodhouse was far enough away that no one would recognise her.

'She got herself in the family way. Why the bloody hell do you think?' The woman sneered. 'It weren't for the fun of it. Didn't want everyone round here talking about us like that.'

'Have you spoken to her since she went there?' It had been a while; there must have been some contact.

'Oh aye, I pick up the telephone every day and we have a natter.' She snorted. 'Course I haven't. Don't have time to write letters. She wouldn't answer if I did, anyway.'

Lottie tightened her lips. 'Mrs Hill, do you have any idea why she might have run off, or where she might have gone?'

'Not really. But once our Jos gets an idea in her head there's no shifting it.' She shrugged. 'Been that way since she was little.'

'Do you have any idea at all where she might have gone?'

'Not really.' She reached into the pocket of her apron, took out a packet of cigarettes and lit one, just as Cathy put three mugs of tea on the table. The woman heaped in two spoonfuls of sugar and took a long drink. 'I'll tell you what, I'll swing for her if she's done owt daft.'

'What about the baby's father? Could she have gone to him?'

'Possibly,' Mrs Hill admitted. 'She'd never say who it were, though, not even when her dad took a belt to her.'

'No idea who it could be?'

'One or two.'

And they could easily deny it, Lottie thought. Not much help at all.

'What about her friends? Who are they?'

'You'd do best talking to Elizabeth Townend and Eileen Donnelly, then. Thick as thieves, the three of them.' She gave a dark glance. 'I'll warn you, though, they wouldn't tell me owt.'

'Where do I find them, Mrs Hill?'

The sun had a little warmth behind it as they walked over to the Burton's factory in Burmantofts. Street after street of houses and factories, the smell of soot in the air

'What did you think?' Lottie asked.

'That kitchen was covered in grease,' Cathy complained. 'I can still feel it all over my hands.'

'About Mrs Hill, I meant.'

'I think she's more scared than anything else. Packing the girl off to the home like that seems a bit of a surprise. I hadn't expected her to care so much about reputation.'

But everyone cared in their own way, Lottie thought. And some of those ways were unexpected.

The building was huge, and still growing, judging by the labourers they saw laying bricks and mixing cement. Inside, the sound of the machines filled the air like a swarm of flies; there were hundreds of women with their heads down, sewing the suits to go on sale in shops the firm had all over the country. Business was good. The noise only quietened as they were shown into a hushed waiting room.

'Not bad, this place, is it?' Cathy said, inspecting the posters on the walls. 'Look, they've even got a social club. Nights out, day trips. Canteen. Why can't we have things like that?'

'Maybe you should apply on the way out. At least you wouldn't have to wear a scratchy skirt.' It came out harsher than she'd intended and she tempered it with a wink.

'Maybe I will. At least I wouldn't have to put up with Moaning Minnie on morning parade. She gets on my wick.'

Time passed, the clock on the wall ticking away the minutes until the door opened and a young woman showed them to a room down the corridor. It was sparsely furnished with a table and some old chairs, and metal filing cabinets lining the walls. A storage room for old paperwork, Lottie guessed.

Two girls sat waiting nervously, glancing around as the door opened. Lottie smiled, trying to ease their fears. But their eyes were on Cathy. She wasn't surprised or envious; it was usually the way. Cathy had a look that attracted gazes, that small twinkle that made her seem as if she knew secrets.

'Who's Elizabeth and who's Eileen?' Lottie asked. She knew her voice sounded too jolly; couldn't be helped.

'I'm Eileen,' one of the girls replied in a small voice.

She should have guessed. Red hair gathered in a scarf, freckles on her nose. She looked so young. They both did.

'I'm Constable Armstrong. Don't worry, you haven't done anything wrong.' She could see the relief. 'But you both know Jocelyn Hill.'

'Jos?' Elizabeth Townend asked in surprise. She was short, with dark brown hair carefully covered, eyes wide, a broad face and heavy lips. 'What about her?' The girl had a wary, suspicious voice.

'Do you know where she'd gone?'

'Course,' Elizabeth snorted. 'Got herself up the spout and her mam and dad sent her off to have it.' She rolled her eyes. 'Everybody knows.'

Lottie looked at Eileen. She was staring at the floor, picking at a piece of skin by her fingernail. 'Jocelyn disappeared last night.'

She saw the brief look they exchanged. Shock, she decided; they didn't know anything.

'Why?' Eileen asked.

'We don't know,' Lottie replied gently. 'Have either of you talked to her since she went into the home? Any letters or anything?'

They both shook their heads. It was as if Jocelyn had left the world when she entered the house. Like vanishing into a convent.

'Do you know who the father of her child is?'

The question brought an embarrassed silence.

'Do you?' Lottie asked again quietly.

'She wouldn't never say,' Eileen answered, blushing as she spoke.

'We asked,' Elizabeth interrupted, 'but she just laughed and said she couldn't tell us.'

'No guesses?' Cathy asked with a grin. 'Come on, you must have done that.'

'We thought it might be my brother.' Elizabeth coughed. 'But she said it weren't. Not even warm.' She shrugged. 'So we really don't know. Honest.'

It was frustrating but it felt like the truth. A dead end. Lottie hated to go back to the station with nothing; it made her feel as if she'd failed. Mrs Maitland would look at her with disappointment, although the woman wouldn't say a word.

'Is there anyone who might be able to help?' Cathy said it before she could.

'Maybe Mrs Brown,' Eileen suggested after a few seconds.

'Who's she?'

'The midwife,' Elizabeth said. 'Over on Lavender Walk. I know Jos went to see her, back when she found out she were up the duff. We went with her and waited on the corner. She were in a right strop when she came out, wouldn't say why.'

But Lottie could guess. Midwives delivered babies. They also stopped women coming anywhere near term, doling out the herbs and potions that caused abortions if the gin baths and other remedies didn't work. She must have refused to help Jocelyn. That was a start.

'Right,' she said as she rose. 'Thank you. And look after yourselves.'

'Do you think you'll find Jos?' Eileen asked. There was a tremor in her voice.

'I'm sure we will,' Lottie assured her. 'You just leave it to us.' She paused for a fraction of a second. 'Is there anything else you can think of?' One after the other the girls shook their heads. 'All right. If you think of anything just send us a message at Millgarth. We'll come and listen to you, I promise.'

The corridor stank of boiled cabbage and custard, drifting up from the canteen below. Lottie wrinkled her nose and held her breath until they were outside. It took her back to Barnbow, all the smells of cooking as they came out of the sheds, sour enough to put her off her dinner half the time.

'I don't know how you do it.' Cathy interrupted the memories.

'What do you mean?'

'You're so good at getting them to talk.'

'Not really. I just ask questions.' She shrugged. It was nothing special. It wasn't even as if she was especially nosy normally; she didn't know all the doings in her own street and didn't care. But when it came to work, she was curious. She enjoyed it. It was like working through a maze or a puzzle and she'd always enjoyed that.

'You have the feel for it.'

'Right now I'm just worried about Jocelyn Hill.'

If the girl hadn't shown her face somewhere by evening all the beat bobbies would be asking and looking. A missing pregnant girl was cause for alarm.

It wasn't difficult to find the midwife. Everyone for streets around knew her. She'd probably delivered most of the children in the neighbourhood. There was no lavender on Lavender Walk. Not much of anything except grimy brick and cobbles.

They'd barely turned into the street when a door opened thirty yards along and a girl came out, dressed in a short skirt that came just below her knees and a cloche hat jammed over short hair. She turned the key in the lock behind her then glanced around, eyes widening to see the two policewomen.

Lottie recognised her immediately.

'Margaret Simmons.' It came as a shout. Before the words were out the girl was running, heels clattering on the pavement as she dashed away. Lottie began to follow but she already knew she didn't have a chance. She'd never been fast.

But Cathy was quick. As soon as the girl began to move she was already running. Within ten yards she was gaining ground, feet pounding, legs and arms pumping.

Lottie smiled and stood, watching. Cathy had told her once she'd been a champion sprinter at school, as fast as any of the boys. Now she could believe it. Even before they reached the postbox at the end of the block, Cathy had hold of the girl and was taking out her handcuffs. She didn't even look winded.

'Maggie.' Lottie shook her head as she approached. 'You should have known we'd catch up with you.' Never mind that it was just a pair of gloves from Schofield's, or that they'd been looking for someone else on the street. Make her think she'd been nicked.

Cathy beamed proudly. 'What should we do with her?'

'Do you want to take her down to Millgarth?' Lottie asked. 'I'll take care of the other thing.'

Maggie glared. 'I thought you came for me.'

'You're not important enough,' Lottie told her. 'You just showed your face at the wrong time.'

'Come on.' Cathy had a grip on Simmons's arm. 'You'll like being back in jail. You can see some of your old friends.'

The outside of number twenty-one was spick and span, windows gleaming, paintwork washed. The front door gleamed. Mrs Brown was houseproud.

Lottie didn't expect to learn much. Abortion was against the law. Admitting anything to do with it was a ticket to jail. No one was that stupid. But she had to try.

Mrs Brown was dumpy, sleeves rolled back to show heavy forearms. A fleshy, jowly face, with eyes that seemed to have seen everything, and wavy hair the colour of old iron. She glanced at the uniform.

'You'd better come in,' she said.

Back into the kitchen, the centre of the house, probably the only room always in use. A kettle was steaming on the hob, apple peelings on newspaper in the middle of a battered deal table. By the back door, a large old leather bag. The tools of the trade, Lottie thought.

The woman sat down with a deep sigh. 'Right,' she said, 'what do you want?'

What was the best way to do this? By the book wasn't going to work. Woman to woman? All she could do was play it by ear.

'You probably haven't heard yet,' Lottie began, 'but a girl's gone missing.'

Mrs Brown cocked her head. 'Oh aye? What's that got to do with me?'

'She came to see you a while ago. I wondered if she might have been back, or if you know where she's gone.'

'What's her name, then?' She pulled out a packet of Black Cats, lit one and blew smoke at the ceiling.

'Jocelyn Hill.'

The laugh sounded like a cackle, mouth open wide to show half the teeth missing.

'She's run off from that home, has she? I thought she might, she never wanted to go in the first place.'

'It was her mother's idea, wasn't it?'

Mrs Brown nodded. 'Out of sight, out of mind, and no little 'un to embarrass everyone. But she's not been back here, luv. All I could do for her is deliver the poor little thing, and that won't be for a few weeks yet.'

'Could she have gone to see the father?'

The woman shrugged. 'Who knows? She never told me who he were. Didn't ask, not my business. That it?'

'Yes.' Another dead end. 'You didn't hear any rumours or gossip about the dad, did you?'

Mrs Brown pursed her lips. 'There's always gossip when a girl ends up with a bun in the oven. Maybe there was something about Ray Coleman. Maybe it was someone else. I don't really remember.'

'Thank you.'

A name. A thread, if nothing more. But she couldn't do anything about it. If a man was involved, one of the male constables had to take over. Those were the rules. She hated them; she was capable and wanted to be able to follow the investigation. She was a copper; she wasn't about to faint with an attack of the vapours. But there was no choice but to obey if she wanted to keep her job. At least she'd have something to report.

Still, she thought as she strolled back to Millgarth, it hadn't been a bad day for the policewomen. They were on the trail of the missing girl and they'd put a shoplifter in the cells. That should make Mrs Maitland very happy.

CHAPTER TWO

LOTTIE gathered the plates off the table, took them into the kitchen and returned with the teapot.

'You won't believe what Mrs Maitland said this afternoon,' she said to Geoff.

'What?' She saw the interest in his eyes, the pleasure he took in her, and remembered again why she'd fallen in love with him. He might have his failings, but he truly cared about her.

'She wants me to go with one of the male constables tomorrow.'

'That's good, isn't it?'

He didn't understand her job. Geoff had encouraged her to apply, pushed her when she'd had her doubts, even trained her in unarmed combat so she could defend herself, but he'd never seen quite why she wanted to become a policewoman. His world at Dunlop was very ordered, controlling an office of clerks and typists, making sure the world of tyres ran smoothly.

'Good?' She grinned with satisfaction. 'It's never happened before.'

She'd scarcely been able to believe her ears when the matron told her. It felt like the biggest thing that had happened since she'd been sworn in. The anticipation rippled through her.

On the tram home she'd already looked forward to the next morning, scarcely noticing her stop or the walk up from Chapeltown Road to their house on Oak Road. She knew she'd only be working with Constable Tennison for a few minutes, listening while he questioned Ray Coleman about Jocelyn Hill, but even so, it was a huge step forward. For women on the force, but even more for *her.*

'You're sensible enough, Armstrong,' the matron had said. 'I think you can be trusted.'

'Yes, ma'am. Thank you.'

Lottie hung up her uniform, slipped on a comfortable dress and started to cook tea. But everything seemed to happen without thought; her mind was fixed on the next morning. Being a proper copper. Part of her hoped that they wouldn't find Jocelyn overnight. Terrible, and she knew it. Even so…

She finished the washing up and settled down with the new issue of *Good Housekeeping*. On the wireless the news from the BBC was just finishing. Geoff had built the set the year before, endless evenings in the kitchen with a set of plans and a soldering iron. It was cobbled together, far from perfect, but it worked. A bit like their marriage, she thought with a quiet smile.

'Do you fancy doing something tonight?' Geoff asked. 'The pictures?'

'Would you mind if we stayed at home?'

Normally she'd have jumped at the chance. *The Thief of Baghdad* had just opened at the Tower. But not tonight; her mind was too fixed on the morning. If they went to see a film she'd never be able to concentrate. It would just be a waste of money.

'Of course not.' He gave her a bright smile.

She was at the station long before Mrs Maitland. Lottie waited, cradling a mug of tea. She was aware of the blatant stares and the sly glances of the uniforms as they left after roll call. Never mind, she told herself. Only to be expected. They're men.

'You're miles away, luv.'

The voice was deep, seeming to rise from the ground, and wryly amused. She looked up quickly to see a broad man towering over her. He was in his fifties, hair cut brutally short. But his eyes were warm and he was grinning.

'You must be Armstrong,' he continued. 'I'm Constable Tennison. You might as well call me Henry, every other bugger does.'

She stood, taking the large hand he offered. 'Charlotte Armstrong,' she said. 'Lottie.'

'Soon as your guv'nor shows up and gives us the nod we'll go and talk to Coleman.' He grimaced. 'They haven't found that lass yet.'

'Do you know him?'

'All his life,' Tennison answered with a nod. 'And he knows me. I've clouted him round the ear a few times when he was a nipper, done him for truancy.' He shrugged. 'He's not a bad lad. Only twenty now, so he was a bit too young to fight. Lost two brothers in the war, spent the years running a bit wild. And you know what it's like these days. There's nothing in the way of jobs for the likes of him.'

'It's no better for the girls.'

'I know that, luv. I see it every day. I know Jocelyn and her friends too. Poor lass. I hope we find her sharpish. Maybe Ray can help.'

Mrs Maitland marched briskly round the corner, took out a key and unlocked her office. As she opened the door, she said, 'Enter.'

Tennison raised an eyebrow at Lottie and followed her into the room. They stood at attention while the matron removed her hat and took her seat behind the desk.

'You both know this is unprecedented,' she said seriously. 'The first time a male and female constable have worked together. The station inspector and I only sanctioned it because it's urgent that we find what's happened to Miss Hill. I don't need to remind you that she's been missing for a day and a half now, and no sign overnight. So I'm willing to pursue every avenue, however unorthodox.' She paused for a second. 'Still, no matter what, I expect the two of you to conduct yourselves properly. Armstrong, remember that Constable Tennison is in charge, and the honour of the women police constables rests on your shoulders. If he gives you an order, you will obey it. Understood?'

'Yes, ma'am.'

Mrs Maitland looked at them both, then nodded. 'Dismissed.'

Cathy was waiting outside, learning against the wall, ready to report for duty. She gave a broad wink, assessed Constable Tennison, and hissed, 'Tell me *all* about it later,' then slid through the open door.

'Blimey,' Tennison said once they were outside, 'that matron of yours is something, isn't she? What does she do, chew steel girders for breakfast?'

'You saw her on a good day,' Lottie told him. 'Wait until she wants to tear a strip off you.'

He grimaced, fitted his helmet on his head, rolled his shoulders back and said, 'Right. We'd better see a man about a girl.'

'Where does he live?'

'Unless he's moved in the last month, he's with his mam and dad on Everleigh Drive.' It was just a few minutes' walk from Jocelyn's house, tucked away off York Road, across from the baths. Tennison grinned at her. 'Think you can walk that far?'

'Cheeky devil. How do you want to handle Coleman?'

'Just a quiet word,' he answered thoughtfully. 'To start with, anyway. We don't even know he's the father of her baby.'

'He'll deny it. Men always do. When I was at Barnbow—'

'Oh, a Barnbow canary, were you?' He smirked.

'I was.' She bristled. 'And proud of it. Why?'

'Doesn't matter,' Tennison said. 'Go on.'

'As soon as a girl was up the spout we'd take bets on whether the lad would admit it was his. Almost every one of them tried to wriggle out of it for a while.'

He stayed silent. But there wasn't much he could say, Lottie thought; he was a man.

'Do you reckon you'll know if he's lying?' Tennison asked after a while.

'Maybe.' Would she, Lottie wondered? Would she be able to see the guilt on Ray Coleman's face? 'Is that why they want me there?'

'Like as not.' He glanced around. 'I don't see a sergeant and I'm going to trust you to say nothing.' He took out a cigarette and lit it, cupping it out of sight in his hand. 'Young Ray's going to be embarrassed with a woman there. Maybe it'll make him tell the truth. Seems to me it doesn't matter whether the bairn's his or not. She hasn't said, has she?'

'No, she won't tell anyone.'

'And what we need is to find her. We'll just hope that Ray can help us. If he feels some responsibility, so much the better. Maybe it'll make him shape up. I did when my first was born.'

'How many do you have?'

'Three. Two now.' She could hear the change in his tone and knew what was coming. 'Our Robert died on the Somme. Broke his mother's heart. Me, I'm glad the other two were girls. God only knows what might have happened otherwise.' Tennison gave a small cough. 'What about you?'

'We can't,' Lottie explained. 'My husband had an injury.' She shrugged. 'It doesn't matter.'

He didn't say anything, just offered a short nod. That was better than most; people generally stumbled over awkward apologies. To her it had become a fact of life. But Tennison was in his fifties, about the same age her father would be if he was still alive. He'd seen a thing or two.

'It's along here,' he told her after a couple of minutes. Tennison dropped his dog end and ground it out on the pavement, then adjusted his helmet. 'Ready?'

Someone must have seen them coming; Ray Coleman answered the front door himself. He looked younger than twenty, with fair hair, not even really shaving yet, just some light down on his upper lip. Skinny, a jumper over his shirt, a pair of trousers that had seen better days. No boots on his feet and socks that had been darned umpteen times.

'Constable,' he said in a nervous voice. He gulped, his Adam's apple jumping. 'Do you need something?'

'Just a chat,' Tennison said gently. 'We can do it here if you like, or maybe inside over a cup of tea.'

'Yes.' He moved aside, letting them through. No need to show them the way in a house like this. Ray's mother was in the kitchen, already putting a kettle on the hob. There were no modern conveniences here. The house had probably looked much the same thirty years before.

Mrs Coleman disappeared as the tea was mashing. Not a word had been said, they'd simply taken their places around the table. Ray lit a cigarette, his foot tapping quickly on the floor. Tennison sat back, hands over his ample belly. He leaned forward as the door closed.

'Little birds keep saying you know Jocelyn Hill.'

'That's right,' Coleman agreed. 'You know, say hello, walk to the shops, like that. Until she went away.'

'And you wouldn't know anything about her going away?' Tennison smiled.

'Me?' The boy looked cornered, a fox with the hounds approaching. 'No. Why would I?'

As lies went, it was pathetic. The blush was flooding up his face.

'Are you sure about that?' Lottie asked. She gave him time to answer, pouring the tea and pushing the cups across the table. 'There's nothing wrong with being friends, after all.'

'Yes, we're friends, I suppose.'

'Maybe a bit more, eh?' Tennison suggested with a wink. 'You know why she went away.'

'I know what everyone says.' Coleman's face was bright red.

'Perhaps you had something to do with it.'

The idea seemed to floor him. 'Give over, Jos wouldn't look twice at me. Not… you know. I wasn't her type.'

Lottie believed him. There was something in his voice, disappointment, a little pain. He carried a torch for her and she didn't even notice.

'What was her type?' she asked.

He didn't answer at first, spooning sugar into the cup and stirring it. Then, 'She liked them a bit older. With some money. But she kept that quiet. Her mam didn't know. No one round here did. She sneaked off in the evening.'

Tennison opened his mouth to speak. Lottie shook her head slightly at him.

'Did you ever follow her, Ray?' she continued.

He bit his lip and nodded. 'I just wanted to know where she was going. I…' He shrugged. He didn't possess the words. Or maybe he didn't want to admit them to himself.

'When was this?'

'The night before last. I saw her near her house.'

'Where did she go?' Without thinking she reached out and patted the back of his hand. It was pure instinct. His eyes widened in surprise.

'The Market Tavern.'

She knew it, a stone's throw from Millgarth station. The Madhouse, everyone called it, although she'd never heard why.

Tennison gave a quick cough. 'Did you see her come out again, Ray?' he asked.

'Can't have been more than ten minutes.' She could hear the frustration in his voice. 'She came out with a man and he helped her into a motor car. Then they drove away.'

How could a lad with no job hope to compete with someone who owned a car?

'Do you know what type of car it was?'

'A Standard Pall Mall,' he answered without hesitation.

In spite of everything, she had to smile to herself. Only a man would know something like that. Only a man would care. Still, they had a lead now. There weren't many vehicles on the roads; it should be easy to find the driver. But a few more questions might yield something better.

'Had you seen the driver before?'

'No. But…' he hesitated. 'He seemed like he had everything. Like he knew everything. And Jos, she just looked at him with these big eyes.'

'Thank you,' Lottie told him. 'You might be helping her. You heard she was missing?'

He nodded. 'Everybody knows. That was one reason I followed her. She was supposed to be at that place, not round here.' His voice trembled.

'Don't you worry, we'll find her,' she assured him. 'Maybe she'll realise things are better closer to home.'

'By God,' Tennison said in admiration as they walked back down the street. 'Where did you learn to do all that?'

'What?'

'Get them to talk. You should be a detective.'

She laughed. 'And pigs will fly. Come on, he wanted to tell us, you could see it in his face. He loves her, he wants to see her safe as much as anyone.'

'If you say so,' he said doubtfully. 'That touching his hand, what made you do it?'

'I don't know. It just seemed to be what he needed. Why? Was it bad?'

'It was ruddy marvellous.' He smiled at her and glanced at his wristwatch. 'What time are you due back on patrol?'

She looked at him. 'I don't know. As soon as we're done, I suppose. Why?'

'Oh, I just thought we could drop in to the Market Tavern before you went back, that's all.' He glanced at her from the corner of his eye, a sly grin on his lips.

'Go on, then,' she agreed quickly. 'As long as it stays quiet. Mrs Maitland will have me off the force if she finds out.'

'I won't say a word, cross my heart.' He winked. 'For a lass, you're all right, you know that?'

She nudged him in the ribs, hard enough for him to feel. 'And I've come across worse blokes than you.' Her eyes were laughing. 'So who's this rich man, do you think?'

'Haven't a clue, but someone's bound to know. You won't find many Standards in Leeds, they're not cheap. Whoever owns it has a bit of brass.'

She'd gone into pubs with Geoff, a few times with gaggles of girls from Barnbow when they enjoyed a night out. A cocktail bar with Cathy. But never anywhere like the Market Tavern. It was early enough in the day to stink of stale beer and old smoke, dust motes hanging in the air.

A few hardened drinkers slumped in the corners, shunning company; a man listlessly mopped the bar. The spittoons hadn't been emptied and the brass needed a healthy polish.

'Morning, Bill. Is Nancy about?' Tennison said, looking around the faces in the place.

'In the cellar, Henry. She'll be back in a minute.' He stared at Lottie, the look becoming a leer as he licked his lips. 'Who's the bird?'

'That'll be Woman Police Constable Armstrong to you.' There was an iron edge to his voice. 'Unless you fancy a belting into next week. Not from me, from her. And don't go thinking she wouldn't dare.'

Bill bowed his head and seemed to deflate into himself.

At Barnbow the men had flirted. Some of them had tried it on, hands free when they thought they could get away with it. But she'd been one girl among many, plenty of them prettier and more happy-go-lucky. Since she put on the uniform it had been worse, as if she was fair game. Plenty of comments, someone trying to grab her breasts on a crowded tram. Even one of the coppers at work had fancied his chances, thinking he could drag her into a cupboard. A sharp knee had ended that idea and kept him off work the next day. Since then they'd treated her warily around the station. Everyone knew what had happened; no one ever spoke about it.

Footsteps echoed on stone stairs. A door opened and a woman filled the opening. She was large, tall with wide shoulders. Big-boned in every way, around forty, but she carried it handsomely, wearing expensive, stylish clothes, make-up carefully applied to hide the wrinkles, her hair cut to suit her broad face.

'Well, well, well, look who's blown in.' She had a voice like a contented purr, low, pleasant, but with the edge of teasing. 'Where have you been keeping yourself, Henry?' Her eyes turned to Lottie. 'This must be one of them WPCs.' She nodded approval. 'The uniform suits you, dear. And Henry wouldn't be dragging you in here unless you could hold your own.'

'I've got a question for you,' Tennison said. The attention, and everything that lurked beneath it, didn't seem to bother him. 'About someone who drinks in here.'

Nancy took a Woodbine from a packet on the bar and lit it. 'Well,' she said finally. 'Spit it out. I don't have all day.'

'He drives a Standard,' Lottie said quickly. 'Probably in his twenties or so. Very likely thinks he's the bees' knees.'

The woman laughed. 'You're not backwards about coming forwards, are you? You're looking for Ronnie Walker. Comes in here a couple of times a week. Likes to think he's hard stuff because he's slumming it. What's he done?'

'Maybe nothing,' Tennison said. 'We need to talk to him and find out.'

'You need to take a look in Headingley. Somewhere round there.' She stared at Lottie. 'What's your name, luv?'

'WPC Armstrong.'

Nancy sighed. 'Your real name. Like he's Henry and I'm Nancy.'

'Lottie.'

The woman extended a large hand and Lottie shook it. 'You'll do. You need anything, come and ask for me.' She nodded at Tennison. 'You don't need to wait for him. And no one will hurt you in here. Not unless they want to answer to me.' She grinned, showing a set of discoloured teeth. 'And they don't, believe you me.'

'You went in the Market Tavern?' Cathy put her hands on her hips. 'Come on, tell me all about it. I keep hoping someone will take me in there.'

They were walking through County Arcade, all the old glamour looking a little faded and dreary, the black and white tiled floor sad and grubby.

'There's not much to tell,' Lottie told her. 'It's a dreary place. We weren't even inside for ten minutes.'

'What about the woman?' Cathy asked eagerly. 'I've heard about her.'

'Nancy? She's lovely. Big, but… it suits her.'

'Are they keeping you on the investigation? What did Mrs Maitland say?'

'The case has gone to the detectives.'

She didn't want to say more. After her hopes had been raised for a few hours, they'd been dashed again. Still, that was to be expected. Outside the matron's office Henry had given her a sympathetic look and a shrug before heading back to his beat. It was the way of the world.

Evening report was almost complete when Mrs Maitland looked at her. Her next words seemed to come out grudgingly.

'Inspector Carter wants you to report upstairs to CID before you leave.'

CHAPTER THREE

FOR a moment her stomach seemed to turn liquid. Why did CID want her? Had they heard she'd gone in the Market Tavern? No, she decided quickly; Maitland would have relished taking care of that herself.

'Go on. Don't just stand there with your mouth open.'

She gave Cathy a short, confused look, then left, heels clicking along the corridor then up the stairs. At the CID office she knocked on the door and entered.

One man was there, sitting behind a desk and smoking. Sergeant McMillan. She coughed and saw him cock his head towards her. He was a slim, handsome man in a well-tailored pinstripe suit, a thin, dark moustache on his upper lip.

Full of himself, she thought. That was what everyone said. Too cocky by half. But the rumour was he'd been a war hero, and he was supposed to be good at his job.

'You must be Armstrong.'

'Yes, Sarge.'

'Stand at ease.' He stubbed out his cigarette. 'You've been working on this Jocelyn Hill thing.'

'That's right, Sarge.'

'Tennison brought me up to speed.' His smile turned wolfish. 'He told me you met Nancy Smith. Says she took a shine to you.' His tone was gently mocking.

'She was pleasant enough, sir.'

'Nancy doesn't like too many. You've been favoured.'

'Yes, Sarge.' She really didn't know what to say. She had no clue what he wanted, no idea where this was going. It didn't feel as if he was going to reprimand her.

'Tennison says you're a natural with the questions.'

'Thank you, sir.' She felt herself reddening at the praise.

'How would you like to work with CID on this Hill case?'

'Sir?' For a moment she was certain she'd misheard. Work with CID?

'We're going to find her and we'll need a woman to sit down and talk to her, to find out what's happened. Maybe even to talk to people along the way.' He took out another cigarette and lit it. 'What do you say? If Henry's right, you're just who we need.'

'I...' She felt tongue-tied. It was impossible to believe. This was exactly what she'd hoped for when she joined the force. But she'd stopped believing it could ever happen. Lottie dug a fingernail into her palm, just to be certain she hadn't fallen asleep on the tram and started dreaming. She was still here, still facing Sergeant McMillan. And he was still smiling hopefully at her.

Lottie took a deep breath. 'Yes, Sarge,' she said. 'I'd love to.'

'Let's make a start, then.' He pulled an old mackintosh and a trilby off the rack and led the way out of the station's back door to the street. A small Peugeot coupé stood at the kerb.

'In you get,' McMillan told her with a grin. 'We're going to give your friend Ronnie Walker a surprise. See if Miss Hill's there.'

She could see Cathy pacing by the gate, waiting, a raincoat buttoned over her uniform.

'I just need to talk to my partner,' Lottie said. 'I'll only be a minute.'

She could sense his impatience as she walked away. But Cathy deserved to know.

'Well?' she asked. 'What did they want?'

Lottie let the words flow out, still scarcely believing them herself, and Cathy squealed loud enough to make people turn. She hugged Lottie tight.

'That's wonderful. But you'd better make sure you tell me everything.'

'I will.' The reality was starting to sink in. She began to grin and couldn't stop.

'If you're working for that Sergeant McMillan I might have to scratch your eyes out.'

Lottie glanced back at the man waiting in the Peugeot and bit her lip, eyes twinkling.

'You rotten cow!' Cathy was laughing with pleasure. 'Do you get to wear plain clothes, too?'

'Uniform. The sarge thought that might be a step too far.'

'Tell him he can dress me up any time he likes.'

Lottie couldn't remember the last time she'd been in a motor car. Carole's wedding, perhaps, when she'd been a bridesmaid. For a moment it felt like luxury, then she remembered the job.

'I want to put some pressure on Walker. We need to find Jocelyn. She's been gone far too long in her condition.'

At least they were worrying about her; that was something. The story would be in the papers soon, maybe even the late edition of the *Evening Post*.

'What do we know about him, Sarge?' she asked as he overtook a lorry.

'Not a lot,' McMillan admitted with a sigh. 'He's twenty-two, the family's well off. I stopped at the Market Tavern and had a word with Nancy. Seems he likes to go down there and slum it with the criminals a couple of times a week.'

'Did she say anything about Jocelyn?'

He shook his head. 'Not a word. But that place is busy at night. Half the crooks in Leeds spend their evenings there.'

'Really?' She'd heard it was rough but not that bad. 'Why don't you close it down?'

'Better to know where we'll find them than have them scattered all over the city.' He gave her that cocky grin again. 'Makes our job easier if we want to nick one of them.'

He kept driving, past North Lane and out along Otley Road, until they were leaving the houses behind and seeing fields.

'Close now,' McMillan told her. 'And don't worry, they're not out in the middle of nowhere.'

A turn on to Spen Road, then another sharp left and he pulled up.

'That's it.' He pointed at number four. It was a tall, detached house, three stout brick storeys, the front gate open, the drive empty. Neat bay windows downstairs, the inside hidden by net curtains. 'What do you think?'

'Looks like they have a pretty penny.'

'The father has some company in Hunslet and the mother's from a family that owns a bit of East Yorkshire.' He turned in his seat. 'I have a suggestion, Armstrong.'

'Yes, Sarge?' Tactics, she wondered? A way to approach Walker?

'When it's just you and me, why don't you call me John and I'll call you Lottie? It is Lottie, isn't it?'

'Yes, S... John.'

'Better.'

'I don't think we're going to get a chance to talk to Walker, though,' she pointed out. 'He's supposed to drive a Standard and there's nothing in the drive or on the street.'

'Observant,' he said approvingly. 'I like that. But there's going to be a maid or mother inside who can tell us where he's gone.

He won't have brought Jocelyn back to a place like this, you can stake your pay packet on that. If she's with him, he has a little love nest somewhere.'

'Oh.' He was right, of course. For a second she felt stupid. But this was McMillan's business and he was supposed to be good at it. It was her first time; she was bound to make mistakes.

As it was, all she had to do was stand there. The maid called the only family member who was at home, Walker's younger sister, Irene. She leaned on the door jamb, looking as if the whole world bored her even as she simpered at the sergeant. Her parents were away for a couple of days at York races.

The girl could have stepped out of a woman's magazine. The bob, the silk dress, the shoes, the kohl to highlight her eyes, were all exactly right. Everything perfectly in fashion and she had the figure to carry it well. But another couple of months and she'd probably be shopping for something in the next style. Gamine, with big, dark Lillian Gish eyes, she was flawless. Yet McMillan seemed immune to her.

Irene didn't know where her brother had gone.

'All I can tell you is he came home terribly late last night and went off again straight after breakfast.'

'What about yesterday?'

'I suppose it was the same then,' she answered after a moment. 'Yes, it was, I remember now. But Ronnie's always done what he wanted.'

She sounded sulky, Lottie thought. Bored.

'Does he have places he likes to go? A set of friends?' McMillan asked.

'Well, of course,' Irene Walker told him as if it was the most obvious thing in the world. 'Dancing, cocktails. He sees Brian Dover quite a lot. Do you know Brian?'

'No,' McMillan said with a smile.

'There's him and a few others. They were all at school together.'

'What about the Market Tavern. Has he ever mentioned that?'

She shook her head. 'I don't think so. Why?'

'It doesn't matter. Do you know where we can find Mr Dover and some of his other friends, Miss Walker?'

She returned with a pair of addresses written on a page torn from a notebook. At the bottom was a telephone number.

'I added that in case you needed to get in touch about anything,' she said. No blush, forward as you like, Lottie thought.

'Thank you.' He tipped his hat to her and turned away.

Before she followed him, Lottie leaned closer to the girl and whispered, 'There's a ladder in your stocking.'

As Irene lifted a leg to check, she strode off to the car, a small smile on her lips. It was terrible, she knew. But true. And rather satisfying.

'What do we do now?' Lottie asked as McMillan drove back to town. In the distance, down towards the river, she could see smoke from all the factories hanging over Leeds.

'Ah,' the sergeant said, and she knew it wasn't going to be good for her. 'Back to the station and find out about those names Miss Walker gave me.'

'You didn't mention Jocelyn Hill to her. She might have known something.'

'Would you trust her with a secret?' He lit a Black Cat cigarette and blew out a thin plume of smoke.

'No,' Lottie agreed. 'She just about threw herself at you.'

He chuckled. 'She gave us the information, that's what matters. I think my wife will find it funny.'

'You're married?' That had stayed quiet. Cathy would be disappointed.

'Since just after the war. We have two boys and a girl.' He nodded at her wedding ring. 'You too, by the look of it.'

'Yes.' She smiled. 'No children, though.'

'Sometimes I wish we didn't have children. I love them really, but it's non-stop.' He paused and glanced at his watch. 'I know your shift's over. Do you need to get home to your husband?'

'He'll be wondering what's happened to me,' she admitted.

'Would you mind if I dropped you off in town and you took the tram? I want to track down this friend of Walker's and see him.'

Lottie could taste her disappointment. She'd wanted to be there, to be part of it all, especially when they found Jocelyn. They'd need a WPC there for that.

'My husband won't mind. Just let me tell him.'

'You can ring him from Millgarth.'

'We don't have a telephone.' She could leave a message with Mrs Bradley down the street. But then the whole neighbourhood would know her business. 'It's just off Chapeltown Road.'

Geoff sat at the table, jacket on the back of his chair, sleeves rolled up, braces dark against his white shirt. He looked at her, bemused.

'This is what you wanted, isn't it?'

'Yes. You know it is.'

'Then why are you hesitating?'

'I…' It was the sense of duty, she thought. To him, to their marriage.

'Is he coming to pick you up?'

Lottie's eyes flickered to the clock. 'In an hour.' McMillan had wanted time to find Brian Dover and talk to him first. Better she wasn't there, he suggested with a dark grin.

'Get some food inside you,' Geoff told her. 'It might be a long night.'

She leaned forward and kissed him. How many men would encourage their wives like that? No wonder she loved him.

The sergeant was five minutes early. She'd been watching from the front window, a mug of tea going cold in her hands, as he pulled up. Lottie dashed out. He was sitting at the wheel eating a sandwich.

'This is my supper,' he told her. 'I'll be done in a tick.'

She could hear the soft, constant noise of the Peugeot's engine and feel the vibrations in the metal and the seat.

'I've been thinking about Jocelyn and Ronnie Walker,' she said.

'Go on. Don't mind me eating; I'll still be listening.'

She took a deep breath before speaking. He'd probably already considered everything, but she still needed to say it and hope she didn't seem too forward.

'Walker must have had a shock when Jocelyn showed up at the Market Tavern. He probably thought he was rid of her, and then she turns up again, big as a house.'

'Maybe. But we know the two of them came out and drove off in his car.'

'That's what the lad who followed her told me,' Lottie said.

'I had a word with someone who was in the Market that night,' he told her. 'He saw her, remembered her because she looked ready to drop her baby. Everyone noticed her, he told me. My man doesn't know Walker, but he said she was talking to a chap for a few minutes, then they left together. All very pleasant, no cross words.'

'Funny that the landlady doesn't remember if it caused such a stir,' Lottie said sharply.

'I wouldn't worry about that. Nancy tends to recall things only after her memory's been prodded a few times.' He gave her a wry grin. 'She's perfected the art of saying nowt. Brian Dover didn't have much to tell, but he claims Ronnie's been spending more time at the Market lately, and talking about his tough pals as if he wants to become one of them himself. Having Jocelyn walk into the place like that won't have helped his standing.'

'True,' she agreed. 'Did he have any idea where to find him?'

'No,' McMillan admitted with a sigh. He crumpled the empty sandwich wrapper. 'That's better. When we were in the trenches we used to talk about what we missed in England. For me it was always tongue sandwiches. I'd eat them every day if I could.' He put the car in gear. 'Come on.'

'Where are we going?'

'To talk to a couple of criminals.'

CHAPTER FOUR

THE gramophone needed winding. Even as Lottie walked down the dark street she could hear the music becoming slower and slower. It was that new jazz record, *What'll I Do*, one she liked to whistle on patrol. She made a face as the sound ended.

Lottie knew they were in Armley, one of the poorest areas of Leeds, but she had no idea a road like this existed here. Running down a hill off Town Street, even at night it seemed quite different from the rest of the area. She could hear leaves rustling in the trees and smell the grass. The cobbled road led to a row of well-tended cottages. It was like an undiscovered little village, she thought. She heard a cranking sound from one of the houses and the music started again, at the proper speed this time.

McMillan strode ahead of her, past the houses and down the hill, hands pushed into the pockets of his mackintosh, moving in and out of pools of light from the street lamps. She followed, still glancing around with pleasure, taking in all she could see. She could happily live down here.

The sergeant turned down a drive and Lottie hurried behind. Suddenly she was staring at the back of a large old stone house that had been hidden from view. Lights showed in the windows. McMillan was looking around impatiently.

'His name's Bert Newsome. Let me do all the talking,' he said quietly. 'He's probably going to be surprised to see a woman here. Let's hope it makes him say something he hadn't intended.'

'Crime must pay well,' she said, looking at the building.

'This used to belong to a mill owner. He bought it for a song during the war.'

'He wasn't in the army?' Lottie asked, surprised; even criminals had been patriotic.

'Medically unfit.' She could hear the disgust in McMillan's voice. He rubbed a thumb over his first two fingers; money had changed hands. 'Poor eyesight. That was the report.' He knocked hard on the back door.

She nodded, attentive as she heard footsteps on the tiles and the face of a maid appeared.

'To see Mr Newsome. Tell him it's Sergeant McMillan and Constable Armstrong.'

The girl's eyes widened with astonishment as she saw Lottie in uniform, then she nodded and hurried away. The door was still open and the sergeant stepped inside as if he owned the place, glancing around the kitchen.

The house might be grand, she thought, but they hadn't done much to this part of it. Still the old blackleaded range and the stone sink. The only modern touch was a geyser for hot water.

The footsteps again, and the maid led them through to a parlour that overlooked a long front garden. Another view to surprise her. It wasn't decorated on a budget. All the furniture was good quality, quite new, and everything thoughtfully arranged; that had to be a woman's touch.

The man waiting for them was younger then she'd expected, no more than forty, with a ready smile and an easy manner. Dressed in a beautifully cut pale grey lounge suit, his hair short, he didn't look like any kind of crook she'd imagined. More like a businessman who'd done well for himself. His eyes seemed amused as he watched them.

'Sergeant,' he said. 'A pleasant surprise.' He gestured at one of the chairs. 'Have a seat. And miss.' He gave a small bow that could have been mockery; it was impossible to tell. 'Now, what can I do for you?'

'Ronnie Walker,' McMillan said. 'Ring any bells?'

Newsome shook his head and took a cigarette case from his jacket. 'No. Should it?'

'He likes to hang around the big men a little. Been seen at the Market Tavern buying drinks for Archie Brennan and Seth Johnson.'

'I daresay they won't mind who stands them a drink.' A flash of a smile that vanished in a second. 'But no, I don't know your chap, sorry. Maybe I should if he's always that generous.'

'So you'd have no idea where I could find him?' McMillan seemed perfectly comfortable, sitting back in the chair, legs extended.

'Not a clue.' Newsome cocked his head. 'You said Archie knows him?'

'That's right.'

'I suppose I could telephone to him and ask if he knows where the man might be. As a favour to you.'

Newsome left the room, making sure the door was completely closed behind him, then a muffled voice from the hall. She glanced at McMillan. He was grinning, enjoying himself, and gave her a wink.

'He's in Manchester for the day,' the man said when he returned. 'Not due back until late. He's going to ring me in the morning.' Newsome gave a small shrug. 'Sorry. I can let you know tomorrow, if he has the information.'

'That's fine.' The sergeant stood. 'Tomorrow will do.'

'Would you care to go out of the front door, Sergeant?' The man planted his words deliberately.

'We're fine with the back. Wouldn't want your neighbours to get the wrong impression.' He tipped his hat. 'Good evening.'

'Well?' McMillan asked as they strolled back up the hill. He lit a cigarette and blew out smoke. 'What did you make of him?'

'Apart from the fact he was lying through his teeth, you mean?'

He laughed. 'You noticed that, too, did you?'

'He knew exactly who Ronnie Walker was. I think he wanted to be sure anything he said wouldn't come back on him. And I think he has the information. He wanted to see how badly you needed it.'

McMillan whistled softly through his teeth.

'You should really join CID. You're quicker than most of the ones we have.'

Lottie flushed with pride. It would never happen but the praise was wonderful to hear.

'He rang…'

'Archie Brennan. Newsome will be on the blower to me in the morning, I can guarantee you that. But it won't be more than a hint. That way we'll be in his debt a little but we'll still have to do the digging.'

'Is that how it works?' she asked.

'Sometimes. Give and take, negotiate with the enemy. No one ever said policing was a clean business.'

'Did my being there make any difference?'

'Definitely. Usually we're daggers drawn when we meet. He controls half the prostitutes and protection rackets in Leeds. Today he was polite as you like. I think he let us know he could find out about Ronnie to try to impress you with his generosity.'

'I never feel terribly impressed with crumbs.' She was quiet until they reached the car. 'He's married, isn't he? Newsome, I mean.'

'Useful crumbs,' he reminded her. 'And yes, he is. She's his second wife. The first died in the influenza outbreak after the war. Why?'

'I just wondered. The place looks like it has a woman's touch, that's all. Except for the kitchen.'

'They probably hardly ever eat there. You can find them in restaurants most of the time. More or less have their own tables at Powolny's and King Edward's.' He shook his head and gave a frustrated sigh.

'Now we'd better hope Jocelyn turns up overnight. The longer it is, the more chance of a body.'

'Do you think she's dead?'

'Honestly?' He lit a cigarette as he drove down the hill, all the lights of night time Leeds in the distance. 'I hope not,' he said finally. 'Now, I'd best get you home. There's nothing more you can do until morning.' McMillan smiled at her. 'You've made a good start. Trust me on that.'

'Well, I'm not surprised he said you'd done a good job.' Geoff began to chuckle. 'Honestly, you're the most capable girl I've ever met. I used to see you at Barnbow, taking charge of everything—'

'Me?' That wasn't how she remembered things. She'd been efficient once she learned the system, but glad to defer to the women who ran things.

'You,' he insisted. 'Honestly, it was one of the first things I noticed. You looked so confident it scared me a little. You can handle this.'

Lottie blinked in astonishment. Geoff had never said anything like this before. He been behind her joining the police, in trying things, but never praise like this.

'Do you mean that? It's not just something to make me feel better?'

'Of course I mean it,' he told her, and she couldn't doubt the words or the look in his eyes. 'You'll probably end up as the first woman detective.'

That worked for the evening, but by the time she was marching down Sholebroke Avenue to catch the tram Lottie felt nervous. She'd had beginner's luck. She hadn't even needed to do much, just be there. What if she made a hash of it all today? Sitting on the bottom deck as the tram rattled its way along the tracks, she glanced out of the window at the people they passed. Were they all terrified too, she wondered?

She'd taken a little extra time over her appearance, brushed her hair carefully and caught it up with pins so it wouldn't stray. Rubbed all the tiny shreds of lint from her jacket.

'You look splendid,' Geoff told her with a kiss and a wink. 'I love a girl in uniform.'

'Get away with you.' But it made her smile for a moment.

No reporting to Mrs Maitland. Straight up the stairs, ignoring the usual looks and the comments whispered behind hands. Shoulders back, she entered the CID room. The conversation stopped.

All four men turned. It was Sergeant McMillan who recovered first, moving forward with a smile.

'This is WPC Armstrong,' he explained. 'I've asked for her to work with me on the Hill case.' Lottie nodded at the faces. 'These are Detective Constables Logan and Tyrell—' the two younger men with cigarettes dangling from their fingers '—and this is Inspector Carter.'

'Sir.'

Carter had a sweep of thick, dark hair, heavily pomaded, thin, bloodless lips and heavy eyelids.

'Welcome, Armstrong,' he said, but there was no warmth in his voice.

'Could you give us five minutes?' McMillan asked. A wink and the smallest nod.

Cathy was waiting for her by the toilet, eager for all the details.

'You met a real gangster?' she asked when Lottie had finished. 'Was he the way they are in the pictures?'

'He was just like a businessman. If I hadn't been told I'd never have known.'

'What about the girl?'

'Irene?' Trust Cathy to ask about her.

'Yes. Was she pretty?'

'Very. The thing is, she was trying so hard to seem grown up and sophisticated. You won't believe it, she wrote down her telephone number for him.'

Cathy's eyes widened. 'She didn't! My God, what did he do?'

'He was smooth as you like. Just thanked her and left. Anyway,' she added with a smirk, 'he's married. He told me. Three young children.'

'What?' Her head jerked up and she sighed. 'Oh well, that's him off my list.' But her regret only lasted a moment. 'I suppose you're abandoning me again?'

'I think so.' She wasn't certain what was happening yet, waiting on tenterhooks.

'I suppose I'll have to soldier on whilst you and *John* get all the glory.' Cathy straightened her uniform skirt. 'I'd better get to work.' Her tone softened. 'Don't pay me any mind. I'm pleased for you, I really am. You deserve it.'

'Newsome telephoned a few minutes ago,' McMillan said as they left the station. 'Walker supposedly has somewhere on Blackman Lane.'

'Did he say where?'

'I told you, a hint's as far as he'll go. That's his idea of co-operation. We need to go up there and look. Ask whoever's on the beat.'

'I might have a better idea, sir.'

The space behind the Royal Hotel stank. The bins overflowed and there was a strong stench of urine from somewhere. Lottie paced around, waiting and trying to be patient. The sound of traffic was muffled and distant. A train went by on the embankment, the second in ten minutes, making the earth under her shoes shake as it passed.

Finally the door at the back of the building squeaked open on rusty hinges and a heavyset woman emerged. She was dressed in a man's double-breasted suit, correct down to the collar and tie, shoes polished to a high gloss, short hair in a brutal shingle cut and pomaded down. Blinking in the light, she lit one of her Turkish cigarettes.

'Hello, Auntie Betty,' Lottie said. 'I haven't seen you in a while.'

At first McMillan refused to go in. They sat in the car on Lower Briggate and looked across the street at the place.

'They'll know I'm a copper as soon as I walk through the door,' McMillan objected.

'Well, I can't. I'm in uniform,' Lottie reminded him.

He pushed the brim of his hat back. 'It's just...' He shook his head and a look of distaste crossed his face.

'Because they're different, you mean?' She chose her words very carefully.

'Yes. It's wrong, inverts and mannish girls. It's not natural.'

'Sarge,' she began patiently. 'John.' What was the best way to put it? 'This is the quickest way to get the information. Betty's lived up on Blackman Lane for years. She knows the place inside and out. Two minutes and she can tell me where we can find Walker.'

'How do you know her, anyway?'

'Her niece had a few problems. WPC Taylor and I helped sort them out. Betty came to see us out on patrol and said how grateful she was.'

He glanced at the entrance to the Royal Hotel. 'All right,' he agreed reluctantly. 'We'll do it like this: you go to the ginnel at the back and wait. I'll pop in, have a word with her, say you need to talk to her. Be as quick as you can. We'll meet back here.'

'You're looking well, Lottie.' Betty smiled. Everyone called her Auntie, a strangely sexless figure, more man than woman and ending up neither. She was a fixture behind the bar, serving drinks for the homosexuals and lesbians who spent their money there, always ready to advise them on their problems but never finding answers to her own.

'So are you.'

'That poor man you sent in looked terrified.' She gave a chuckle. 'Kept looking around like someone might eat him.'

'He's harmless, Auntie. Just scared, that's all. Did he tell you I need your help?'

'Yes.' She stared at the cigarette as she turned it in her thick fingers. 'Something about Blackman Lane.'

'We're looking for someone who has a place there,' Lottie said. 'I don't know if it's a flat or a room.'

'What's his name?'

'Ronnie Walker. He's in his early twenties.'

'Doesn't ring a bell,' the woman answered slowly. 'They come and go so fast these days.'

'He drives a Standard sedan.'

'Oh, *him*.' Her face brightened. 'Number seventeen. He has the attic. What's he done? Why are you after him?'

'I can't tell you, Auntie. And please don't say a word.'

'Lips locked,' she promised. 'And I'll throw away the key.'

'Thank you. For everything.' She leaned forward and gave Betty a quick peck on the cheek, seeing the glimmer of loneliness in the woman's eyes.

'Number seventeen,' Lottie announced with a smile as she closed the door of the Peugeot. 'I told you Betty would know.'

'God, she's an odd creature. Gave me the creeps, dressed like that.'

'She's lovely.' Lottie turned on the seat to look at him. 'Without her we'd be hunting around and trying to find Walker's address. I hope you won't forget that.'

'I know,' he said quietly as he wove through the traffic on the Headrow and Woodhouse Lane. 'I know. It's just… well, it doesn't matter.' He gave her a tight smile.

'Isn't that a Standard?' She pointed at a parked car on Blackman Lane. There were no more than a handful of vehicles, along with a Matthias Robinson's delivery lorry.

'That's the one,' McMillan agreed. 'Right outside the house, too. The attic, you said?'

'That's what Betty told me.' She wanted to remind him who'd given them the information.

'Let's take a gander. If we're lucky, your Miss Hill will be here and we can finish this right now.'

The front door of the house was unlocked. They climbed the stairs slowly, one flight, then pausing on the landing before taking the second. At the top, the door stood ajar.

Something felt very wrong.

'Let me go first,' the sergeant whispered. He trod carefully, barely making a sound. He hesitated for a fraction of a second before grabbing the door handle and easing it down. Lottie had barely started the climb when she heard him shout, 'Get in here now!'

CHAPTER FIVE

SHE dashed up the steps, pushing the door wide. Light came through a pair of dormer windows, showing the couple lying a few feet apart on the floor. McMillan was kneeling, fingertips against Walker's neck, feeling for a pulse.

There was blood all around, on the carpets, soaked into the floorboards, a spray of it across the walls. All over the clothes and the skin of the young man and the young woman. The air smelt like iron. Flies were buzzing everywhere.

She didn't even pause to think. All the training she'd received when she joined the force took over. Breathing through her nose, Lottie dropped on to her knees next to the girl and checked for any sign of life. For a moment she couldn't feel anything, and she opened her mouth, ready to speak. Then it was there. Only faint, but regular: a tiny beat, and the slightest rise and fall of her chest.

'She's still alive.' Her voice was focused. Lottie took the girl's hand in her own and squeezed it gently. 'We're here now,' she said. 'Police. Don't worry, we'll look after you.'

Her hand moved over the bulging belly. A stab wound. Was the baby still alive? She didn't have any way to tell. But all the blood…

'Walker's dead,' McMillan told her, getting to his feet. 'We're going to need an ambulance for her.'

'I'm not sure if the baby's alive or not. Jocelyn needs someone with her.' She reached into the pocket of her uniform and threw him her police whistle.

They waited outside as the ambulancemen worked their way downstairs with the stretcher.

'Would you mind going to the hospital with her?' McMillan said. There was pleading in his eyes.

'Of course not,' she told him and saw the relief on his face. She wanted to be there, anyway. In case. To see it through, to try and help Jos stay alive. The baby too, if there was still a chance. Then she wanted to find who'd done this.

'I need to stay here,' he continued as if he needed to explain. 'The fingerprint boys will be arriving soon and the crew from the coroner's officer.' His voice tailed away.

'I'll be with her,' Lottie assured him.

He nodded, distracted. He'd smoked cigarette after cigarette, lighting one from the end of the last. She'd even had one herself, a way to calm the shakes that began once she started to understand everything in front of her.

One murder. Two if Jocelyn didn't pull through. Three if the baby was dead. Not that, she prayed.

All she could do was hold the girl's hand on the journey. For the first time, Lottie had a proper chance to study Jocelyn's face as the vehicle speeded along to the infirmary. So young, she thought. Not a line on her skin. Eyes closed. Her hair tangled and dull. She hadn't even stirred since they found her. Her hands had been put together over her breast, above the two slashes in her belly. Lottie put her mouth close to Jocelyn's ear.

'Don't you give up,' she said softly. 'We're almost at the hospital now. They'll take care of you. And the little one.'

As soon as they reached the infirmary a pair of nurses took charge, escorting the stretcher quickly along the corridor and through a door marked No Admission. Even her policewoman's uniform wouldn't make her welcome beyond that.

Five minutes while a harried clerk took down the few details Lottie could give her. And then the waiting. Barren, uncomfortable wooden chairs ranged against the plain walls. After a few restless hours she begged use of a telephone and rang Millgarth.

She needed to let Geoff know she'd probably be late. Very late, most likely. Cathy should be back from patrol, probably dolling herself up for a night on the town. Lottie had to wait while they searched for her.

'Where are you? I can hear all sorts of noise in the background.'

'The infirmary. Do you think you could do me a terribly big favour?'

'The infirmary?' There was panic in Cathy's voice. 'Are you hurt? Is something wrong?'

'Calm down. I'm fine.' She quickly summed up the day. 'Do you think you could go and see Geoff and tell him I need to stay here? None of the neighbours are on the phone. I know it's a lot to ask…'

'No, I'll do it,' Cathy offered without hesitation. 'What about the baby?'

'I don't know yet.' She hesitated, thinking of the girl's face in the ambulance, pale, bloodless. 'Really, I don't. They won't say a thing. I don't even know if Jos is going to pull through.'

'Don't worry about Geoff. I'll tell him.'

The pair of them had met before; Cathy had visited after work one Saturday.

'Tell him to go and get fish and chips for his tea. Better than him trying to cook anything.'

Another hour passed. Two. By now she could see evening through the windows. Her back hurt from sitting for so long. A nurse took pity and brought her a cup of tea.

'Just wet and warm,' she whispered with a shake of her head. 'But that's how Sister likes it.'

'Do you know… ?'

'The girl? She's still in theatre. The surgeon's doing all he can.' She gave a soothing, practised smile. 'He's very good.'

'The baby?'

'I don't know. I'm sorry.'

Then she was alone again. No one to talk to, nothing to read. She was too scared to slip away and find something; someone might come with news. Instead there was nothing but the slow tick of the clock.

Finally, close to half past nine, she heard the slow pace of footsteps and a man appeared in the door. Bald, haggard, a face weighed down by jowls, and a grim, cheerless mouth.

'I'm Mr Curtis. You brought the girl in?' He had his hands thrust deep into the pockets of a coat that had lost its whiteness, stained with patches of blood.

'Yes.' She stood, staring at him. 'WPC Armstrong. How…?'

'I was able to save her,' he answered gravely. 'She's not out of the woods yet, though. She's going to be seriously ill for several days. She lost a great deal of blood.' He hesitated. 'I'm afraid the baby was already dead when she was brought in.'

'I see.' She felt a dullness rising in her chest. Somewhere inside she'd believed both of them would survive.

'There was nothing I could do,' Curtis said, as if he needed to explain. 'I'm sorry.'

'Can I see Jocelyn?' Lottie asked, but he shook his head.

'She won't wake until the morning. Even then I wouldn't expect much from her for a while. You might as well go.'

'Thank you.'

After so long in a small waiting room it felt strange to be walking through town. Along the Headrow, towards Millgarth. She felt exhausted, drained inside. Ready to go home and sleep for hours. First, though, she needed to report in and hope McMillan was there.

He was the only person in the CID room, his trilby perched right on the edge of his desk. The sergeant raised his eyebrow in a question when he saw her. She gave him the news and watched him bite down on his lower lip.

'God,' he said quietly. 'But she's going to survive?'

'That's what the surgeon said.'

'I'll send someone down to stand guard.'

'Have you managed to find anything?' Lottie asked. She stifled a yawn with the back of her hand. 'Sorry.'

'Nothing from the fingerprint men yet. I've had constables doing a house-to-house in the area but no reports. Two of my men are digging into Walker's background. That might give us something. I went out to tell the family. His parents are back from York.'

'That must have been awful.'

'It's the worst part of the job.' The sergeant shrugged. 'Still, someone has to do it. If they knew why anyone would want Ronnie dead, they were keeping their mouths shut. Even that sister of his was quiet.'

'Do you think he was involved in something?'

'He must have been. Why else would someone want to kill him?'

'I suppose I'm off the investigation now?' Lottie asked. The thought had gnawed at her all the way back from the infirmary. No woman police constable could be involved in something as serious as this; WPCs worked with girls and women in trouble. Not death.

'You? Why?' He cocked his head. 'Has someone said something?'

'But it's a murder case.'

'True,' he agreed. 'Double murder. And it's also the attempted murder of a young woman. As far as I'm concerned that makes you still a part of it. No one's told me any different.'

'If you're sure…'

'I'm positive. Without you we might never have got to Miss Hill in time. Of course I'm sure. And if anyone objects, I'll have a word them. Even your Mrs Maitland.'

Lottie smiled. 'Thank you.'

'Now go home,' he told her. 'You look all in.'

'I'm supposed to be off all weekend, but I could come in. Jos will be waking up. I'd like to be there. If you don't mind, that is.'

'I think it's a good idea,' he agreed, and ran his palms down his cheeks.

Lottie had one hand on the doorknob when a thought struck her. 'Has anyone told her mother?'

'I sent the beat officer over.' McMillan's voice was weary. 'Let's put it this way: she didn't drop everything and rush over to the hospital.'

Waiting for the tram a man edged up to her, head bowed, holding an old army blanket like a shawl around his shoulders.

'Do you have a penny for an old soldier?' he asked. She could see the humiliation on his face and gave him tuppence from her purse. That could have been Geoff, she thought, or her cousin who'd died in the first months of the war, his body never recovered from the shell hole in no man's land.

On the tram she almost dozed, and her legs felt like lead as she walked along Sholebroke Avenue. She could see a glimmer of light through the curtains in the front room as she unlocked the door.

Lottie paused, the key in her hand, as she heard Geoff's laughter. Full-throated, open. So different from the quiet man she saw every day. Then a woman's voice said something, and her body stiffened.

She kept a smile on her face as she entered the room. A fire was burning in the hearth to warm the couple sitting at the table. Geoff, in his shirtsleeves, wearing a sleeveless V-necked jumper. His eyes were merry as he turned to look at her.

And Cathy. Wearing her favourite frock, the one from the market that shimmered like silk. Playing cards in one hand, a cigarette in the other. She started to rise, then sat again.

'I thought I'd just pick up the fish and chips on the way here, and when I explained, Geoff asked me to stay. You don't mind, do you, Lottie?' She gestured at the cards. 'We were playing pontoon.'

'I didn't fancy a night in on my own,' said Geoff. 'Cathy said she didn't have anything special to do tonight, so I thought…'

'Oh, give over.' She waved down the explanations as she sank into the easy chair and sighed. 'You did right to make an evening of it.'

Of course it was innocent. Stupid to think it might be anything else, even for a moment. Not with Geoff's injuries. And it had been so lovely to hear him laugh like that, like an early Christmas present.

All Lottie really wanted was to sink into sleep and push the world away for a few hours. She'd seen too much today. Pain, blood, death. But she wasn't going to have that luxury yet. Not until she'd told them.

Cathy made the tea, a strong, proper brew, and Lottie drank gratefully. She took off her shoes, finally starting to feel as if the day was behind her.

'Well…' she began.

At five Lottie crept out of bed. She'd been awake for an hour, lying between the sheets with her mind racing, turning towards the clock, watching time pass so slowly. In the bathroom she shivered, washing and starting to dress, lacing up her brassiere at the side until it felt snug.

Saturday morning and for once she wasn't officially on duty. No uniform today. Instead she selected a blouse, a slip, and a brown woollen skirt that reached to mid-calf, pleated just below the knee.

A cup of tea as she stared out into the darkness of the early morning. Thoughts of Jos had woken her. The girl on the floor, blood all over her. In the ambulance. As they took her away in the hospital. So helpless, so alone now, with the baby dead.

Her heels sounded sharply against the pavement as she walked down to the tram stop, a good coat to keep out the dawn chill, a felt hat pulled down tight over her hair, and a determined look on her face. She'd left a note for Geoff. So much for a quiet Saturday.

At the infirmary she had to ask before she found Jocelyn Hill. She was in the corner of a ward, screens around the bed, a constable sitting close by, feet planted firmly on the linoleum. Not someone she knew.

'Can I help you?' he asked. A firm voice, too used to hearing lies.

'I'm WPC Armstrong.' She nodded at the bed. 'I found Miss Hill and came with her in the ambulance.'

He stared at her, his eyes showing nothing. 'If that's right, who were you with and where were you?'

'Sergeant McMillan. And it was on Blackman Lane. Number seventeen, up in the attic if you want me to be exact.'

The copper grinned. 'Sorry, but you wouldn't believe some of the lengths people go to.' He stuck out a hairy hand. 'Tom

Peters. They dragged me over from Wortley to sit here. I knew we had some lasses on the force but I've never met any of you.' He paused for a second. 'They've given you a better uniform than us, any road.'

'I'm Lottie Armstrong,' she told him quietly. 'Has she woken?'

'Stirred about three o'clock. The nurse came and gave her something. She's been sleeping ever since.'

'I thought I'd sit with her for a while.'

'Be my guest,' Peters said. 'Since you're here, I'll stretch my legs for a minute and see if I can find a cup of tea. Do you want one?'

'That'd be lovely. Thank you.'

The chair scraped lightly over the floor as she sat and looked down at Jocelyn. The girl's eyes were still closed, but her breathing seemed stronger and there was a little colour in her cheeks.

Jos's hand lay on top of the blanket. Small, thin fingers, the nails bitten down raggedly. Lottie covered it with her own, squeezing lightly. A moment later the girl stirred, her arm moving slightly. Not conscious yet, but just below the surface. And for now perhaps it was better that way.

Ten o'clock. She'd just seen the hand turn the hour when Jocelyn started to struggle awake. Eyelids fluttering, trying to open, her hands scrambling at the sheet.

'Shhh,' Lottie said, reaching out and stroking the girl's skin. 'It's all right. It's all right. You're safe.' Jos blinked, trying to move her head, to see, to understand where she was and how she'd got here. 'You're in hospital. You're going to be fine. I'm a policewoman. You're safe here.'

Panic flickered in her eyes as she opened her mouth to speak.

'How?' It was a dry croak.

'Someone attacked you.' Lottie tried to keep her voice even, serious but soothing. 'You and Ronnie. Do you remember?'

Then it came, the fingers pulling away, moving over her belly. Eyes widening. And the screaming started. By the time the nurse dashed in, Lottie had hold of Jos's wrists, trying to stop her from flailing too wildly.

'Oh God. Keep hold of her, I'll get something.'

The girl fought, and the screams wouldn't stop. Then the nurse jabbed a needle in her arm and in a few seconds she slumped, eyes rolling up under the lids. Lottie stood back, breathing hard, the sound still ringing in her ears.

'That'll knock her out for a couple of hours,' the nurse said. 'What happened?'

'She remembered yesterday. Someone killed her baby and her boyfriend and she's still alive.'

'Poor little thing. No wonder she was yelling.'

Not long after midday Lottie sensed the girl stirring. This time she was ready, leaning close and whispering even before Jos surfaced.

'I know,' Lottie said. 'I know. It's terrible but you're going to be all right. You're safe now. I'm here with you.'

No screaming this time. Just the confusion and the realisation of all she'd lost. The tears ran down Jocelyn's cheeks and Lottie wiped them tenderly away.

'I'm sorry. You remember it all, don't you?'

The girl pointed at the jug of water on the table. Lottie poured a glass and raised Jos's head so she could drink, sipping at first, then small gulps.

'I'm a police constable. I was in the flat yesterday. I came with you in the ambulance.'

'My baby…'

All she could do was shake her head and let the girl grip her fingers tightly.

'I'm sorry. They did everything they could.' Before the tears could begin again, Lottie pushed on. 'Who did it? It's important, please, we need to know. Can you tell me what happened?'

'We...' Jos gathered her breath. 'We were in the room.' The girl stared straight ahead as if she was seeing it all happen again. 'There were... footsteps. Ronnie...' She gestured for the water again and drank once more. 'Ronnie opened the door and they stabbed him. He's dead, isn't he?'

'I'm sorry. He is.'

'Oh God.'

Lottie needed to keep asking questions. She needed the information.

'They?' she pressed. 'How many of them?'

'Two. I didn't even have time to shout before they were on me.' A long, hopeless silence. 'That was it.' The tears began again, running down her cheeks. Lottie took a handkerchief from her bag, dabbing softly at the girl's face.

'What did they look like?'

'Just... ordinary.'

'Were they young?'

'About Ronnie's age,' Jos answered after a while. 'They seemed like they were enjoying themselves.'

'Did they have dark hair? Fair? How were they dressed?' She kept her eye on the girl. They needed every scrap of information she could give, but Lottie dared not push her too far.

'I...' Jocelyn closed her eyes together and bit her lip hard as a wave of pain passed through her. 'One fair, one dark. The dark one was fat.' Another tear trickled down. 'He kicked me after.' Her hand touched the emptiness of her belly.

'Had you seen either of them before?'

She shook her head slowly. The girl was fading. Lottie waited until Jos's breathing was even, tucked the girl's arm under the covers and moved quietly away.

'Did you get owt?' Peters asked.

'A little.' She sighed. 'God, I can't imagine going through what's happened to her.' She glanced around the ward, seeing it properly for the first time. Women of all ages, some coughing, some huddled in the blankets, a few staring off absently. Everywhere the acrid, stinging smell of carbolic.

'I'll keep an eye on her. Don't you worry.'

Lottie smiled and patted him on the arm as she left.

Outside, all the noise of Saturday overwhelmed her. She had to stand still for a second. People filling the pavements, buses, motor cars. The stink of exhaust fumes catching in her throat. After the hospital it seemed like an explosion of life.

'Busier every week, isn't it?'

Lottie turned. McMillan was at her shoulder, staring at the street. He was unshaven, still wearing yesterday's suit, a ring of grime on his shirt collar. His face looked almost grey with tiredness.

'Don't creep up like that,' she told him. 'You startled the life out of me. How long have you been there, anyway?'

'Just arrived.' He nodded at the Peugeot parked by the building. 'Peters rang in earlier and said you'd come by.' He grinned at her. 'Wanted to know if he should chuck you out.'

She snorted, then her face turned serious. 'I had to be here. I told you.' He nodded his understanding, and she went on, 'I feel…' It was hard to put into words. 'Responsible for her, I suppose.'

'Come on. I'll buy you a cup of tea and you can tell me all about it.'

Lyons on Bond Street was busy with shoppers. Families at the tables, children wriggling around restlessly. The hat pegs were a mix of bowlers, caps, straw boaters. Lottie waited while McMillan found a table, sliding in as a couple was leaving. He ordered a pot of tea and two toasted teacakes from a harried waitress.

'Was she able to tell you much?'

Lottie recounted what Jocelyn had said. McMillan scribbled notes, looking up as she finished.

'He *kicked* her?'

'Yes. Do you know them?'

The sergeant shook his head. 'There's not enough to go on from that. We've been asking all over but we haven't found anything yet.'

'What can I do?'

'You've already done it.' He took a sip of tea and lit a cigarette. 'I mean it. You were down here first thing. You sat with her. It sounds like you asked the right questions. You've done a wonderful job, Lottie.'

'But?' He was leading to something more; she could feel it.

At least he had the good grace to look embarrassed. 'The inspector says it's a job for CID now. I'm sorry. I tried to tell him how valuable you'd been.'

She cut him short.

'It's fine.' Part of her had been expecting it. Sooner or later it was inevitable but the words still hurt. She blinked, reaching in her handbag for a handkerchief. She'd left it at the infirmary, balled up in Jocelyn's hand. 'Excuse me, please.'

Hidden in the women's loo, she dabbed at her face and applied fresh lipstick, breathing slowly as she watched herself in the mirror. She'd had a few hours of real police work. That was more than she'd ever really expected. Be grateful, she told herself. You know what it's like now, and it's hard graft.

She tried to smile, but there was no heart in it. Never mind; at least Cathy would be glad to have her back on Monday.

McMillan stood as she returned. A proper gentleman, she thought.

'I really did fight to keep you,' he insisted.

'Thank you.' She believed him. 'I don't suppose there was ever really much chance, anyway.'

'I told you yesterday, you're better than most of the detectives we've got. I'll keep working on the inspector.'

What else could she say?

'I'm sorry,' Lottie told him. 'I need to go.'

'Of course…'

She was miles away, lost in what ifs, maybes, and disappointment. Lottie didn't even notice the tram arrive until someone nudged her; she had to scramble in her purse for pennies as she took a seat.

It was a decision that was always on the cards. Never mind that the sergeant thought she could do the job. Men had decided that women weren't suitable. Women weren't even as valued as regular police constables. Instead they kept order with women and children.

Lottie breathed out slowly. She was angry. She'd had that taste of proper policing and she'd enjoyed it. She wanted more. But wasn't that always the way, wanting what you couldn't have?

Geoff was in the kitchen, pieces of the wireless scattered over the table. Solder dripped on to an old tin lid and the room smelt as if something was burning.

As soon as he saw her face he put everything aside, came over and held her tight. No questions, just the long hug she needed more than anything right now.

This was why she loved him, why she'd married him. She didn't always need to spell things out for him. He understood and he cared. That was worth more than almost anything she could imagine. He'd wait until she was ready to tell him and let it all spill out. Then he'd be there to hold her again.

On Sunday they worked in the back garden, digging up most of the potatoes and cleaning away the debris from the raspberry canes before going over the ground.

'It's probably too early to get it ready for winter, really,' Geoff said, but he did it anyway. He was wearing his old battledress jacket, like so many men up and down the country. In the kitchen a joint was roasting. By the time it was ready they'd have worked up a good appetite.

Her back ached from the digging, but they'd done a good job. The earth looked dark and rich. Another month or so and it would be ready for some manure.

She enjoyed days like these, the autumn sun the colour of lemon, a hint of early sharpness and mist in the air. It wasn't quite her favourite season, but a close second. And for the last two hours she'd barely thought about the Hill case.

Lottie sighed as she sipped at a cup of tea. For a moment the image of Jocelyn in her hospital bed slipped into her mind, but she pushed it firmly away. There was nothing more she could do. In a few minutes she'd start the rest of the Sunday dinner. Carrots and potatoes they'd grown themselves, straight from the ground. And Yorkshire pudding, of course, the way her mother had taught her to make it, with the fat so hot it sizzled. That was one thing her mother could do well. Geoff would work a little longer then pop down to the pub for a pint. The routine they'd developed. Perhaps it would seem boring to someone like Cathy, but it was comfortable to them. As snug as an old cardigan.

'WPC Armstrong reporting, ma'am.'

'WPC Taylor reporting, ma'am.'

Lottie felt Cathy looking at her from the corner of her eye. There'd be a flood of questions as soon as they were alone.

'Back with us, Armstrong?' Mrs Maitland asked. The woman was relishing this, Lottie brought back to earth after rising above her station.

'Happy to be home, ma'am.' She forced herself to smile.

The woman nodded. 'No special orders today. You know what to do. Dismissed.'

The door had barely closed behind them before Cathy was opening her mouth to speak. Lottie put a finger to her lips. Outside.

Monday. Time to walk around Quarry Hill and Marsh Lane. The slums and the stench. Some of the houses were already empty and boarded up, awaiting demolition. It was a start. The whole area needed to be razed, she thought. There was more prostitution round here than anywhere else in Leeds; that was what she'd been told.

Not that they ever saw much of it in the hard light of a Monday. Mostly worn-down women trudging to and from the wash house with their laundry. They'd found a girl loitering once and taken her in, but that was their only success.

'Well?' Cathy asked as they waited to cross the road. Not a question, more a demand.

'Inspector Carter wants CID working on the case.' Lottie tried not to sound bitter but it still seeped through.

'Why? I thought your sergeant wanted you to help.'

'He did. I even went down to the hospital on Saturday and got a description when Jos woke up. But…' She pressed her lips together and shook her head.

'It's not right,' Cathy told her.

'I know. Life isn't, though, is it? Come on, we'd better get moving.'

It was the same as every other Monday, but it felt different. Not as satisfying. She went through the motions, chatting with faces she knew from the area. Inside, though, she seemed empty. Even the gossip and talk with Cathy didn't have the same spark.

It'll pass, she told herself. She was simply feeling blue, a bit sorry for herself. Soon enough she'd be back in the routine.

Yet by the time her shift ended she felt no better. The hours had dragged and her heart hadn't been in it. With a coat over her uniform and a hat pulled down on her head she came out of Millgarth and sighed.

She'd had one small taste of real policing, nothing more than that. It couldn't have affected her *that* deeply. Another day and she'd be back to the old Lottie.

A car horn honking over and over disturbed her thoughts. She glanced across in annoyance and saw McMillan in his Peugeot waving at her. For a moment she was tempted to turn away; that would be childish, she thought. Instead she opened the door and leaned in, smelling the tobacco and his hair pomade.

'Do you have a few minutes?' he asked. 'I'll give you a lift home, if you like.'

She didn't reply immediately, not sure what to say. Part of her wanted to jump in the motor car and hear if he'd found the men. The rest wanted nothing to do with him.

For a second or two she wavered, then settled on the seat and he put the car in gear.

'I'm sorry, really,' he told her. 'The inspector's wrong. I told him again today.'

'You told him?' She could hardly believe that. You didn't disagree with a senior officer.

'Yes.' He made it seem completely normal. 'I was up at the infirmary.'

'How's Jos?'

'Physically she's starting to mend. But her mind… I saw too much of that during the war.'

She understood what he meant. All those men with the empty eyes of shellshock.

'What can you expect?' Lottie said. 'After what happened to her…'

'I know,' he agreed solemnly. 'I was hoping she might be able to tell me more.'

'You haven't found them?'

'Between you and me, we don't even have a clue where to start. I thought she might have remembered some little thing. Anything.'

'She hadn't?'

'She wouldn't even talk to me.'

'Maybe she really doesn't remember anything else,' Lottie said.

'That's the problem. I don't know and she won't say.'

'Why won't she talk to you?'

He blew out smoke. 'Because she wants you. Said you were kind to her.'

For a moment she felt a thrill of pride. Then she remembered what had happened afterwards. 'I'm sorry.'

'I had another word with the inspector. He's finally given in and said you can go and talk to her in the morning.'

'What?' It was the last thing she'd expected. 'I'm working with you again?'

'Just to question Miss Hill,' he said. 'That's all. He's going to have a word with your guv'nor first thing, then you can go over to the hospital.'

'Do you mean it?' Daft question, she knew. He wouldn't say it otherwise.

The car headed up Chapeltown Road, caught behind a slow tram.

'Of course.' He smiled at her. 'Bright and early tomorrow. I just wish it could be for longer.'

For now she wasn't even going to think about that. She was back on the case for a little while. That was something. Suddenly she remembered.

'Can you park here? I need to get something for tea.'

It was so mundane she just had to laugh.

CHAPTER SIX

SHE'D gone over her uniform with a sponge and a stiff brush before quickly dressing and eyeing herself in the mirror. Geoff had already left for work. Parting the bedroom curtains she watched him stride down the street, briefcase in hand, and Lottie's heart filled again.

He'd been so happy for her when she told him the news, twirling her around the hall until she was giggling like an idiot.

'Well done!'

'Stop it,' she told him as she laughed. 'I didn't do anything.'

But she would.

'You look like a cat who's been given a gallon of cream.'

'I'm back on the Hill case.' She saw the astonishment on Cathy's face, eyes widening in disbelief. 'It's only for a couple of hours, to talk to her again.'

'You lucky dog. I don't know how you wangled that.'

'That makes two of us.' She stood straight, one hand on the matron's door handle. 'Ready?'

Sergeant McMillan was waiting outside the CID office, already wearing his raincoat and twisting the trilby in his hands.

'Ready when you are,' Lottie said.

He smiled and led the way to the Peugeot. 'Quicker than walking.'

At least he looked refreshed, the deep circles gone from under his eyes, some colour to his face, a faint aroma of bay rum on his skin.

'Has there been anything more overnight?'

He shook his head, gearing down and overtaking a lorry on the Headrow. 'If anybody knows, they're keeping quiet.' He grimaced. 'We'll just have to hope Miss Hill can give you something more.'

'What about Ronnie Walker?' Lottie asked. 'He liked to spend time with criminals.'

'To hear them talk, none of them liked him. Kept him at arm's length.'

'Do you believe that?'

'Oddly enough, I do,' McMillan answered after some thought. 'Walker was an outsider. He had money. They didn't trust him. The way I heard it, he was like an eager little boy, wanting some of their glamour.'

'Glamour?' she asked sharply. There was nothing glamorous about the crime she'd seen. Shoplifters, prostitutes: nothing but sadness.

The sergeant shrugged as he parked next to the infirmary and switched off the engine. 'Who knows? But I'm relying on you now.'

'I'll do what I can,' she promised.

'You're good. Don't forget that.' He pulled a copy of the *Daily Mail* from his mackintosh. 'I'll be out here.'

'Hello, Jocelyn.'

The girl was sitting up in bed, her back heavily propped with pillows. Her hair had been washed and brushed, but her eyes were dull.

'You. You were here on Saturday.' Recognition. A faint smile. That was good.

'That's right, I was.' Lottie sat on the empty chair and smoothed down her skirt. 'I'm WPC Armstrong. In uniform today, though. You look a little better.'

'Do I?' A dull expression. 'I wish I felt it.'

'The sergeant said you wouldn't talk to him, Jos.' She took a breath. 'We need to find who did this to you. And to Ronnie.'

'I'd never seen them before. I said that.'

'What about Ronnie? Did he seem to know them?'

Long seconds passed before she answered.

'I… I don't know. It was all so *fast*.'

Lottie tried to frame her words. The evening before she'd gone through it all in her mind. There were things she didn't understand at all.

'Tell me something. Why did you wait so long to run away from the home? And what made you go to Ronnie?'

A small spark fired in Jocelyn's gaze. 'It was the first chance I had. The old bag watched us like a hawk.' There was anger under her words, a dry bitterness that seemed to bring her alive. 'I hated it there. Me mam knew, but she made me go. Said I'd be out of the house if I didn't. That Mrs Allen, she went out for a few minutes so I left.'

'I know you went back to Cross Green. Why did you go looking for Ronnie?'

'I didn't know where else to go. I mean, the kid was his.' She raised her chin, expecting a challenge. 'I couldn't go home. I knew he'd be in that pub. He didn't want me, either. He'd made that clear months ago. But I wasn't going to let him off.' She stared. 'It was only right.'

'Yes.' Just a word to encourage the girl, to keep her going.

'I talked to him. Let him know what was what, that he had to do his bit. He got me out of there and drove me to his flat.'

'What were you going to do?'

'I don't know.' Jos's shoulders slumped a little. 'He said he'd get some money for me, like that would make it all right. He told me I could stay there for a few days.'

'How much time did he spend with you?'

'Not a lot. He had to go home to his family.' The disgust made her thoughts clear. 'But he thought I should still, you know… told me that at least I wouldn't get pregnant from it.' Her mouth hardened.

'And then the men came…?'

'Yes. Ronnie had just arrived. Said he'd got some money for me. Told me he was going to take me to Manchester. No one would know me there, I could start over, say I was a widow or something.'

'What did you do?'

'I refused.' For a second she blazed. 'Said I wasn't leaving Leeds. Then five minutes later…' She didn't need to finish.

'The men who came, Jocelyn. Is there anything else you've remembered about them?' Lottie asked. 'Anything at all.'

'The thin one had a moustache.' She traced a line over her top lip with her fingertip. 'Just a tiny one, a bit like Douglas Fairbanks.' She paused a second and stared. 'And he had very sad eyes.'

'Who used the knife?'

'The fat one.'

'He seemed to enjoy it?'

A small nod, and the first tear trickled. More would follow. But she had to try for every last piece of information.

'How were they dressed?' she asked urgently.

'Suits. Cheap ones. Caps.' She was blinking hard; in a moment the flood would come.

Lottie reached across and hugged her. 'We'll find them,' she whispered, keeping hold until the girl nodded. 'I have to go and pass this on.'

'Can you come back sometime?' She sounded hopeful, like a little girl.

'Of course I can,' Lottie assured her. 'Of course I can.'

'It's not much more,' McMillan said doubtfully when she gave him the descriptions. 'We already had most of that.'

'Not the moustache,' she pointed out. 'And we didn't know how Jos ended up at the flat.'

'The bit about him having some money and wanting to take her to Manchester interests me.'

'Did you find any money?'

The sergeant shook his head. 'Not on him, in the flat or in the car. The killers might have taken it, of course.'

'Or he could have been lying.'

'Yes.' He lit a cigarette. 'No one said they'd lent him any. He'll probably have a bank account; I'll need to check that.'

'So he could have been planning to take her to Manchester and dump her there.'

'It's possible.' He shrugged. 'But it still doesn't help us find the killers.'

'How many people knew about the flat?' Lottie wondered.

'Some of the criminals in Leeds, obviously,' McMillan answered and made a sour face. 'Still, it would hardly do to say he was living with Mummy and Daddy, would it?'

'I suppose not,' she agreed.

'I don't know.' He flicked the cigarette out of the car window and put the car in gear with a sigh. 'It was worth a try.'

'What now?'

'I keep on looking. And I take you back.' She could see him watching her from the corner of his eye. 'I'm sorry, but that's the arrangement.'

'It's fine,' she told him. But she'd hoped that someone in the brass might have changed their minds.

'You've helped, believe me. I'd keep you working on this if I could. I've told you that.'

'I know. Can you drop me off at City Square, please? On Tuesdays Cathy and I cover the railway stations and the Dark Arches.'

McMillan raised an eyebrow and turned on to Park Row.

'Those places must keep you busy.'

'Sometimes.'

The truth was their patrols had become too effective. The prostitutes and pickpockets made sure they were out of the way whenever the policewomen came around. They'd tried varying the times and days they patrolled the area, but as soon as they were spotted the word passed and people vanished. It was a game they couldn't win. They still had to play it, though.

He pulled over behind a lorry and Lottie opened the door.

'Thank you again,' McMillan said. She gave him a weak smile then marched away, back straight.

'That was quick.' Cathy still had her notebook in her hand, watching a girl amble away through the Arches towards Holbeck. She'd turned at the sound of footsteps.

'A new one?' Lottie nodded at the figure in the distance.

'She says she has a room at the Crown and a job at Dodgson's in Hunslet Mill. Not sure I believe her. She didn't look like she had two farthings to rub together. I daresay we'll see her again. Anyway, what happened?'

She stared at the girl Cathy had talked to until she disappeared round a corner. 'I talked to Jocelyn, found out a little bit more. That's it, really. A thank-you and it was all over. Back to the real world.'

'You haven't missed much. That's been the most excitement I've had today.'

'I think I've seen her before,' Lottie said slowly. 'There's something in the walk. I can't think where, though.'

'Are you sure? She didn't look familiar to me,' Cathy said.

'Maybe I'm wrong.' She looked at her watch. 'I suppose we'd better get on.'

'There's a shoplifter to keep an eye out for, too. She's been seen at the Pygmalion and Matthias Robinson.' She flicked through the notebook until she found the page. 'Early thirties, brunette, long wavy hair, quite big.'

'Oh, with a description like that we'll have her by this afternoon.' Lottie snorted.

They started to walk, pace for pace, down Swinegate towards the bridge across the river. It was a grey day, a small chill on the breeze, the sense of autumn bearing down and another year passing.

The time passed quietly and quickly. She slipped a couple of Thorne's toffees from a paper bag in her pocket and gave Cathy one. It would last them until dinner at the station café. They were finishing the circuit, coming back down Whitehall Road, trying to decide between eating at Lyons or Craven Dairies. New Station was in sight, Cathy chattering away.

'I meant to tell you, I found a lovely dress pattern yesterday after work. A Butterick's one, only a tanner. It'll look—'

Lottie jerked her heard round, following Cathy's gaze to see a boy dart across the street in front of a van.

The driver didn't stand a chance. His brakes shrieked and the back of the van swung round, but it was too late. The lad was flung in the air, landing hard on his back.

Before Lottie could even react, Cathy was already sprinting. Traffic had stopped, the world seemed to have gone silent.

As soon as she began to blow her whistle, things came alive again. Drivers climbed out of their cars.

Cathy was on her knees, cradling the boy's head in her lap. He was still breathing, crying out in pain, one leg bent out at an unnatural angle, blood pooling around his left hand where the fingers were crushed.

Lottie heard a scream and saw a woman dashing across the pavement, clutching a brown paper parcel across her chest. She moved quickly, putting her arms around the woman and holding her back from the child. His mother; from the terror on her face she couldn't be anyone else.

'It looks worse than it is,' Lottie said quietly, her voice even and soothing, hoping she was right. 'There'll be an ambulance here in a minute. You can go to the hospital with him. What's his name?'

'Billy. Billy Kennedy.'

'WPC Taylor's looking after your Billy, Mrs Kennedy. She knows what to do.' She kept her grip until the woman stopped struggling. 'Why don't you tell me what happened.'

'I was only in the shop.' The woman looked over her shoulder as if she could turn back the clock and change everything. 'Billy was outside. I was just paying when I heard the brakes…' She pushed herself forward again, squirming away from Lottie, and falling to her knees beside her son, stroking his face and hair.

The driver of the van was standing by his vehicle. His face was white with shock and he was twisting a cap through his hands.

'I couldn't do anything,' he insisted as Lottie came close. 'He just ran out.' The man raised his eyes to her. 'I tried to stop. He was too close.'

'I know,' she told him. 'We saw it happen.'

'Is he..?' The man couldn't bring himself to say the words.

'Some broken bones, but I don't think he'll die, if that's what you mean.' She glanced over. Billy's face was contorted in pain, but he was talking to his mother. A good sign.

'Thank God for that. I couldn't live with myself.'

'I do need to ask you a few questions.' She took out her notebook.

'Yes,' he agreed quickly. 'Right.'

Everything was in in order. His driver registration had been renewed by the council just two months earlier, his vehicle looked safe enough.

'I've been driving since before the war,' he said. 'I've never had an accident.'

'It wasn't your fault,' she assured him. 'We saw it.'

A constable had arrived to direct traffic carefully around the scene and make room as the ambulance pulled up. Two minutes and Billy Kennedy had gone, his mother with him, off to the infirmary.

Cathy dusted down her uniform skirt. 'Poor lad's more scared of what his dad will do than the hospital.'

'We can't help with that.'

'I know,' Cathy agreed with a sigh. 'Come on, let's get something to eat and I'll go and see how he is.'

It was a dull afternoon on patrol by herself. Not even a tiny incident to spice it up, just plodding the circuit. Plenty of time for her mind to wander, thinking about Jocelyn Hill and the murder.

Not that it gave her any answers. By the time she trudged her way through the market and back to Millgarth she was none the wiser. But how could she be when she didn't have all the information?

Never mind. She'd done what she could. And she would go back to see Jos, exactly as she'd promised. She owed the girl that.

Cathy was waiting outside the station, looking around and trying to seem busy, her notebook in her hand.

'Where have you been all afternoon?' Lottie asked.

'At the hospital with Billy and his mum.' Lottie raised her eyebrows in disbelief. 'Most of the time.' She glanced away.

'And the rest?'

'I started talking to one of the doctors.'

Lottie began to laugh. 'Do you have any idea how terrible you are? You'll flirt with anything in trousers.'

'Not anything… He was lovely. And time just ran away.' Cathy blushed a little. 'Will you cover and say I was with you if she asks?'

'Go on, then. I don't know how you do it.'

'Do what?'

'Get all the men around you.'

'I just find them interesting. Anyway, Jimmy will be home next week.'

'That'll put you back on the straight and narrow for a while.'

'I'll be glad to have him here.' She sounded as if she desperately meant every word.

Lottie knocked on the door, then turned the handle.

'WPC Armstrong, ma'am.'

'WPC Taylor, ma'am.'

Five minutes and they were back outside.

'Is he going to be all right?' Lottie asked. 'Billy, I mean.'

'Broken leg. Two smashed fingers. He's going to be bruised all over. A few weeks in plaster and he'll be running around again like it never happened. He's sweet, really.' There was a strange tenderness in her voice.

'Feeling broody?'

'Sooner or later.' Cathy shrugged. 'Not until Jimmy's home all the time.'

'As long as you make me a godmother.'

'Only if you buy very expensive presents.'

By the time they came out into a shaft of late afternoon sun they were giggling, the day behind them.

'Looks like you have someone waiting for you,' Cathy said.

'Me?' Lottie had to shade her eyes to see. The Peugeot was parked, engine idling. McMillan sat inside, staring directly at her. 'I wonder what he wants.'

'Maybe he fancies you.'

'Give over. I'm married, remember. So is he.'

'Maybe it's nothing, then.' Cathy gave her a small push. 'Go and find out.'

'I didn't know I merited a chauffeur,' Lottie said playfully as she settled on the passenger seat. 'I won't say no. My feet are killing me.'

McMillan hesitated for a moment. 'I'm hoping you can do me a favour.'

'Oh?' She looked at him, waiting for more.

'I'm going to talk to Ronnie Walker's sister again. I spoke to her parents, and she was there but she didn't say anything.'

'She seemed eager enough to talk to you before, as I recall,' Lottie said. 'Even wrote down her telephone number for you.'

'That's why I want you there.' A flush of embarrassment crossed his face. 'I've arranged it with her.'

'You have?' Lottie asked in surprise. 'Would I be doing this officially?'

'No,' he admitted after a second. 'I had to press hard enough to get you this morning. The inspector won't go for more.'

'I could get in trouble. My husband will be expecting me at home.'

'Ring him.' A trace of annoyance in his voice.

'We don't have a telephone.'

'Look, I need your help. I'm certain she knows something. It's a last resort. But she's under twenty-one…'

Not of age. It made sense that he'd want a woman there. But…

'If you're so sure she has information, why not do it officially?' Lottie asked.

'Because her father knows the chief constable and the word's come down. The family's grieving and isn't to be disturbed.' He shook his head, frustrated. 'They want an answer but they won't help us find it. So I'm doing what I can.'

She felt sorry for him. He was caught up by the machinery behind everything when he was trying to do his job.

'All right,' Lottie agreed. 'But if word gets out that I was there?'

'I'll take responsibility,' he said.

She believed him.

CHAPTER SEVEN

McMillan parked on North Lane. Around them, Headingley bustled with shoppers on their way home from work. Queues at the greengrocer and the butcher. Across the street Charlie Brett's fish restaurant was quiet, just opening for the evening.

It was a cottage of dark stone at the far end of the neatly trimmed lawn, the summer flowers in the borders just starting to fade. Inside, the dining room was empty. He chose a table by the window, gazing out at the road.

'This seems like an odd place to meet,' Lottie said as she looked around at the wood panelling on the walls.

'That's why it's good.' He smiled. 'Far enough from where she lives and she's not likely to run into anyone she knows.'

'Clever,' she admitted.

'I've used it before. Two teas for now,' he told the waitress as she arrived with menus.

'Why do you think Irene Walker can help?'

McMillan lit a cigarette and stared at the tip for a moment. 'It's just little things. That night we saw her she seemed a bit too casual about everything. When I talked to the family she'd look away sometimes when her mother told me something, as if she knew it wasn't right. It made me think.' He shrugged. 'It took a while before I could reach her on the telephone. The young lady has a busy social life.'

'Don't they all these days?' Lottie asked.

'Maybe. I'm old, I wouldn't know.' He sipped from the cup, eyes intent on the street.

'What time is she supposed to be here?'

'Half past five.' The same time they'd arrived. She checked her wristwatch. Quarter to six. Not really late yet, not for a girl that age.

But once another fifteen minutes had passed, Lottie was having her doubts. A quarter of an hour more and she was certain.

'She's not coming, is she?'

'Doesn't look like it.' There was a small pile of cigarette butts in the ashtray. 'I might as well give you a lift home. I'm sorry.'

'People get cold feet,' Lottie said as the car pulled up the long hill on Potternewton Lane, the engine straining.

'I know. I'll try and get hold of her again tomorrow. I'm sorry I wasted your time.'

'You weren't to know.' But she was already thinking ahead, wondering what was in the larder that she could cook quickly for tea. She had a tin of baked beans. They could eat those on toast. There were still a couple of Sunday's scones left, too. It wouldn't win any awards, but it would be fine for one night. 'I'm sorry,' she said, realising McMillan had been talking.

'I said I really appreciate you being willing to do this.'

'Pity she never turned up.'

'Armstrong.'

'Yes, ma'am?' Lottie stiffened her back glancing across at Cathy. Mrs Maitland had a face like a storm, lips pressed tight together.

'Upstairs. Now. Detective Inspector Carter wants you.'

'Yes, ma'am.' A tiny shake of her head as Cathy gave her a quizzical look. Had someone seen her with Sergeant

McMillan? But they hadn't done anything wrong; the girl never appeared.

Hand shaking, she knocked on Carter's office door.

'Where were you after your shift yesterday?' No introduction, no shade of warmth in his voice. A pipe sat in the ashtray. His hair was swept back, turning grey, with thick cheeks that hung like jowls.

'Brett's in Headingley, sir. With Detective Sergeant McMillan.' If he was asking the question, he already knew the answer. No point in lying.

'What were you doing there?' His eyes seemed to bore into her.

'We were supposed to meet someone who might have information about the Walker murder, sir.'

'Who?'

'Irene Walker.'

Carter sat back, tapping a pencil in slow time against his blotter. 'And why were you there, Constable?'

'The sergeant asked me, sir. Miss Walker is under age. He thought it would be better to have a woman there, and I'd met her once before.'

'I see,' he answered slowly. 'You know I'd made it clear that your involvement ended after speaking to Miss Hill yesterday?'

'Yes, sir.'

'Sergeant McMillan said he's to blame. He persuaded you.'

At least he'd kept his word, she thought. 'I was happy to agree, sir.' And now she'd be for the high jump. What sort of punishment? A black mark on her record? Suspended?

'How long did you wait for her?'

'Until quarter past six, sir. We arrived at half past five.'

What was happening, she wondered? If he intended to throw the book at her, this was an odd way of doing it.

'I wanted to confirm the sergeant's story,' Carter said slowly. He picked up the pipe, twisting it in his hand. 'You both say the same thing.' He returned it to the ashtray and exhaled. 'Miss Walker left home a little after four o'clock yesterday. She hasn't been back since then and no one's heard from her. And that knowledge doesn't leave this room,' he warned.

'Of course, sir.' She wasn't a gossip. 'But—' Her mind was racing. 'If she's vanished that could mean—'

'It could mean plenty of things. I'm quite aware of that, Constable. Someone could be going after the family. Sergeant McMillan is with them right now'

Lottie wondered why he was telling her all this. There had to be a reason, otherwise he'd leave her in the dark. She waited.

'So far we have a few things. Hints, mostly. It seems that Miss Walker had a wild side.'

'I suspected that when I saw her, sir.'

He took a notebook from his desk, an old school jotter, decorated in ink on the cover with drawings: fashion, décor, the typical imagination of a girl.

'This was in her bedroom, hidden away. It's as close to a diary as we've found.'

'Yes, sir. Might I ask a question?' He nodded. 'How can you be certain she hasn't run away?'

'There's no indication of it. She didn't have a case or anything, according to the maid, and nothing's missing from her bedroom. We're working on the assumption something's scared her or she's been taken. And we're praying it's the first, not the second.' Carter pushed the jotter across the desk. 'There are some things in her book that can only be properly followed up by a woman.' A flicker of distaste crossed his mouth. 'You're not a sensitive type, are you?'

'No, sir.' She tried to stifle a smile.

'Good. Read through that and follow up. You'll need your partner with you.'

'WPC Taylor?'

'Yes. I've cleared it with Mrs Maitland. Report back to me when you're done.'

'Yes, sir.' She couldn't help herself. 'And thank you, sir.'

Carter grunted. 'If it was up to me you'd be out on patrol,' he told her. 'But some of this needs a woman's touch, and McMillan says you're smart.'

'That's very kind of him.' She felt a blush beginning to rise.

'Don't let it go to your head. Anyway, you'll understand what I want you to do when you read this. Remember, we need answers quickly, and I expect you to be discreet.'

It was a dismissal. Lottie picked up the notebook and left, closing the door softly behind her before letting herself smile. Carter might not want it, but she was back on the investigation. Not just her, both of them.

Cathy was waiting at the bottom of the stairs, pacing around. 'What happened?' she hissed. 'Maitland just said to wait for you.'

'We have a job for CID. Both of us.' Lottie held up the notebook. 'Come on, I'll show you.'

They crowded together in the room, chairs side by side as they read. It felt as if they were doing something wrong, hiding away out of sight to poke into Irene Walker's secrets.

She had a schoolgirl's writing, large loops to the letters, tiny drawings off to the side. Some talent as an artist, Lottie thought. She could capture the expression on a face, bring a person alive on the page.

That was interesting, but not as much as the words. Those were like opening a door into a place she'd never imagined.

Irene was a girl who didn't hide her passions. She had crushes on men, crushes on women. Not just the stars she saw on screen at the cinema, but people she met, from shop girls to friends of her father or brother. Every single one of them older, from a few years to a few decades.

A few she'd arranged to meet. Evenings out in town, mostly at the weekend, a Friday or a Saturday night. Details of where they went. But if there was anything more, the girl was coy about that. Lottie turned the page. Blank. Flipping through, she found half the book was empty. Still, there was enough in what she'd written.

'Well,' Cathy said, exhaling slowly. 'That's…'

'The question is, what exactly did she get up to?' Lottie wondered. She went through the pages again, noting down the names. Irene had met four of them, two men and two women. Carter would have his detectives questioning the men. But the man was a prig, that was obvious. He'd want the WPCs to talk to the women. Circumspectly, discreetly.

Olivia Mortimer.

Barbara Tyler.

She read the sections about the women once more, paying close attention to the details. Mortimer was the sister of one of Ronnie's friends, part of the set that ran around Leeds, the one Irene was a little too young to join. There was probably no more than two or three years between them, but Irene seemed to feel it as a huge gulf, one she wanted to bridge. As if she had to prove something, Lottie thought.

'Barbara Tyler,' Cathy said thoughtfully. 'That name rings a bell from somewhere. I just can't place it.'

Tyler was older; that was obvious from the way the girl described her. No age was mentioned, yet a quick sketch by the entry in the diary showed someone slim, fashionable, probably in her early thirties. That would still make a big gap in knowledge, sophistication, in living. One that was apparently very attractive to the young woman.

'I know,' Cathy said suddenly, mouth wide. 'Barbara Tyler. She's the fashion writer for the *Leeds Mercury*.' She turned to stare at Lottie. 'It has to be the same one, doesn't it?'

'Very likely.'

Carter listened. But he wouldn't look at Lottie when she talked about the entries in the diary. When she suggested catching Tyler at work, he was hesitant.

'It's one place we can be certain she'll talk to us, sir. She'll have her own office.'

'You need to be very delicate,' he said finally. 'This might be nothing more than a young girl's imagination. Everyone knows they have flights of fancy. We don't want to accuse anyone.'

'Of course not, sir,' she agreed brightly. But everything Irene put in her book had the ring of truth. That should have been obvious to anyone.

'Very well,' he agreed begrudgingly. 'But if Miss Tyler complains…'

The *Mercury* shared an office with the *Yorkshire Post* on Albion Street; the receptionist was surprised to see a pair of policewomen walk in. When they asked for Barbara Tyler, at first she didn't know what to say.

'Is she here?' Lottie asked.

'Yes. Yes, of course.'

'Could you let her know we'd like to talk to her, please?'

It would be all through the building in a few minutes, rumours rising. What did the police want with her? Lottie didn't care. They had a job to do and a missing young woman to find while she was still alive.

The office boy led them along corridors. The smell of printers' ink seemed to be fixed deep in the walls. Dark stains on the linoleum and a feel of dirt in the air. The lad kept glancing back nervously. Lottie smiled at him and he turned away quickly, embarrassed.

He knocked on a door then stood aside for them to enter. The window in the office looked over an alley behind the building and across to a brick wall. Hardly an inspiration for fashion, Lottie thought.

The woman behind the desk matched the sketch in Irene Walker's diary. The same tilt to the nose, the arch to the eyebrows. Barbara Tyler rose, extending a hand and looking confused.

'Forgive me,' she said. 'Please have a seat. I'm just surprised to see the police here.' She attempted a smile. 'Have I done something wrong?'

She was an elegant woman, tall enough to be imposing, dark hair cut in a neat, fashionable bob. Probably in her mid-thirties, make-up carefully applied to hide the wrinkles by her eyes and mouth. No wedding ring, but a thick bangle of brightly coloured stones and a scarab pendant on a gold chain. A dress that looked like real silk, with soft geometric patterns on the material, and a flowing scarf as thin as gossamer. The scent of Chanel drifted as she moved.

Dresses and blouses hung from a picture rail. Illustrations of clothes were pinned to the wall, copies of *Vogue* piled on top of a bookcase. Lottie watched as Cathy looked around, entranced.

'Miss Tyler, I believe you know Irene Walker?'

'Irene?' He eyebrows knitted together as she frowned, then cleared. 'You mean Jane's daughter. Yes, I suppose I know her a little.' She leaned forward, sensing gossip. 'Why? Does this have something to do with her poor brother?'

'Yes,' Lottie said. 'It's in relation to that. I'm sure you can understand.'

'Of course.' She wouldn't mention murder; that would dampen the answers. And the omission wouldn't be a real lie, just stretching the truth.

'Tell me, have you ever had an evening out with Miss Walker?'

'An evening?' She blinked. 'I'm sorry, I'm not sure what you mean.'

'Maybe a meal, some cocktails.'

'No,' Tyler replied warily. 'I see her here and there, but that's all.' She hesitated for a moment. 'There was one evening I ran into her and we had a drink and a little chat, but that's all. And that's only because I've known her mother for ages. I suppose Irene was six or seven when I first met her.'

'Do you remember how long ago you had your chat?' There were no dates in the diary, no way to even guess when something had happened. Or might have happened: Irene's tale was very different. 'And where?'

'Where?' The question took her by surprise. 'I don't know, it could have been a dozen places. Doesn't she remember?'

'I'm just looking for confirmation,' Lottie told her. The white lies flowed so easily they surprised her. 'When was it, do you recall?'

'A fortnight, maybe?' She thought, staring at the wall, then shrugged. 'Something like that, anyway. You have to understand, I'm out a great deal. It's part of the job.'

'Of course.'

'I don't think I talked to Irene for more than five minutes. Ten at most. Just the usual things, what she was up to, her family.' She pinched her lips together. 'I don't see how this affects…'

'Just questions we need to ask,' Cathy said, taking her eyes from the clothes. 'Do you often see Irene around when you're out?'

'Here and there, I suppose,' the woman admitted after a few seconds. 'Leeds isn't that big. People tend to go to the same places.'

'Is she with anyone special? Or part of a group?'

'I really don't know; I never paid attention.' She narrowed her eyes. 'What's happened?'

'Nothing.' Lottie smiled. 'We have to check things.' They weren't going to get more without giving something in return or letting an important word slip. Better to stop now. At least they were coming away with Barbara Tyler's story, very different from Irene's record of a long evening of food, drink and talk. The question was, which one was telling the truth?

'Is that a Doucet?' Cathy asked as they stood, tilting her head towards a frock half-hidden behind a woman's fitted suit.

'No,' Tyler answered wistfully. 'No one's going to send me a real Doucet. A friend of mine who's a dressmaker ran it up from a photograph. Lovely, isn't it? Just rayon, not silk, unfortunately.'

Out on Albion Street Lottie breathed deeply. After the ink and the perfume, the smell of exhaust and soot was like fresh country air.

Cathy glanced over her shoulder at the building as they strolled away. 'She wasn't expecting us, but she was very cagey, wasn't she?' She paused. 'I'm not certain, but I think I believe her. Did you see her eyes? She didn't look guilty or if she was hiding something.'

That was true enough. But telling a lie was easy enough; Lottie had just proved that herself.

'We still need to find this girl Olivia and talk to her.'

'Do *you* think Barbara Tyler was telling the truth?' Cathy asked.

A few more paces before Lottie answered. 'I don't know.'

Irene could have built a whole castle on a few minutes' quick chat. Girls did that, especially if they had crushes. She remembered what it was like. Still, she'd sensed as grain of truth when she read the diary. Something wasn't quite right. For now she didn't know quite what.

At the station Lottie sat at a desk, pen in hand, trying to write her report for the inspector. The summary of the interview was there, everything Tyler had said about meeting Irene Walker.

But so far she hadn't managed to add a conclusion. Finally she sighed and dipped the nib in the inkwell.

Miss Tyler told her story straightforwardly. But she wasn't able to add any details – not where they ran into each other, or when. Not even what they talked about. That's plausible, but according to Irene they were discussing details of their personal lives. Honestly, I can't tell yet which account is true.

It would have to do. It was true. Still, she felt she'd failed. No definite answer, simply doubts.

As she began to climb the stairs to Inspector Carter's office, McMillan came down.

'Have you found her?' Lottie asked, but he simply shook his head.

'Nothing.' He took her by the elbow, leading her towards an alcove. 'No one's heard a word. I was talking to the parents all morning. They're frantic.'

'Of course they are.' For God's sake, how else would they feel? A son just murdered, and now a daughter who'd vanished.

'They don't understand why anyone would want to go after her.'

'They didn't go after *her*, though, did they? This is about something else, isn't it?'

'It looks that way,' he agreed soberly. 'This changes everything. About Ronnie's murder, too. We were looking at people he knew. That's why we were getting nowhere. Now we're digging into the family.' He gave her a wry smile and nodded at the paper. 'Is that the report on the women from Irene's diary?'

'One of them. We haven't talked to Olivia Mortimer yet. Cathy's finding an address for her.'

He took the report from her hand. 'It's just like the men she's supposed to have gone out with. They both say it was innocent, just ran into her in a club or at a party. Seems like she made it all up.'

'She's young. That happens.'

'Let's just hope she's still alive,' he said quietly.

'Yes.'

'I need to go,' McMillan told her. 'You give this to the inspector then get out and see that last girl. I bet it'll be the same story, but…'

'Yes, Sarge.'

He was already moving away. 'Sorry. Too much to do.'

She left the report on Carter's desk and found Cathy reading the diary again.

'Anything new?'

'Not that I can see.' She closed the book. 'Olivia is at home. I telephoned and a servant answered. Very snippy.'

'Did you tell her who we were?'

Cathy shook her head. 'We'll take her by surprise.'

No car to take them there, just a journey to Hyde Park on the tram as far as Leeds Girls' High School, then a walk back to

North Grange Road. Big, solid houses with long drives and cultivated front gardens. Plenty of money.

There was a Crosley parked in front of the Mortimers' house, the paintwork and chrome gleaming in the light. A beautiful motor car, Lottie thought as she brought the brass knocker down on the door.

The servant eyed them warily. She was in her fifties, boss-eyed, with a large nose and a mouth that curled down at the corners.

'We'd like to see Miss Mortimer,' Lottie told her. 'Olivia.'

The woman snorted, then grudgingly moved aside to let them enter. 'In there,' she said, pointing at a door. 'I'll tell her.'

The room smelt of wax. Afternoon sun through the window caught the dust motes in the air. An empty grate, old furniture made of dark wood, well used. A pair of hunting scenes on the wall. Everything looked as if it had been moved from elsewhere in the house, Lottie decided; a high-class, tidy junk room.

The door opened and she turned her head. Another thin girl, this one no wider than a rail, with pale skin and short, fair hair. How did they get this way, she wondered? They were all like sticks these days. She was about twenty-two or -three, tall, standing straight. A dress that was real, shimmering silk, and a challenging look in her eyes.

'Betty said there were a pair of policewomen here to see me. I didn't believe her.' She cocked her head, looking confused. 'I can't imagine what you want here.'

'Just a few questions,' Lottie explained. 'But they're quite important.'

'That sounds… intriguing.' She picked up a cigarette from a box on the table and lit it. 'Go on.'

'Do you know Irene Walker?'

'Poor Ronnie's sister? Of course I do.' Her eyes widened. 'What's she done?'

'She hasn't done anything, Miss,' Cathy said quietly. 'We just need some information, that's all.'

'Of course.' The girl sobered. 'Yes, I know Irene.'

'Have the two of you ever gone out anywhere together?' Lottie asked. 'A nightclub, maybe?'

'Two or three times.' Olivia Mortimer smiled. She had young, white teeth. 'She's rather sweet. Very eager for life.'

'In what way?'

'Oh… experiences. She wants it all and as soon as possible. She's fun, is Irene.'

'What kind of places have you gone to with her?'

'I remember I took her to the cocktail bar at the Majestic.' A hint of a smile at the memory. 'It was the first time she'd been in one. A couple of nightclubs once. Oh,' she added, 'and slumming, of course.'

'Slumming?' Lottie stared at her curiously.

'A group of us would go in some of the worst places we could find. We started in the Market Tavern—'

'Was Ronnie Walker with you?' Lottie interrupted.

'I don't think he was. Not that night. We knew he went there, wanted to see what it was like.'

Frosty, she imagined, once a rich crowd entered.

'Anywhere else?' She was taking down the details in her notebook. At least this report would have something in it.

'Irene and I went to a place I'd heard about from a chum.' Olivia lowered her voice to a whisper. 'Do you know about the Royal?'

'Yes. You took her in there?'

'It was just a quick drink and then we left. It scared me, if you really want to know. Those people…' She mimed a shudder.

'What about Irene?'

'She was looking around. Eyes wide but *very* interested. I've never been anywhere like it. God knows what it did for her. She wanted to learn, but really she didn't know anything. A babe in the woods.'

'Did you go anywhere else?' Lottie didn't let anything show on her face, even when Cathy looked sharply at her.

'One or two places, I don't remember.'

'Would you say the two of you were close?'

'Close?' She repeated the word, considering it. 'I can't say we were, no. I enjoyed her at times, but that's all. It was a bit of a laugh introducing her to the wicked world, but that passes, doesn't it?' It wasn't a question that needed an answer. 'Does that help you find who killed poor Ronnie?' She frowned. 'I don't see how it connects, though.'

'It's all part of our investigation, Miss Mortimer.' Lottie smiled. 'Tell me, do you know where else Irene liked to go? Her friends?'

'I think she mentioned a couple of friends she'd made at school.' Olivia frowned. 'I don't know, really. She came out with our set when she could. Her parents weren't too keen.'

'Thank you.' Lottie began to rise, sensing Cathy standing beside her. What she'd given them could be important. Or it could be nothing at all.

They'd just missed the tram. Lottie set the pace, walking fast, her face set, arms swinging, as Cathy kept pace.

'God, I feel like I need a bath after a few minutes with her.'

'She just has too much time and money,' Lottie said. 'No purpose in life.'

'She and Irene Walker sound like a pair.'

'Possibly.' She thought of the shameless way the girl had flirted with Sergeant McMillan. 'Or the student might have passed the teacher.'

'What?' Cathy paused and turned. 'What are you talking about?'

'It's just an idea. If Irene was that taken with the Royal she might have gone back on her own.'

'At her age? She'd probably be too scared.'

'It's only a thought, like I said. But it looks as if one of the things in the diary was true.'

'Makes you wonder about all the others?' Cathy asked slowly.

'I don't know. I'm probably a terrible detective. But people wouldn't be likely to admit they'd do those things with an underage girl, would they? I can't even decide if Barbara Tyler was telling the truth.'

'You've done very well so far. They talk to you.'

Lottie blushed. 'Let's see what Inspector Carter says when he sees the report. He'll probably have an apoplexy.'

He scanned it quickly, then in more detail, asking a couple of questions before sitting back and playing with his empty pipe.

As soon as they walked into the station Lottie had felt the atmosphere: hushed, concentrated. One of the men on the beat had found a coat in a bin by the canal. Irene Walker's parents had identified it from a small, mended tear in the lining. Now they were searching the water and everyone expected the worst.

'Did this Mortimer girl tell you the full truth?' Carter asked.

'I believe so, sir.' Lottie stood at attention, Cathy by her side.

He nodded, let the report flutter to the desk and tapped it with a stained fingernail. 'The Royal.'

'Yes, sir.'

'McMillan says you know someone there.'

'I do, sir.'

'Filthy place. I keep telling the magistrates to take away the licence but they won't do it.' Lottie stayed silent. 'It's not too far from the river,' Carter said thoughtfully after a few moments.

From Lower Briggate to the water? It was no more than a couple of hundred yards.

'True, sir.'

'Go and talk to this... person you know. Find out if Miss Walker visited at other times.'

'Yes, sir.'

'And for God's sake be discreet. We don't want this all over the papers. We're trying to keep a lid on everything for now. We'll release the news of the girl's disappearance this evening.'

'Yes, sir.'

'See what answers you can find before then.'

'Looks as if we're going to see Auntie Betty,' Cathy said once they were outside Millgarth. 'She's not going to be happy.'

There was no other way. No McMillan around to go in and pass the word. They had to march straight into the Royal Hotel.

'Ready?' Lottie asked. She took a breath and adjusted her uniform.

'I suppose so.'

The conversation stopped as they entered the women's bar. Heads turned to watch them. Betty scowled as they approached.

'This had better be important,' she warned. 'Business is going to fall off for a week now.'

Lottie heard the scraping of chairs and the soft footsteps as people left.

'Do you think we'd be here if it wasn't, Auntie?'

The woman was wearing a check suit, shirt and a tie with a broad Windsor knot in a pattern of vivid reds and blues.

'Spit it out, then. The sooner you're gone, the sooner things can get back to normal.'

'A girl called Irene Walker. Does the name mean anything?'

She pursed her lips and shook her head slowly. 'No. But I don't know every customer by name.'

'She's young, Auntie. Tries to look older.' She thought back to the time she'd seen the girl and imagined how she'd look with proper make-up. 'Very stylish. Good clothes. Brown hair, bobbed. Probably five feet three. Very slim.'

'She's not my type, but there are some who'd love her.' Betty ran a hand over her chin. 'We get one or two young ones in here. Mostly they're just curious. They'd run a mile if someone talked to them.'

'I think this one might have been more serious.'

'There was someone. Sat over there, watching.' She nodded towards a table in the corner. 'Ended up talking to Hannah for a long time.'

'How long ago was this?'

'A week? I don't know, I lose track.' She sounded exasperated. 'Why does it matter, anyway?'

'We need to find her.' Betty stared but Lottie wasn't going to give her more than that. 'Who's Hannah and how do I find her? It really is important. Urgent.'

'I don't know how to get hold of her.' Before Lottie could protest, Betty held up a hand. 'I'm not lying. I don't. I've no idea how to get in touch with most of the people who come here. The one who could have helped you left right after you came in.'

She looked around anyway, only seeing a couple of faces, drinkers beyond caring.

'What's her name?'

'Alice Sutherland. You're in luck. She's someone I *can* find.'

CHAPTER EIGHT

ALICE Sutherland had a room upstairs at the Royal. The place hadn't been a hotel for years, just a bar, the remainder of it empty. The staircase was cluttered with junk, dust flying up under their feet as they climbed and making Cathy sneeze. Thick cobwebs clung to the corners, layer on layer.

They followed the corridor, shoes sounding sharp on the bare boards. Lottie knocked on the door of number three hundred and sixteen, and waited as it opened an inch and a surprised eye peered out.

'Hello, Alice,' she said with a smile. 'Auntie Betty sent us up. I'm hoping you can help me.'

The room was clean, old and weary but surprisingly neat, free of the mustiness that filled the rest of the building. The window sparkled, looking out over the courts and yards off Lower Briggate.

Alice Sutherland was a tall, trim woman, with intelligent, curious dark eyes in a small face, surrounded by long, wild hair. Perhaps she was forty, Lottie decided, maybe even a little older; it was impossible to be certain. She had a slightly remote air, as if she wasn't quite of this world. But Auntie Betty had warned them she was strange.

'Half the time it's like she's not here and you won't get any sense from her,' she said.

'What about the rest of the time?' Cathy asked.

'Sharp as a tack. Just odd. Something you ought to know,' Betty added as they turned away. 'Alice owns this place.' She waved a hand around. 'Inherited it all. I pay her rent for the bar.'

'You're kidding,' Lottie said.

'I'm completely serious. She's just, I don't know, eccentric. Oh, and she likes women.' She raised an eyebrow and smiled. 'Your friend is just her type.'

Cathy stayed close to the door of the room, quiet and wary.

'Help?' Alice said. 'How?' she cocked her head. 'Are you the police?'

'Yes,' Lottie said. 'We are. I believe you know Irene Walker.'

'Irene?' The woman's eyes widened with fear. 'What's happened to her?'

Lottie felt the hair prickle at the back of her neck. There was something in the way Alice spoke.

'Why would you think something had happened to her, Miss Sutherland?'

'I talked to her.'

'When?'

Alice's eyes narrowed as she thought. 'The day before yesterday,' she answered hesitantly, then gave a nod. 'Yes. Late in the afternoon. She came up here and we talked.'

'Here?' Lottie asked in surprise. 'How did she know where to find you?'

'She'd been here before, of course.' She said it as if it was the most obvious thing in the world. 'Twice.'

'What did you talk about?'

'She seemed very scared. She tried to tell me, but it was all so garbled. She was so pale. Shaking.'

'Can you try to remember?' Lottie could hardly breathe. Her chest was tight. 'It's very important, Miss Sutherland.'

'That they'd killed her brother and they were after her to make her father pay. It just seemed so impossible…' She stopped and stared at Lottie. 'It's true, isn't it?'

'We don't know.' At least she could give a truthful answer to that question. No white lie. 'What was she wearing when she visited?'

'I don't know. She had her coat on the whole time. A mackintosh, camel-coloured.'

The one they discovered down by the water.

'How long was she here? Did she say anything else?'

'Only a few minutes. She said she had to go while she still could. That was very bizarre.' She cocked her head quizzically. 'Don't you think so?'

'Yes.'

'All her words were a jumble.' She paused. 'That's how it seemed, anyway.'

'What time on Wednesday was she here? Late afternoon, you said.'

'I don't know, I wasn't keeping track.' A small, hesitant smile. 'Five, maybe. Or half past.'

When Irene Walker was supposed to be meeting McMillan in Headingley.

'Thank you.'

Now she could take something worthwhile back to Millgarth.

'You said Irene had been here twice before?' Cathy asked quietly. Alice turned to look at her.

'That's right. The first time was when we met downstairs and we came up here. Then she was back a few days later.'

'How long did she stay?'

'A while. I don't see what business it is of—'

'Do you know how old she is?'

The woman shrugged. 'I didn't ask and she didn't say.' Her eyes flashed a challenge.

'Thank you,' Lottie said quickly. She turned and mouthed, 'Enough!' at Cathy. 'We appreciate the help.'

'You know—' Cathy began as soon as they were outside.

'I can guess.' Lottie cut her off. 'It doesn't matter for the moment. We have something concrete. Carter's going to want to know.'

He listened intently.

'She *lives* at the Royal?' he asked when Lottie had finished.

'Yes, sir. Owns it apparently.'

He shook his head in disbelief. 'Well, I'll be… Still, we have something definite. You've done very well,' he admitted reluctantly.

'Thank you, sir.' She could sense Cathy still seething beside her. Say nothing, she'd told her before they entered. Right now it didn't matter what Alice and Irene had done.

'Go down to the canal, down by Crown Point Bridge. See if you can help at all. They've been searching the water down there.'

'We should have told him,' Cathy said as they walked down Wharf Street and towards the Calls.

'Later, I said. He has too much on his plate right now. He wouldn't want to know at the moment.'

What they'd do, she didn't know. And right now she didn't care. She was involved in a proper investigation, officially part of it. She was helping. She'd already made a difference.

It was easy to locate the group of policemen on the bank of the canal. A boat was tied up alongside, bobbing lightly on the water. Three men inside were talking, and one of them looked up and pointed, chatting with the uniforms as he did. He turned his head as the women approached.

The sergeant in charge frowned when he saw them. Davis, Lottie, recalled, the type of man who believed he knew everything.

'Look who's here,' he said loudly, and the three constables beside him glanced over.

'WPCs Armstrong and Taylor reporting. Inspector Carter sent us over, Sarge.'

'Sent you over?' He looked suspicious. 'Why's that, then?'

'To see how we could help, Sarge.'

Davis chuckled. 'Teas for everyone and a round of sandwiches would be a start.'

She put a tight smile on her face, determined to keep her voice even.

'Beg pardon, sir, but I don't think that's what he had in mind.'

'Well, luv, you'd do better to let real coppers take care of the policing. We don't need the tart patrol around here, no matter what the inspector thinks.'

Tart patrol? Lottie breathed in sharply but said nothing. She hadn't heard that one before. But it was no worse than some of the other names they'd been given. And it didn't stop them doing a good job.

'So you don't need us here, Sarge?'

'Of course I don't.' His temper flared for a second. 'Stupid idea sending you down at all.'

She knew all the men were paying attention and relishing her discomfort. She wasn't going to give them the satisfaction of making it obvious.

'Right, Sarge, we'll leave it to you and the boys, then.' She turned and marched away, her face burning, Cathy at her side. In the distance she heard Davis's voice quite clearly:

'Must be bloody mad, sending a couple of bints down here thinking they could do something.'

They strode on.

'I'll swing for him,' Lottie hissed.

'He's not worth it,' Cathy told her. 'There's half a dozen like him on every corner.'

'I know.' She sighed. 'It's just… he doesn't even know it, but we've done more on this than he has.'

'Even if he knew, he wouldn't care. Come on, forget him, he doesn't matter.' Cathy laughed. 'He'll still be a sergeant when we're running the force.' It made them both burst out laughing. Not unlikely; impossible. But a wonderful thought. 'Look, it's almost the end of shift. Too late to do any work. Let's take our time before we report to Maitland.'

Why not? They'd earned their pay today, several times over.

She'd never felt happier to unlock the front door. Home. Upstairs she changed into a cotton frock in the new style with the dropped waist, combed her hair and put on lipstick, then sat on the edge of the bed with her eyes closed, feeling the calm of the place surround her.

The day had been so good, so exciting. Until the end. Davis and the others had ruined it all. She'd felt so proud, then he'd burst the bubble. Tart patrol, indeed.

He was right, that was the problem. WPCs dealt with women and children. Most often with prostitutes. But they still did something worthwhile. She did some good.

Don't let it get to you, she thought. That's what he wants. What they all want.

Lottie sighed. In the kitchen she lit the gas on the new cooker they'd rented after the big home show in Leeds the year before, waited till the kettle boiled and mashed the tea.

She felt comfortable here, more at home than she'd ever been in her mother's house. She'd been glad to get away from there and into digs when she started at Barnbow. It wasn't just the freedom; it felt like the first time in her life that she'd been able to breathe. And if that made her a bad daughter, well, maybe she was. But she had Geoff now.

Lottie smiled, cup in her hand, staring out of the window and down the street. She liked her evenings with the four walls around her. They made her feel comfortable and safe. She'd taken up knitting the winter before. Not that she'd managed anything recognisable yet, but this year she'd try a jumper for Geoff. And a few times she'd made dresses from patterns. Cooking, sewing: the skills girls learned at school. There was a pile of darning waiting for her now. She'd make a start on it later. Perhaps.

Tripe and onions for tea, with mashed potatoes and peas. A can of peaches for afters with some condensed milk. Geoff ate hungrily, talking blithely about his day. She didn't know how he'd been before the war, but these days nothing seemed to worry him too much. He let it wash over and past him.

'So are you really back on this case?' he asked when she told him what had happened. Everything except the encounter with Davis. She'd keep that hidden away, out of sight.

'I'm not sure.'

And really, she didn't know what might happen tomorrow. She daren't even guess.

A little before six he turned on the radio, tuning in the BBC through the static until the sound of Big Ben rang out for the news.

Lottie sat, slowly sipping at her tea as she listened. The newscaster had the usual sort of voice, rounded and smug, completely different from anyone she'd actually met. He skated over the growing unemployment, the sad state of the economy. Then an item that made her sit up sharply.

'Police in Leeds have reported that a girl is missing. Irene Walker, aged eighteen, was last seen the day before yesterday. Her brother Ronald was brutally killed a few days before, and the authorities believe the two incidents may be connected. Anyone with information is asked to urgently contact Leeds Police.'

'Well,' Geoff said as he looked at her. 'It's all out now.'

'It means they haven't found her yet,' Lottie said hopefully. Carter had said he'd release the information during the afternoon. At least they hadn't discovered a body in the canal. She might still be alive.

She didn't even notice the rest of the news as her mind skipped through the afternoon, remembering fragments of conversations and weighing them to see if there was something she'd missed. Anything at all that might help them find Irene. But there was nothing she'd overlooked.

Lottie stirred as Geoff turned off the radio.

'I've been thinking…' he began with a shy smile. 'What would you say about us getting a motorcycle?'

The question took her by surprise. They had their bicycles, and rode out into the country when the weather was good. The year before they'd taken a cycling holiday, four days up in the Dales that left her legs aching for days. But she'd never heard him even mention a motorcycle before.

'Why?'

'We could go to all sorts of places. With a sidecar for you. We can afford it.'

She didn't know how to respond. 'Are you sure?' It was the best she could manage. A silly question. He was well paid, she brought home a wage. They didn't spend much.

'Positive, I've gone over it.' He smiled enthusiastically. 'And the engines are straightforward. I'd be able to do all the repairs.'

'It sounds like you've already made up your mind.'

'Well.' Geoff gave a laugh. 'I know a chap who has one. He's been singing their praises for months.'

'And he's convinced you?'

'I thought perhaps we could take a look on Saturday. Go to a showroom.'

'That's fine,' she agreed. He was like a little boy, the excitement so obvious on his face. 'It could be fun. And only one way to find out, isn't there?'

CHAPTER NINE

STANDING outside Millgarth, Lottie took a breath and stared up at the building. The windows were grimy, unwashed for years, the stone dark from generations of Leeds soot. It had probably looked grand when it was built. Now it was simply there, part of the fabric of the city. Worn, useful, not quite cared for, but home to her now, in a curious way.

She had no idea what she'd be doing today. More on Irene Walker's disappearance? Back on patrol with Cathy? The tart patrol. That still stung.

'Armstrong,' Mrs Maitland said. 'Sergeant McMillan wants you upstairs. Taylor, you're on your own today.'

'Lucky dog,' Cathy whispered as they left the office. 'Even if he is happily married.'

'We talked to the Walkers till we're blue in the face,' McMillan said as they clattered back down the stairs and out to the Peugeot. 'They're completely broken by what's happened—' He held up a hand before she could speak. 'I know, anyone would be. But I can't get anything out of them about *why* it's happened. Who's after them and why. They know, I can see it in their eyes, but they're too scared to tell me.'

'Why do you want me there?'

'I need you to sit down with Mrs Walker. See if you can get her to open up to you. We still have no idea where Irene is, if she's even dead or alive. Every copper in Leeds has his eyes open for her. The mother's going through hell. You might be able to start her talking.' He stared at her. 'I'm not kidding. We're desperate. I've tried everything I know short of bullying.'

'I'll do what I can.' It was a tall order. 'One thing.'

'What?'

'On the way out there, could we stop by the infirmary? I'd like to see Jocelyn Hill. Just for five minutes.' They'd gone this long without finding anything, a short while longer couldn't make any difference.

He shrugged. 'As long as it's quick. I mean it, Lottie, we need something very soon.'

The girl's hair was brushed, her eyes alert. Her face showed some of the ache and the pain, but she seemed more settled and comfortable.

'I said I'd come back,' Lottie told her. 'I'm afraid I can't stay, though. How do you feel?'

'A little better. It still hurts.'

Inside as well as out, Lottie was certain. The wounds that didn't show

'Have they said how low long you'll be in?'

'A few more days. I suppose I'll have to go back to my mam and dad's after that.'

'Maybe it won't be too bad.' Hopeful words. Probably wasted, though; she'd met Jos's mother. There'd be little love and sympathy in that house. She reached out and lightly squeezed the girl's hand. 'Chin up.'

'I did remember something else,' Jocelyn said quietly. 'About when it happened.'

'What?' She leaned closer, her eyes intent on the girl's face.

'The thin one, with the fair hair. He had a wart on the back on his hand. Right here.' She rubbed the spot with a fingertip. 'I know it was a wart, my little brother gets them. And the other called him Don. I heard it just before I passed out.'

'Don? Are you sure?'

Jocelyn nodded slowly. 'It came back to me.'

'Thank you.'

'Is it right what they're saying about Ronnie's sister? That she's vanished?'

'Yes. We're trying to find her.'

'God. How could anyone do that? Their parents…'

'I don't know. We'll find out who did it.' She stood. 'You get some rest. And you know something?'

'What?'

'When you get back to Cross Green you might find there's someone who's happy to see you.'

For a moment Jos looked confused.

'Ray, you mean? Ray Coleman.'

'Yes. If it hadn't been for him we might not have found you.'

'But he's just a boy.' The corners of her mouth turned down.

'Sometimes that's not a bad thing.'

'You got that out of her?' McMillan was impressed. He parked on the street across from the Walker's house. A constable stood guard at the end of the drive.

'She remembered it.'

'Doesn't matter. We can use it. Now let's see if you can use your magic on Jane Walker. Get her on her own and press her. Gently, though.'

'What's she like?'

'Quiet,' he answered after a moment. 'Not surprising. She's been crying a lot.'

It wasn't what she wanted to know, but she'd find out soon enough. The servant led them through to the morning room. A fire was burning, even this early in the season, making the room hot and close. The air of tension and despair was so thick she could almost cut it.

Mrs Walker was huddled in on herself, looking cold in spite of the warmth. Her arms were tightly folded across her stomach and she seemed to be staring at nothing. There was a shocked softness to her face, with deep shadows under red-rimmed eyes. Her hair was fashionably short, but unwashed and dull. She wore a cardigan pulled over a blouse, a skirt reaching down to her calves.

Her husband sat in a chair on the other side of the hearth, back very straight. Benjamin Walker had a bristle of grey hair across his scalp, a thick moustache and a fixed, determined expression. Suit, tie, everything formal and ordered. Lottie felt someone watching her. She turned her head, seeing McMillan's pleading expression.

'Hello, Mrs Walker. I'm WPC Armstrong.' She knelt by the woman, placing a hand lightly on her arm. 'Do you think you could show me Irene's room?'

Jane Walker nodded lightly and rose. She moved like an old woman, shoulders slumped, arms still clutched around herself. Lottie followed her up an oak-panelled staircase that smelt of beeswax, down a hallway and into a bedroom that looked out over a long back garden.

'Here.' It was the first word she'd said, husky, empty.

The room was colourful, bright silk scarves hanging from the back of the door, a fashionable dress in red and gold on a hanger, still with a price tag. Bed, wardrobe, dressing table with a jumble of cosmetics spilling across the top. Nothing that seemed to show who Irene Walker really was.

'That sergeant already looked in the drawers,' the woman said. 'I watched him.'

If he'd found anything useful, apart from the notebook, he'd have told her. She stared at the mother, seeing her whole history in her eyes. Strict upbringing, obedience drilled into her with discipline, cowed even before she was married then far more after so many years wearing a wedding ring.

'What's Irene like?'

'She wants to be grown up so badly.' Jane Walker gave a sad little smile. 'She thinks that will make everything fine. She'll learn.'

'No magic answer, is there?'

'No. She thinks I don't know about a lot of the things she does. But mothers hear.' She sighed, staring at Lottie. 'I just want her back safe and sound, that's all.'

'We'll bring her home.'

The tears were brimming. Lottie reached out and hugged her, feeling the other woman's head against her shoulder, her body shuddering as she sobbed silently. A son dead, a daughter vanished: who could keep all those feelings inside?

It lasted five minutes and more. Lottie stroked and patted her back as if she was a child, feeling everything drain out of Mrs Walker. But she needed to release it. Finally the shaking slowed and the crying became tiny snuffles.

'Come on, sit down.'

They sat on the bed. Lottie kept an arm around the woman's shoulders. Jane Walker fumbled in her sleeve, bringing out a small handkerchief, dabbing at her eyes and rubbing her nose.

'We're trying to find her,' Lottie said. 'But we need all the help we can get. You understand that, don't you?'

'Yes.' It came out tentatively, then a little more firmly. 'Yes, of course.'

Lottie kept her voice gentle. 'We can't bring Ronnie back, but whoever did that must have taken Irene. If we know why, we can find them.'

'I can't.' Her mouth closed to a thin, pale line.

'Someone killed Ronnie. Someone has Irene. We have to find them, Mrs Walker.' She was close. Lottie could feel the tension in the woman's body. 'They're your *children*.'

She could hear Jane Walker's breathing, sense her mind working, trying to build up the courage to speak.

'I believe my husband owes a great deal of money,' she said finally.

'Who to?'

'He won't say.' Her fingers kneaded the handkerchief. 'He won't even tell me *if* he does. But I'm sure of it. Benjamin has a business. His factory makes boots. He used to export all over the Empire. The government bought a lot during the war. Since then…'

Lottie knew the story. She'd read it so many times in the newspapers. The colonies had developed their own industries. British goods had become more expensive. All over the country, factories had closed their doors, men were on the dole. She saw them every day when she was on patrol, looking hungry and cowed.

'It's failing. I honestly believe it is,' Mrs Walker finished.

'Couldn't he sell it as a going concern?' Lottie wanted to take her time, to tease it all out, to get everything she could.

'Who'd want to buy it? One look at the books and they'd know the truth. I can see it in his face, even if he won't say a word.'

'What about the bank? Can't they help him?'

She shook her head. 'Why would they lose money by helping a business that's going to end up bankrupt? No one would.'

'Do you think he's borrowed money from someone?'

'Oh yes.' Her voice was chillingly certain. 'He thinks I don't know how bad everything is. But I've looked at the figures when he's not here.' She stared at Lottie. 'I'm not a fool. He won't admit it, but borrowing is the only way he can keep going. I told him a year ago we should sell this place, but he won't do it.' She frowned. 'Pride. Stupid bloody pride.' She began to cry again, pressing her fists against her face, as if they could contain all the sorrow.

'How certain are you?'

'Positive. Benjamin always said he could make it work if he only had a little more money. But all it did was make the world fall apart.'

Lottie tried to frame her words carefully. How could she say it without reproach? 'You should have told us everything after they killed your son.'

'Told you what?' she asked sharply. 'All I have are my suspicions. I can't prove a thing and Benjamin is never going to admit it. He didn't when Ronnie was murdered. He hasn't since they took Irene.'

Lottie squeezed the woman's hand. 'We can find her and bring her back. Then we can hang the killers for your son's murder.'

'You can't stop them.' Her voice was empty.

'Talk to your husband,' Lottie told her. 'Persuade him to tell Sergeant McMillan everything he knows. It's the only way. He has to.'

'I've talked and begged until I lost my voice. But if he does that, he's shown he's a failure. Everyone will know.' She snorted. 'And Benjamin Walker could never accept that.'

For God's sake, Lottie thought, wasn't his daughter's life worth more than his pride? What kind of man would put his pride ahead of his own children? She could feel her anger rising and tamped it firmly down.

One life lost, maybe two, all because of a man's pride. 'I have to tell Sergeant McMillan,' Lottie said.

'I know.' Her voice was solemn. 'He still won't pry a word out of Benjamin. I can tell you that right now.'

'Whoever took your daughter and killed your son doesn't have anything to lose. You understand that, don't you?'

Jane Walker raised a pair of terrified eyes. 'That won't make a scrap of difference to him. Believe me.'

'The sergeant will find out.' He had to. She stood, helping the woman to her feet. 'Come on. It's time.'

She waited at the bottom of the stairs, hearing male voices. Mrs Walker clattered down behind, head held high, jaw clenched tight.

'I'll take Mr McMillan outside and tell him,' Lottie explained. 'After that it's up to him.'

They stood on either side of the Peugeot. The sergeant rested his elbows on the roofs, moving a lit cigarette through his fingers as he listened.

'All she really has is suspicion,' he said once Lottie had finished. 'No proof.'

'She's certain. It fits the facts, you have to admit that.'

'Or she made it fit them.'

'Come on, you don't believe that. You're the one who brought me out her to talk to her,' she reminded him. 'That's what she told me. And I believe her.'

He tossed the end of the cigarette into the gutter, took out another and lit it.

'I need to talk to the inspector,' he said. 'Walker has clout. If I start on him…' He shrugged.

'And meanwhile someone has Irene Walker,' Lottie said coldly.

'I'm well aware of that, Constable,' he replied. 'Get in. We'll go back to Millgarth.'

They barely spoke on the journey. She could feel his frustration and anger, but nothing she had to say would help.

In the car park she walked away, patting her hat down over her hair.

'Lottie,' he said.

'Sarge?'

'Thank you.'

'Part of the job.'

CHAPTER TEN

SHAFTON Street, over in Holbeck. Cathy was already there. Back-to-back houses in blocks of eight, a gap for the outside privies, then more houses.

Number thirty-seven was exactly the same as its neighbours. The only thing to mark it was the crowd of women gathered across the street, talking and watching the front door. Lottie felt their eyes on her as she strode up and knocked hard.

A few seconds, the snick of the lock, and she was in the front room, standing next to Cathy. The room smelt of mould, a stain of damp over the distemper up by the ceiling.

'The doctor telephoned the station just before I left. He'd been called in first thing this morning. Bad case of septicaemia.'

Lottie glanced at her. They both knew what that meant. An abortion that had gone wrong.

'Where is she?'

'Hospital. It took forever to get an ambulance here. She's only sixteen, poor thing.' Even younger than Jocelyn Hill. Cathy frowned and shook her head. 'I tried to talk to her but she was off her head with pain. The doctor had given her something but it didn't seem to help much.'

'What about the family?'

'Mother's gone with her. Three sisters and an aunt.' She nodded towards the scullery. 'They're all in there.'

'Father?' Lottie asked. 'Husband?'

'Father's at work.' Cathy sighed. 'They sent the youngest but he hasn't come. Can't afford to lose the money. The girl doesn't have a husband. That's why she was having the abortion.'

They'd seen it before. They'd probably see it many times in the future. That didn't make it any easier. No one talked about abortions, but they happened all the time. Not just in streets like this or Cross Green; perfectly respectable girls found themselves in the family way, too.

Often there was no problem with it. But when there was… usually the girl died. Left it too late before calling for help, too many complications.

'Is she going to survive?' she asked.

Cathy shook her head and shrugged. 'It didn't look good. I'm just going over to the hospital. I'll leave you to question them.'

'Right.' She took out her notebook. 'Better give me the details.'

Hannah Moorcroft. Born July ninth, 1908. Spinster. Unemployed. There was nothing more to tell.

'You didn't get the midwife's name?' Lottie asked.

'Haven't had a chance. I'd better go.'

'Watch yourself.' She grinned. 'There's a coven waiting across the street.'

'I'll think pure thoughts.'

'There's a first time for everything.'

Three girls. Jocelyn Hill. Irene Walker. Now there was Hannah Moorcroft. Lottie took a breath and walked into the scullery.

The girls wore pinafores over their dresses. The oldest was perhaps fourteen, the others younger, probably just too old for school. Eleven and twelve, maybe. The woman sitting at the old, wobbly table had an austere air of religion. She was dressed all in black, from her small hat to the boots on her feet, her only decoration a worn gold wedding ring. A face covered with lines, cheeks sunken where she'd lost most of her teeth and a fierce, fixed expression in her eyes.

'I'm WPC Armstrong.'

'Evelyn Richards.' The woman gave a small nod. 'Hannah's mother is my sister. I live just over on Rydall Place.' A few streets away, next to the factory. But she'd know the area.

Lottie pointed to the teapot keeping warm on the range. 'Is there another cup in that?' It was always a good way to begin. It put people at ease, let them feel busy, in charge in their homes, even in the worst situation.

'Honor,' Mrs Richards said, and the oldest girl moved to fill a cup and set it down by the milk jug and sugar bowl.

'I think you know what I need to ask,' Lottie said after taking a sip. Long enough in the pot to be strong but not stewed.

'You three, out for a few minutes,' Mrs Richards ordered the girls. 'It's grown-up talk.' As they filed out she raised her voice. 'But don't you go far.'

The back door slammed; they were alone.

'Who?' Lottie said.

The woman shook her head. 'I don't know. And before you start, I'm chapel and I don't approve of what our Hannah did. Not how she got it or how she got rid.' She waited until Lottie nodded her understanding. 'The first I knew was this morning when young Harriet come for me.'

'You live around here. You know what goes on.'

'Not that, though.'

'The midwife?'

'Mrs Brady?' Her gaze was firm. 'Never. Not in a hundred years.'

'Someone did it.'

'You'll need to ask Hannah, unless the Lord takes her for what she did. Or my sister. But from the look on her face when I walked through that door I doubt she knows, either. I'll tell you this, though: there'll be the devil to pay with her da.'

'Who was the baby's father, Mrs Richards?' The woman's eyes flickered; she knew. 'Well?'

'Bobby Denham. You'll not find him round here now, though. Ran off to join the merchant marine as soon as he discovered our Hannah was in the family way and we've not seen a sign of him since. That were six weeks ago. So he's had nowt to do with this.'

'How far along was she?'

'Three months, near as. Poor little lass.' It was heartfelt, but full of the kind of fatalism she'd seen before. Hannah Moorcroft would probably die. That was in God's hands. And if she did she'd be going to a better place. Maybe it really did help people cope.

'Do you have any idea who could have done it?'

'I don't, luv, and that's the truth.' She looked Lottie straight in the eye.

There was nothing more to be learned here.

'You said Mrs Brady's the midwife around here. Where does she live?'

'Brown Lane East, just off the moor. But I told you it weren't her.'

Lottie smiled as she stood. 'I believe you, don't worry. Maybe she'll have an idea or two.'

She was at the corner when she heard the footsteps and turned. The oldest girl from the Moorcroft house. Honor. The resolute look had gone from her mouth. It was all fear now.

'Is Hannah going to die, Miss?'

There was no point in giving false hope.

'I don't know.' The girl's face fell. 'I haven't seen her. They'll do everything they can at the infirmary. You know what happened, don't you?'

'Course.' But that was no surprise.

'Do you know who did it, Honor?'

The girl shook her head. 'All I know is she went out yesterday afternoon. When she came back she said she didn't feel too well and went to bed. It got worse during the night and she started screaming with pain after me dad left for work. That's when mam sent for Auntie Evie and the doctor.'

'Why don't you show me where Mrs Brady lives?' Lottie asked. The girl brightened. She needed company, a little warmth. 'Tell me about your sister.'

'Not much to say. She's daft half the time. But she's pretty and I love her.'

'What about Bobby Denham?'

'He's a waste of breath.' Honor snorted. 'Everyone saw it but our Hannah. He was good-looking and he always had a bob or two to spend. Thought he was the bees' knees and she lapped it up.'

'What happened when she told him she was having a baby?'

'She came back over the moon. He'd promised he'd be over the next day and talk about the wedding. Morning comes and everyone's saying he's scarpered. I told her she was better rid of him but she just cried her eyes out.'

Pregnant, humiliated. No wonder she wanted an abortion.

'That's Mrs Brady's over there,' the girl said. 'Number five.'

'Thank you.' She needed to give Honor some hope, if nothing more. 'I know the people at the infirmary. They're very good, they'll do everything they can.'

'Yes.' A tight, scared nod and the girl was running off.

There was no answer at number five when she knocked.

'She's over at the Bartlett's,' a neighbour told her. 'Delivering twins.'

'Do you know how long she'll be?'

The woman gave her a withering look. 'As long as it takes. They're not trains, they don't come on a timetable.'

Stupid question. 'I'll try her again later.'

Cathy was still at the hospital. Lottie gave her report to Mrs Maitland then stood in the queue, waiting for her tram. People pressed all around, some giving her uniform curious looks, most too absorbed in their own thoughts to notice.

She'd always wanted a job that would test her. Barnbow had been exacting, but once her shift was over she could leave it all behind her until the next day. She'd hoped that she'd find what she needed as a policewoman. But most of the problems were easy, solved in a few minutes, hours at most. Then again, what they covered was limited. Tart patrol, she thought angrily. But it had all changed with Jocelyn Hill. Since the moment they'd gone to the home for unwed mothers, everything seemed different.

They filled her thoughts: Jos, Ronnie, Irene and Jane Walker, now Hannah Moorcroft and her sisters. All their pain and fear. She was involved. It might only be for a short while, but it made the job seem worthwhile. Even the guilt she felt at their misery was fine.

Walking up Sholebroke Avenue she heard a handbell in the distance as the muffin man made his rounds. The orderliness of it made her smile.

The paper lay on the table. Geoff might have left it there by accident, but she knew him better than that. It was quite deliberately in the way for her to see. An advertisement for the

BSA Model L. And he was right; she read it. Most of the details meant nothing, it didn't matter to her if it was a three-speed gearbox with a 349cc side-valve engine as long as it started and stopped properly.

The shape was sleek. It looked fast. Just one seat. Lottie tried to imagine how she'd feel in a sidecar. Scared at first, she was certain. But after that… She smiled. He'd been right; it had worked. She was interested.

She left it sitting as she served the liver and onions. The radio hummed and crackled as the valves warmed up and a pale, lemony sun came through the windows.

'Do you want to go on Saturday?' she asked.

'Go?'

She nodded towards the advert. 'To take a look at one.'

He smiled hopefully. 'Do you think you'd like one?'

'I'd like to see it.' That was as far as she was willing to go for now. Probably they'd be driving home with one, but she wasn't going to let him win quite so easily. He'd be ready to go first thing on Saturday morning, waiting for her, as eager as a child going on an adventure.

'Good.' By now he was beaming, the meal forgotten. 'I've been talking to a few more chaps who ride. They say there's nothing like it.'

A little later, standing in the kitchen and drying the plates, she thought about something he'd told her: 'One fellow said that riding is what freedom must feel like.' It seemed an odd phrase. Disturbing. They had freedom, didn't they? Wasn't that what the war had been about?

CHAPTER ELEVEN

THE words came back to her as the tram wobbled its way down Chapeltown Road. She didn't understand them any more than she had the night before. Never mind, she told herself; it doesn't matter.

As soon as she reached the station Lottie asked about Irene Walker. No sign yet. The father was being questioned; he knew something. Thank God, she thought; maybe something will move. Was there news about Hannah Moorcroft? All she received were shrugs and blank looks. The girl hadn't been important enough to remember. From the front desk she telephoned through to the infirmary, waiting patiently to be connected to the ward sister.

Still alive, the nurse told her warily. At first they didn't think she'd last. But she had some strength. A fighting chance; that was as far as she'd go.

'Thank you,' Lottie said.

'That other policewoman…'

'WPC Taylor?'

'Yes.' The sister's voice softened. 'She was here past midnight, just sitting, being there and talking to the mother. I'm sure it helped.'

'I'm sure it did.' Lottie smiled to herself. She knew full well that Cathy had a soft side; she just rarely allowed herself to show it.

Standing in Mrs Maitland's office, Cathy's face showed the long night. Deep smudges under her eyes, her skin pale.

'So Miss Moorcroft is likely to survive?'

'The doctors are hopeful, ma'am,' Cathy said.

'Right, then I want the pair of you following up on this. Ignore the patrol today. Find out who did this so we can arrest them have them up in court.' Mrs Maitland's voice was cold and deliberate. 'Any questions?'

'No, ma'am.'

If Hannah had died the detectives would have taken over the case quickly enough. Alive, she was just another minor problem. But it was theirs. They were going to find out who'd nearly killed her.

'Armstrong, I want to talk to you before you go.'

She waited until the door had clicked shut.

'Sergeant McMillan had high praise for what you did yesterday.'

'Thank you, ma'am.'

'He and Inspector Carter want you available in case they need you again.'

She could feel the flush on her face and the pulse beating fast in her neck. It wasn't all over. They felt she still had something to offer.

'Yes, ma'am.' It came out as a croak. Lottie cleared her throat and repeated, 'Yes, ma'am.'

'The inspector suggested that you telephone to the desk sergeant every hour. If there are any instructions for you, he'll pass them on. Is that clear?' Lottie nodded. 'Then dismissed.'

'You must be over the moon,' Cathy said as they marched over the bridge and into Holbeck. 'You're a popular girl.'

'Let's see if they need me first,' Lottie warned. 'Anyway, we've got more important things right now. Did Hannah's mother tell you anything?'

'Didn't know a thing about the abortion until her daughter came home and started feeling poorly. That's what she claims, anyway.'

'Do you believe her?'

'Yes,' Cathy said with a sigh. 'We talked for a long time. She was telling the truth.'

'What about Hannah's friends?'

'I've got their names. It was too late to start last night.'

'I heard. I rang the infirmary this morning.'

'Oh.' She began to blush, then grinned. 'Hush. You did the same with Jos.'

'We need to talk to the local midwife. No one thinks she did it but she might have some ideas. Start there and move on to the friends?'

'You're the brains.'

'Don't say that,' Lottie laughed. 'You'll scare me.'

Mrs Brady knew nothing. She'd heard; everyone in the area knew, and mouthed a silent prayer when she heard Hannah was likely to survive. She was in her sixties, and wore a dress that reached her ankles; she had powerful forearms and long, delicate fingers.

'I brought her into the world. Her sisters, too, and their cousins. But I've no idea who could have done that. I wouldn't. I couldn't, it's not right.'

'Who might?'

'If I knew, I'd tell you.'

Two of Hannah's friends were at work, the pair of them at Hunslet Mill. Luckier than many round here, Lottie thought. The pubs were full of men from the time they opened, but they nursed their drinks like treasure, making them last, knowing to the last farthing how much they had to spend.

A third friend, Frances Grogan, was at home. No job to go to. She sat at the table in the kitchen.

She knew. It was obvious from the way she shifted on her chair and kept turning away, not looking them in the eye.

'Do you know what happened when Hannah went for her abortion?' Cathy asked. She was sitting across the table, watching Frances move a tea mug over the oilcloth. Lottie stood in the doorway, behind the girl, listening carefully. Not that there'd been anything worthwhile to hear. 'Well?' Cathy said.

'No.'

'Frances... please, look at me.' The girl raised her head slowly. 'Your friend almost died. Do you understand that?' A hesitation and a nod. 'It could still happen. And it'll be a long time before she's well again.'

'I went to the infirmary last night,' said Frances. 'They wouldn't let me in to see her. They said she already had two visitors.'

'I was there with her mother. Tell me, had she tried other things before the abortion?'

'Pennyroyal. She came over when me mam were out. Made some tea from it then drank it until she was sick but it didn't shift anything. And raspberry leaf. Even tried falling down the stairs. Didn't do no good.'

'You know who she went to, don't you?'

A long pause before Frances nodded. 'Miss Jackson. Over in Hunslet. I asked, me cousin told me.'

'Where in Hunslet?'

'Primrose Lane. She... me cousin said she were good. She promised me.' The girl began to cry, shoulders shaking.

'I don't want anything to happen to Hannah. I don't want her to die. She's the best friend I've got.'

'I'm sure Miss Jackson only wanted to help.' Lottie watched Cathy. Her face was gentle and open, her voice soothing. She was good at this, with a kindness that seemed to start deep inside her. 'What's her house number on Primrose Lane?'

'It's a blue door. That's how everybody knows it.'

They'd find it quickly enough. It made sense that the girls would look for someone who wasn't too local. Word spread. Gossip. Hannah had already been humiliated once, by a young man. She didn't need more elsewhere.

A few more minutes, long enough for Cathy to assure the girl that she wasn't in trouble, but still scare her enough to keep her on the straight and narrow.

The women across the street had all gone behind their front doors. Everything was quiet. No little children playing on the cobbles. Only the boom and grind of the factories in the distance and the smell of soot on the air.

At the corner shop Lottie used the telephone to call the station. No, the sergeant told her, amusement in his voice, CID hadn't been asking for her.

'We can probably find a tram to take us over to Hunslet,' said Lottie.

'Let's just walk.'

Lottie glanced at her. Cathy was always in a rush to do everything. 'If you want.'

'I got a letter in the post this morning,' Cathy said after a short while.

'Who from? Jimmy?' Lottie asked. As soon as she said the words she knew it was a stupid question. Who else would be likely to write to her?

Cathy nodded. 'He says this is his last voyage. He's handed in his papers. No more merchant marine. He thinks it's time we settled down properly and started a family.'

'That's wonderful.' She stopped herself. 'Why didn't you say something before?'

'He said someone's been telling his brother things about me.'

'What things?'

'Running around and seeing other men.' Her face crumpled for a moment. 'God, what am I going to do?'

'It's all innocent. That's what you told me.'

'It is,' Cathy insisted. 'Just some company. None of… you know. But how am I going to make him believe that?'

'When's he due back?'

'Tomorrow.'

Lottie glanced at Cathy and found her dabbing away tears. 'I thought this was what you wanted.'

'I know. I *do*.' She sounded lost.

'You'll really have to leave the men high and dry now.'

'Don't, please,' Cathy begged. 'It was just flirting. Fun.'

'I know,' Lottie told her. 'Honestly, I do.'

'Last time he was home he was talking about having children.' Cathy was silent for a while. 'I got a copy of that book.'

'What book?'

Cathy lowered her voice. '*Married Love*.'

It wasn't as if she needed to keep it secret. Most of the women Lottie knew owned a copy or had borrowed one. It must have sold in the thousands and thousands. Millions maybe.

'What about it?'

'Well, I want to keep this job for a little while. And seeing what happened to Hannah… I want to make sure me and

Jimmy are careful before we start a family, that's all.' She paused for a heartbeat. 'If he still wants me.'

Birth control, contraception. Those were the things Marie Stopes's book discussed. The things women needed to know, but so many didn't. It told them to enjoy their marriages but that they didn't have to spend their lives churning out babies, and how to make sure it didn't happen. Lottie had thumbed through a copy. Not that it mattered to her, not with Geoff's injuries, but it was sound advice.

'He wants you. Why would he come back otherwise? He loves you.'

What else could she say? Cathy was bright. And after a while in this job, not much was likely to embarrass her. She had Jimmy wrapped around her little finger; she'd said so often. He couldn't do enough to please her. But by the sound of it she was going to need all her wiles.

'I hope so.'

Time to change the subject, she decided. Get her thinking about something else for a little while.

'You did well with Frances.'

'Did I?' Cathy's face brightened; she looked relieved at the fresh topic. 'I felt sorry for her. You could see how scared she was.'

'We'll see what this Miss Jackson has to say for herself.'

It wouldn't be easy. Unless she admitted it, or Hannah gave evidence, they had no proof. CID wasn't likely to investigate something like this. That set her thinking about Jos again. Then Irene Walker, out there somewhere and maybe still alive. She took a deep breath.

'Once you're used to it you'll like having Jimmy around all the time,' Lottie said.

'Will I?' Cathy sounded doubtful. 'He might believe his brother and kick me out.'

'He won't. Trust me.'

'I never.'

The blue door stood open behind her. Miss Jackson faced them down, arms folded and face set. She didn't care if the neighbours heard. She seemed to want it. Already one or two had gathered to watch.

'Miss Jackson…' Cathy said.

'You accuse me again and I'll have you for slander.' There was a glint of fury in the woman's eyes.

'We're asking you a question.' Lottie needed to keep the peace before things turned nasty. 'Nothing more than that.'

'And I've given you my answer.'

'You have to understand. We were told, we have to check.'

'Aye, and who told you? Probably some flibbertigibbet.' Her voice was loud enough to carry across the street.

'Why don't we talk about this inside?' Without a crowd, the woman might calm down.

'We'll say what we have to say out here.' The woman squared her thin shoulders like a boxer. 'I've nowt to be ashamed of. Not like you two.'

'You've never met Hannah Moorcroft?' Cathy asked, ignoring the comment. 'Never heard of her?'

'Not until you mentioned her. And if I see her, I'll box her ears for her, accusing me like that.'

'You'll have a hard job. She's in hospital with septicaemia.'

It shut the woman up.

'Are you saying I'm responsible?' she asked after a moment.

'We're asking,' Cathy insisted.

'You talk to anyone round here. They'll tell you I've been delivering babies for donkey's years. I bring them into the world, I don't kill them, and I won't have anyone saying otherwise.'

Lottie tapped Cathy on the elbow. There was no point in asking any more. Miss Jackson would deny everything, and they'd end up looking like fools.

'We won't take any more of your time,' Cathy told the woman.

'I should hope not. Shouldn't have been here in the first place, harassing innocent people.' As they started to walk away she raised her voice. 'You know they said I'm a killer? Coming here to accuse me. No proof.'

It was a relief to turn the corner. The voice faded to nothing. Cathy's face looked grim when Lottie glanced at her, face brick-red with embarrassment.

'We're going to have to wait until Hannah can talk.'

'I know,' she said through clenched teeth.

'It was worth a try,' Lottie said. 'She might have felt guilty and admitted everything. Still,' she added with a smile, 'if she's responsible, it'll be a bigger pleasure to take her in.'

'True.' Cathy glanced at her watch. 'Isn't it time for you to ring in again and see if you're in demand?'

Once more there was nothing.

'Would you mind patrolling on your own?' Cathy asked. 'I want to pop over to the infirmary. Maybe Hannah's woken up.'

'Meet for dinner at half twelve?'

'Kardomah? If you haven't been called to action before, of course.'

'Fat chance of that. They just want to keep me dangling.'

'How is she?' asked Lottie later on at the Kardomah.

'They have her on something to help her sleep.' Cathy sipped the cup of coffee and took a bite of her meat paste sandwich. 'The nurse said she'll be fine in time, but she won't ever be able to have a baby.'

'She's going to live,' Lottie said quietly. 'That's something.'

'I know.' Cathy pushed the plate away and started to reach for her cigarettes. 'I forgot. Not when we're in uniform. I have an appointment at the hairdresser after work. She was willing to squeeze me in.'

'To look nice for Jimmy?'

Cathy smiled. 'I'm going to sit him down and have a talk. Tell him the truth and hope he believes me.' She gave a small, wan smile. 'It's all I can do.'

'You'll win him over.' She tried to sound certain. 'Have your talk, then it can be honeymoon for a while.'

'Did I ever tell you what our honeymoon was like? One night in a hotel before he had to rejoin his ship.' She raised an eyebrow.

'Give him months of honeymoon and he'll soon forget the rest.'

They both smiled.

'You know, we could pop back to Millgarth,' said Cathy. 'It's only a few minutes' walk, easier than finding a telephone. I can give Mrs Maitland the report on Hannah.'

The station was just through County Arcade and down the hill. Lottie finished her tea and signalled the waitress for the bill. 'You just want to sneak off into the loo for a cigarette.'

'Me?' Cathy put a hand to her chest. 'I'm shocked you'd even think that. Just give me an extra five minutes when we're there.'

CHAPTER TWELVE

'WHERE have you been?' McMillan asked as he saw her.

'Sarge?' Lottie turned to face him while Cathy marched on along the corridor.

'You were supposed to ring in every hour.'

'I did. But every time, the sergeant said there wasn't any message for me.'

'He said that?' McMillan took a breath. 'Come with me.'

The desk sergeant stood to attention behind the counter.

'What were your orders this morning, Sergeant Berwick?'

'In what regard, sir?' He was a heavy, florid man, a map of broken veins across his nose and cheeks, his top lip hidden under a heavy grey moustache.

'With regard to messages for a woman police constable.'

'That she would ring in every hour and I should pass anything on to her.'

'Then why didn't you?'

The desk sergeant stared daggers at Lottie. 'Because I never received a telephone call from her, sir. I'd have passed any message on otherwise.'

'That's—' she began, but McMillan cut her off.

'What if I say I know that's a lie?'

The sergeant drew himself up. 'Then it would be your word against mine.'

'The inspector will be talking to you. I daresay he'll ask for a statement.'

'Whatever he wants.'

'How many times have you been reprimanded, Berwick. Three?'

'Twice.' The man stayed at attention, staring straight ahead now.

'Then the third time might bounce you off the force.' He took Lottie by the elbow. 'Come on, I've needed you all morning.'

'Why?' She followed him out to the car.

'Jane Walker went out last night,' he told her. 'Guess what?'

'She hasn't come back.'

'You're on the money. We have coppers all over looking for her. I'm surprised you hadn't heard.'

How would she? Whoever told the women anything?

'Isn't there a constable on their house?'

'She told him she was popping down to the shops and drove off. He didn't think anything of it until later.'

'What about her husband?'

'The inspector's been questioning him half the night and most of the morning. Says he doesn't know where she's gone. He thinks she might have gone hysterical under the pressure.'

'What?' Lottie asked with her hand tight on the door handle of the Peugeot.

'You know what he means.'

'I do.' Her voice was cold.

'People do crack up.' He slid into the driver's seat. 'I saw it in the trenches.'

She thought of some of the shell-shocked men she'd seen wandering in town during the war in their blue hospital jackets. They looked lost, overwhelmed by the world. Even now there were plenty of them around, six years after the Armistice. Yes, they did break. Maybe Jane Walker had, too. But it wouldn't have been her fault.

'Where are we going?'

'Back to the Walker's house. I'd like you to talk to the servant, see if she knows anything. I tried, but she just began crying.'

'I'll do what I can.'

'We've talked to Mrs Walker's friends. None of them have heard from her.'

She knew enough to use the door at the back of the house. For servants and tradesmen. She found the woman there, blackleading the range.

'Hello.'

The servant turned sharply, eyes taking in Lottie's uniform. 'You've been here before.'

Her hair was tucked under a starched white cap, her black dress neat and clean, a long apron covered in stains from the morning's work. She had a thin, feral face, with suspicious eyes and a small, pursed mouth.

'That's right, I have.' She sat down at the table. 'I'd like to ask you a few questions.'

'I have my job to do.'

'This is part of your job,' Lottie said. 'You want Mrs Walker and Irene back, don't you?'

'Course.' She bristled. 'What are you saying?'

'You probably know everything that's going on in the house.'

'Some of it.' The woman's voice was wary.

'What's your name?'

'Shelagh. For my nana.'

'How long have things been bad around here, Shelagh?' She needed to start the woman talking, let things build before asking the big questions.

'Months. Sometimes the air between the mister and missus were so thick you could cut it with a knife. I'd walk in where they were and want to walk straight out again, it were that bad.' She shook her head at the memory.

'What was the problem?'

'He owes money. Couldn't help but hear them talking about it. And then that telephone would ring late at night, after I were in bed. Could hear him muttering away on it, trying to be quiet. Afterwards he'd be up a while.'

'What happened after Ronnie was killed?'

'I didn't believe it when one of your lot came to tell us. None of us did. Who'd want to do that? I came when he were ten, he was still a little lad to me.'

'What did Mrs Walker do?'

'She was screaming and crying. Blamed her husband. He knew it was his fault but, well, too late then, wasn't it? He said she had to keep quiet or it would get worse.'

'You heard him tell her that?'

Shelagh lifted her head. 'I don't lie.'

'What was she like when Irene vanished?'

'She's been terrified ever since. You saw her.'

'Do you know where she could have gone when she left here yesterday?'

'I didn't even know she'd left until that copper on the gate came for his cuppa and said she hadn't come back.'

'Where do you think she'd go? You know her.' This was the important question. Lottie held her breath, hoping for an answer.

Shelagh hesitated and glanced away before answering. 'She likes Eccup Reservoir. It's peaceful up there, she says. A good place to think.'

It was somewhere to start. The chair scraped over the flagstones as Lottie stood up.

'What was she wearing yesterday? Do you remember?'

'Your sergeant asked me that. Tweed skirt, blouse, cardigan. And her coat.'

'What colour is her coat?'

'Royal blue.' Shelagh smiled. 'Had it for years, she has. Says it's so bright it always makes her feel better.'

'Eccup Reservoir,' Lottie said as she climbed into the car. 'Evidently Jane Walker likes to go there.'

McMillan banged his palm again the steering wheel. 'Why the hell didn't the woman tell me that? We could have been looking already.' He slipped the car into gear. 'We're going to need some men out there to search.'

Lottie had cycled out to Eccup with Geoff during the summer, carrying a picnic that they ate in a field looking over the water before riding home. But she'd never walked by the reservoir, she didn't know all the roads.

A phone call to the station, then McMillan dodged through the traffic to Alwoodley and beyond.

'There's talk that Walker was a profiteer during the war,' he said. 'Overcharged the government, provided sub-standard boots for the troops. Plenty of motive for hurting him and his family.'

'Mrs Walker and the servant both said he owed money.'

'I daresay he does. I'm just thinking out loud, trying to find connections. We're getting nothing from Walker himself. Just sits on his bloody pride. Excuse my French.'

He became quiet. Soon enough he was driving along a thin, rutted road with dry stone walls on either side, before pulling over near a dusty track.

'It's the other side of those,' he said, pointing at a wide grove of trees. 'Come on, we'll make a start. It's going to be a while before anyone else arrives.'

She followed him down the slope. 'Why do you know Eccup so well?'

He turned his head and gave her a wink. 'I did a lot of my courting out here.'

Suddenly he raised an arm. 'There's something – see it?'

The glint of light on glass. He began to run, stumbling twice but never quite falling.

'It's her car!' McMillan shouted. 'No one inside.'

A Crosley, cream and light blue. Dust from the track covered the coachwork and windows. The bonnet was cold; no one had driven it in hours. And no sign of anyone nearby. Only birdsong broke the silence.

He turned his head from side to side, chewing on his lower lip. 'You go that way, I'll go this. Use your whistle if you find her.'

The path was overgrown. Blackberry bushes with their big, awkward thorns, nettles that crept too close, burrs that clung to the skirt of her uniform. But no sign of Jane Walker, no hint of a royal blue coat anywhere.

Lottie found a dead branch, carrying it to push the brambles away as she moved along the trail. She could hear the call of a magpie, the stutter of a woodpecker somewhere, even a quiet plop on the water as a fish surfaced momentarily.

The dirt under her feet was dry and hard, no footprints, nothing to help her at all. The undergrowth was thick enough to hide an army; anyone could crawl off in there and never be found. It was going to take dozens of men to search the area properly. Two of them walking round, it was simply hoping Lady Luck would smile on them.

They met on the far side of the reservoir.

'Carry on,' McMillan told her. 'Maybe you'll see something I missed.'

He pushed his trilby back on his head and looked up at the sky. High cloud and hazy, thin sun. If they hadn't been working it would have felt like a beautiful autumn day.

At first she saw nothing but the greens and browns of the trees and plants and the long, grey stretch of water. Then, as the path turned, she noticed a place where the grass and bushes were bent, as if someone had forced their way through. Slowly, she followed along, glancing around and looking for… she didn't know what.

About twenty yards away, behind a thick of blackberry bushes, she walked into a copse of beeches. The air was still. Sitting on the ground, her back against one of the tree trunks, was Jane Walker.

Lottie felt for a pulse in the woman's wrist, but as soon as she touched the skin she knew it was hopeless. The flesh was cold and waxy, hard under her fingertips. Jane Walker's eyes were empty, staring off into the branches. Her left hand was stretched out, a brown bottle of pills in her palm, the metal cap missing.

And the blue coat was buttoned tight around her body.

McMillan was out of breath, panting as he looked down at the body. Not even ten minutes has passed since she'd stood and started blowing the whistle, but it seemed like hours. The birds had flown off at the noise, leaving her completely alone with Jane Walker's corpse.

Lottie was careful to disturb as little as possible, moving away, exactly as she'd learned during training. Back then, though, no one had expected a policewoman would ever really see a dead body. Now she'd seen two of them in a week.

'God,' he said sadly. 'Why here?'

'She probably liked it. Thought it was peaceful.'

'But…' he began, then shook his head. 'Maybe you're right. Did you take a look at that bottle?'

'No.'

'Doesn't matter. I can see it later. You think she killed herself?'

'Do you think she didn't?' This was her secret spot, a place she came when she needed to get away from the world. This time the leaving had been permanent. There was no sign of a struggle, no indication that it had been anything but deliberate. Maybe Jane Walker knew there was nothing she could do, and this was the only grace she could find.

McMillan interrupted her thoughts. 'There should be a few uniforms out here soon. They can stand guard until the coroner's van arrives.' He frowned. 'It's going to be a right job getting the body out. Once someone comes I'll take you back to town. There's nothing you can do here.' He took out a handkerchief as he approached the corpse, and used it to wrap the bottle and slip it into his jacket pocket. 'Fingerprints,' he explained.

'There's nothing else,' Lottie told him. 'I couldn't even find the cap.'

Another quarter of an hour until they heard the shouts and the sergeant guided the men over. They didn't talk; she didn't feel like idle conversation and he smoked, leaning against a tree.

Lottie felt as if the wood was closing in around her, pressing down on her lungs. Too much death around, perhaps. Back in the open air she breathed deeply.

'The first few always get to you,' McMillan said as they walked back up the rutted track to the car.

'How many have you seen?'

'Hundreds. Thousands. The war.'

'Of course. Sorry.'

'But enough on this job. Accidents, mostly. Suicides. One or two murders.' He stopped himself. 'What did you do during the fighting?'

'I was a Barnbow Canary.'

'Were you there for the explosion?'

'I started two days later.' The smell of cordite had still been heavy in the air, men removing what was left of room forty-two, where it had happened. Thirty-five women dead, dozens more in hospital. And not a word in the newspapers because of the war effort. She remembered stepping through the gates, feeling the atmosphere and wondering what she'd got herself into. So long ago now that it might have happened to someone else, something she'd read in a book or a magazine.

'My sister was there,' he told her as he drove back down the lane. 'She was injured. Lost her right arm and her right eye.'

'I'm sorry.' What else could she say? It was as if seeing a corpse brought out all the reflections of death.

He shrugged. 'My parents look after her.'

He parked outside Millgarth.

'I need to telephone the coroner,' McMillan said. 'You did excellent work out there. We might never have found her otherwise.'

'They'd have spotted her once they began searching,' she said. It was no more than the truth.

'You did it sooner.' He cast an eye over at the desk; no uniformed sergeant behind it right now. 'I'll get the proof you rang in this morning. We don't need people like Sergeant Berwick in the police. Not if we're going to be a proper force.'

Nothing more on Irene Walker, she learned back at Millgarth. The girl wouldn't know about her mother; maybe she'd never learn, Lottie thought as she left the station to find Cathy. But she'd no idea where her partner could have gone. Following something about Hannah Moorcroft? She couldn't find her as she covered the patrol. No one seemed to have seen her.

But she was there in Mrs Maitland's office as the shift ended.

'Nothing to add, ma'am,' Cathy said. 'I've written everything down.' She nodded at the report waiting on the desk. 'I can't do anything else until I take a statement from Miss Moorcroft.'

'And have you been given any indication when that might be?

'It should be tomorrow, ma'am. She's recovering but they're worried by the infection.'

The woman gave a curt nod then turned to look at Lottie. 'I hear you've been causing trouble, Armstrong.'

The words took her by surprise. 'Ma'am?'

'Sergeant Berwick. He claims you disobeyed orders to ring in every hour.'

'With respect, ma'am, he's lying.'

'I was there when she telephoned,' Cathy added. 'I know WPC Armstrong is telling the truth.'

'I've no doubt you are,' Mrs Maitland told Lottie. 'I've told Inspector Carter you are.' She lowered her voice. 'The sergeant has said many times that he doesn't believe women belong in the police. He doesn't think any of us should be here. I have an assurance that if Berwick is proved to be a liar, he'll be sacked.'

'I used a telephone at a shop,' Lottie said. 'They'll be able to tell anyone.'

'Very good. Write down where you were when you rang and they'll follow up tomorrow.'

'Yes, ma'am.' She scribbled in her notebook and tore out the page.

'Dismissed.'

'I need to dash,' Cathy said. 'I saw a lovely frock in a shop window. I've just got time to try it on before I go to the hairdresser.'

'You'll look a picture for him tomorrow.'

'Let's hope he thinks so. God, I'm scared to see him.' She let out a breath. 'At least old Berwick will get what's coming. I never liked him, always leering at me.'

'We'll see. Off you go, you can't keep a good hairdresser waiting.'

She was waiting for the tram, seeing Jane Walker's body in her mind, the blue coat buttoned tight. Even when the car horn sounded she didn't pay attention until someone nudged her.

McMillan in the Peugeot, staring at her and grinning. She made her excuses as she pushed through the queue.

'What are you doing?' Lottie asked as she closed the passenger door behind her, feeling embarrassed. 'This is becoming a habit.'

'I was passing and I saw you. Thought you might like a lift.'

'That's very kind, but…'

'I'm going back to Eccup. I want to take a proper look at Mrs Walker's car before it's dark.'

'Have you seen her husband?'

'Yes. The inspector's had him most of the day. Kept exactly the same look when I told him. Didn't say a word about it. You'd think… I don't know,' he said with a frown. 'Maybe it's me. I'd fall apart if my wife killed herself.'

'I think most people would,' she told him quietly. 'They'd blame themselves.'

'Whatever he's feeling, he's not showing it.'

They stayed silent as he kept a steady speed through Sheepscar and up Chapeltown Road.

'We're getting absolutely nowhere,' McMillan said finally. She could hear the frustration and anger simmering in his voice. 'Two dead, one missing, another girl in hospital and we still don't have a bloody clue who's behind it.'

'Not even a single lead?'

'I think we've talked to most of the criminals in Leeds and not one of them knows anything.'

'*Someone* must,' she said.

'Walker,' he replied emptily. 'And he's not saying a word. I don't know if his pride is more important than his family or if there's something else going on.'

'What?'

'I don't know. The inspector keeps hammering at him and getting nothing and the rest of us might be banging our heads against a brick wall for all the progress we make. I've never known anything like it. It doesn't make any sense.'

'I'm sorry,' Lottie said, then added, 'Do you think you'll need me again?' Unless they found Irene alive, what could there be for her to do?

'I don't know,' he answered. 'It's probably not what you want to hear.'

'Better to be honest.' She managed a smile. 'You can just let me off on the main road, it's fine.'

He parked in front of the greengrocer, boxes of apples and a few late tomatoes in their crates, a pile of bright bananas in the window.

'You did a wonderful job today,' McMillan told her as she stood on the pavement. 'Outstanding police work. I told the inspector that.'

'Thank you,' Lottie said. 'And thank you for the lift.' She felt flustered, not sure what else to say. She liked the praise but knew the memory of discovering the body in the wood would stay for a lifetime.

Put it away, she thought as she walked up the street. Be ordinary. What could she make for tea? Fry up a little skirt of beef, maybe, some Bisto to thicken the gravy. Potatoes and a tin of peas. Easy and quick.

A few minutes later she was home and changed, an apron over her housedress, peeling potatoes and dropping them into salted water. Everyday things. But however much she tried to lose herself in them, they couldn't banish the thoughts that crept from the back of her mind. Jos, Jane, the image of lost Irene.

She heard the key in the lock and Geoff came through to the kitchen. He was beaming, face flushed, dirt and soot on his cheeks, tie askew.

'My God, what on earth happened to you?' Lottie asked. 'You're…' She didn't even know. There were no injuries she could see.

'Turn all that off and come outside. Come on.' He held out his hand. She took it and followed, curious.

It was there, at the curb. The paint shone glossy green on the fuel tank, the chrome of the handlebars sparkled. And bolted to the side, a dark metal sidecar. She turned to him, not sure what she felt more: joy at the surprise or anger that he'd spent money without asking her.

'I thought we were going to wait until the weekend.'

'I know.' He had the grace to look sheepish. 'But I was just saying that to see if you were interested. A chap at work was selling his, it's only six months old and the price was good.' He held up his hands. 'I know. I'm sorry. But it's a bargain, honestly. Hardly any miles on it.' He beamed, full of pride at his new toy. 'Anyway, we can take it out on Saturday instead of shopping for one.'

Carefully, Lottie climbed into the sidecar. The seat seemed comfortable enough. She was aware of net curtains twitching across the road and smiled. At least there was something for them to see.

'I thought we might go for a spin,' Geoff suggested.

'After tea,' she told him, and wondered what she ought to wear.

She was surprised. He seemed to understand the machine, to control it quite easily. Lottie had wondered how scared she'd be, but by the time they reached the Old Red Lion out along the York Road, she felt comfortable and safe. Just buffeted by the wind.

'Well?' Geoff asked with pride as he dismounted, 'what do you think?'

'It's more fun than I expected. Colder, too.' She'd put on a heavy coat but could still feel it on her face. 'I need goggles or something.'

'Me too.' He rubbed at the grit in his eye. 'Better dress up warm next time. Come on, a quick drink then home again?'

'You shouldn't have spent the money without talking to me first,' Lottie said, picking up her gin and tonic. They'd started the conversation at home but she wasn't ready to let it drop yet.

'I'm sorry.' He gave her a rueful look. 'But you have to admit it was worth every penny.'

'That's not the point,' she said. 'We're married, we're supposed to make decisions together.'

'I know.' He played with his pint glass, looking like a chastened schoolboy. She wasn't really angry, she just wanted to remind him that he didn't run everything.

'Just don't do it again.' She put her hand over his. 'Please.'

'I won't,' he answered with a smile. 'Promise.'

It was dusk as they rode home, the headlight picking out figures on the pavement, the shadows of parked cars. It was different, thrilling. And being so low, just above the road in the sidecar, she felt every bump and dip.

She could get used to this, Lottie decided as he helped her out. And whoever said that about the freedom was right.

CHAPTER THIRTEEN

'YOUR hair looks wonderful.'

Cathy smiled and primped herself. 'Do you think Jimmy will like it? The hairdresser did a beautiful job.'

'He'll love it,' Lottie assured her.

'I bought the dress, too. I'll change as soon as I'm home so I'll be ready.' Her smile started to waver.

'When's he due?' Lottie asked quickly.

'Eight, he said. Look at me.' She held up a shaking hand.

'Talk to him. He'll believe you.'

'God, I hope so.' She didn't sound certain.

'We have a shift to do first. Hannah Moorcroft,' Lottie reminded her.

'She drifts in and out of consciousness,' the ward sister told them. Her uniform was crisp, the apron and cap startling white. She had a brisk manner, used to being obeyed without question. 'Even when she's with us she doesn't make much sense. I can't allow you to interview her.'

'We need to find out who's responsible for her being here.' Cathy's voice was just as firm. 'She's the only one who can say.'

'Not this morning. The doctor hasn't seen her yet. He might want to change her medicines.'

'You do realise that while we're standing here, some other girl could be ending her pregnancy?' Cathy asked. 'That she might end up in the same condition as Hannah?'

The sister sniffed and pursed her lips. She wasn't used to being challenged, Lottie thought.

'You'll still need to wait until the doctor gives his permission.'

'That's fine,' Cathy agreed. 'What's his name?'

'Doctor Harrison.'

'Where can I find him?'

'At his rooms, I'd imagine. In Park Square. He does his consultations before he comes for rounds.'

'We'll go there.' She turned on her heel and marched away, leaving Lottie to follow.

'Snotty madam,' Cathy said as they crossed the Headrow by the Town Hall. The building was black, towering high above them. Lottie glanced up. It had been part of her life since she was a little girl. Going into town with her mother she always wanted to watch the clocks strike the hour in the Grand and County arcades, laughing at the mechanical display of figures. Then it would be along the Headrow to stand on the open space in front of the Town Hall for a minute. What had happened to that child, she wondered? When did she lose that sense of wonder? 'Thinks she owns the place,' Cathy continued.

'It's her ward; what she says is law.'

'Not if a doctor overrules her.'

'If you can persuade him.'

Cathy grinned. 'He's a man. Of course I can.' She realised what she'd just said. 'The last time, honestly. Apart from Jimmy.'

That was the beauty of the policewoman's uniform, Lottie thought. It made people uncomfortable. Within five minutes they were sitting in Doctor Harrison's consulting room. He had expensive rooms in one of the houses on the north side of Park Square, all elaborate flocked wallpaper and dark wood. Older women with fox stoles sat in the waiting room.

He was in his late forties, a man with a hint of Douglas Fairbanks in his looks, dressed in a lounge suit that hadn't come from the Fifty Shilling Tailors.

'How may I help you?' He took a cigarette from a box on his desk and lit it. The heady smell of Turkish tobacco filled the room.

Cathy explained the situation. As she finished, she slowly crossed her legs, smiling as he heard the swish of the stockings. 'We need to talk to her as soon as we can.' Another smile. 'I'm sure you understand, Doctor.'

'Of course,' he agreed, watching her carefully. 'But we have to be certain she's well enough to answer. I'm sure you can see that, Constable.'

'We'd be very grateful if you could arrange something. If she's not too poorly.'

Harrison look at his wristwatch. 'I have rounds in an hour. Why don't you go back to the ward after dinner? I'll leave instructions that you can talk to Miss Moorcroft if she's able.'

'Thank you.'

'It's nothing.' He stood to show them out. 'And if there's anything else I can do to help you…'

'I'll be certain to ask.' Cathy beamed at him.

'See, I told you it would be easy,' Cathy said as they sat in the Craven Dairies restaurant on Boar Lane.

'For you,' Lottie pointed out.

'He's a man. Honestly, give them a kind smile and they're putty.'

'That's what you think. Sometimes they do what they like. Geoff bought a motorbike without even telling me first.'

'You're kidding.'

Lottie explained as she ate her ham sandwich and sipped at a cup of tea.

'I suppose I don't mind too much, really,' she finished. 'I can't remember the last time I saw him looking so pleased.'

'He'll be out tinkering with it every weekend,' Cathy warned. 'There's one down our way. He has his bike in bits so often it never goes anywhere.'

'I'll make sure it's not like that,' Lottie said. 'But I did let him know it annoyed me. He won't do that again.'

'Until the next time.'

Lottie hoped not.

'You talk to Hannah,' Lottie said as they walked into the infirmary, the harsh smell of antiseptic all around. 'You've done all the work on this so far.'

'Don't you want to be there?' Cathy asked in surprise. 'Where are you going?'

'I thought I'd see Jocelyn Hill. They'll be sending her home soon.'

'I'd forgotten. There's been so much.'

'She's where it all starts,' Lottie said. 'Her and Ronnie.'

The ward was spotless, the nurses busy changing one of the beds. The girl sat in bed, hands above the covers, staring at nothing. Her hair was washed, brushed until it shone, and there was colour in her cheeks.

But what was she like inside? Did she manage to sleep at night? Lottie couldn't know, she'd never know. And there was little she could do.

'Hello, Jos.'

Jocelyn turned her head quickly. 'Hello.' No expression on her face, no pleasure. But at least no pain.

'You're looking better.' She settled on to the chair.

Jocelyn shrugged. 'I suppose so.'

'Home soon?'

The girl's mouth drooped. 'Tomorrow. Do you remember Ray?'

'Of course.' The young man who'd set them on Jos's trail. The one who carried a torch for her.

'He's coming for me. Bringing some clothes.' She smiled. 'Said we could take a taxi an' all.'

'You could do a lot worse than him.'

'I know. But… well, no one's going to want me now. Not after, you know.' Absently she rubbed her stomach, where the baby had once been.

'You wait,' Lottie told her. 'Ray's hardly running away, is he?'

'No,' she agreed. 'Have you found Ronnie's sister yet?'

'Not yet.' Lottie hesitated. Should she tell the girl about Jane Walker? The news would be out soon enough. 'Her mother killed herself.'

'What?' Her face contorted. 'Oh God, no.'

'I'm afraid so.'

The tears began, and Jos dabbed at them with the back of her hand as she apologised. But few of them were for Jane Walker, Lottie thought. Some for Ronnie; most for her murdered baby. It would be a long time before those stopped flowing, if they ever did.

'Is there anything else you've remembered? Even a little something? It might help us. We don't want anyone else hurt, Jos.' But the girl just shook her head, hair swinging like a curtain. Lottie stroked her arm. 'You just look after yourself. And give Ray a chance. He thinks the world of you.'

She was a few yards away when Jocelyn said quietly, 'I don't know what it means but there might be something.'

'What?'

'You know how you remember things when you're not expecting it?' Jos asked, looking down at her hands.

'Yes.' Was this how information happened, she wondered, drip by drip?

'Last night, just before I went to sleep, something popped into my head.' Lottie didn't interrupt; better to let her say it in her own time. 'It must have been after I thought I'd passed out, after the fat one stabbed me and kicked me. Or maybe I was on the edge, I don't know. Suddenly I could hear him saying "You'll have to tell Donough you banged up the car."' She looked up. 'That's all. I'm sorry.'

'Donough?'

'Yes. I'm sure I didn't imagine it. I've never even heard the name before.'

'That's wonderful. Thank you.' She didn't know if it helped, if it even meant anything. But it was one more piece for the puzzle. Perhaps McMillan would understand. 'Please, look after yourself.'

At the switchboard they let her use the telephone. A new desk sergeant at Millgarth, a voice she didn't recognise, then McMillan was on the line.

'Donough?' he asked when she'd finished. 'You're certain?'

'That's what Jos told me,' Lottie said. 'Why?'

'It's—' he began. 'Never mind. Are you still at the infirmary?'

'Yes.'

'Stay there. I'll come and pick you up.'

'All right,' she replied, but he'd gone. For a moment she stared at the receiver, then put it down gently. She'd find out soon enough.

'I've been looking all over for you.' Cathy was standing outside, hiding a cigarette in her cupped palm.

'McMillan's on his way over. He wants me for something.'

'Very mysterious. I got a name from Hannah.'

'Miss Jackson?'

'Mrs Manningham. I've never heard of her. No address. She didn't remember, or she didn't want to say. Somewhere in Hunslet, that's all. How long will you be?'

'I don't know,' Lottie told her. 'I don't even know why he wants me.'

'You love it. He can't resist you.'

'Oh, give over.' She smiled and shook her head. 'But it looks like you'll get to find Mrs Manningham without me.'

'I'll tell you all about it later.' The Peugeot pulled up at the far end of the car park and the horn sounded. 'His Master's Voice. You'd better go.'

'What's so urgent?' she asked as he pulled out on to Great George Street.

'What did Miss Hill tell you?' McMillan asked as he drove. A cigarette hung from his mouth and he squinted against the smoke.

'I already said.'

'Word for word.'

'"You'll have to tell Donough you banged up the car." That's what Jos said she heard. Who is he, anyway?'

'James Donough,' he said with a smile. 'The type of man you spend a career hoping to get in court.'

'I don't understand,' Lottie said.

'We've been certain for years that he's behind a number of things. It started during the war. The thing is, he's clever.

He keeps everything at arm's length. There's never anything to connect him. It's all done through companies, nothing to prove he's involved.' He grimaced. 'It's modern crime and he's good at it.'

'What do you want me to do?' Lottie asked. She didn't understand why he'd brought her along.

'He's a widower, but he's bound to have staff. Grand house: you understand. Talk to them, especially the women.'

'I can try,' she said doubtfully. If he was that clever, he wouldn't be letting the servants know his business.

'This is the closest I've come to having anything on him.'

'But you don't,' Lottie pointed out. 'Not really.' Something a woman might have heard, spoken by a man they hadn't found. It was thin as gauze and he knew it.

'I'm going to make him think we have more. Try and put the wind up him a little. If you get the chance to plant a few seeds with the servants…'

'I will.'

Far Headingley. She felt she could almost smell the money in the air. Big, well-kept houses. Large, expensive motor cars in the drives, the fronts gardens lovingly tended.

'Welcome to the world of the rich,' McMillan said.

She went to the back door, knocked, then walked into the kitchen. A new gas cooker stood next to the old range. A geyser for hot water by the stone sink. The old world and the new, side by side.

A woman in a black dress and white apron bustled into the room, soles hard on the flagstone floor, stopping suddenly when she saw Lottie.

'You almost gave me a heart attack.'

'I'm sorry,' she began, then stopped, taken aback. 'Aren't you Andrea Baldwin?'

'I am,' the woman admitted as she stared. 'Do I know you? You're dressed like a copper.'

'I'm a policewoman. Lottie Armstrong.' The woman looked none the wiser. 'Lottie. Lottie Thomas when you knew me.'

Barnbow. There'd been thousands of them there during the war, making the shells. Andrea had been in Shed 40, there since the fighting began and the first of the girls were employed. The two of them had shared digs for two months late in 1918 after Lottie had left her previous lodgings. Never friends, but they'd known each other, gossiping over meals, travelling to and from work together.

'Lottie?' She seemed to peer, not quite believing. 'Go on, it can't be.' She laughed. 'You, a rozzer? I'd never have expected that.'

'I couldn't have pictured you as a domestic, Andrea. Not after the factory.'

The woman's smile vanished. She shrugged, putting a pile of tea towels on the table. 'Didn't have much choice. No work around, they told me it was take a job as a servant or starve.'

'What's it like? Big place.'

'There are three of us so it's not too bad. I'm the housekeeper, I live in, up in the attic. Mr Donough could be worse, I suppose. Why are you here, any road?'

'Your employer. My detective sergeant thinks he's a criminal. Behind all sorts of things, evidently.'

'Mr Donough?' Andrea asked in disbelief. 'He can't be. Come on, sit yourself down. I'll put the kettle on.'

She'd worked there almost a year, it turned out. There'd been other jobs after Barnbow. Another factory until the soldiers were home, working in a shop for a while and then a mill. But that had closed and she'd joined all the others, too many people chasing too little work.

'Are you serious about Mr Donough being a crook?'

'That's what the sergeant said. Don't be fooled by the uniform, I don't have much in the way of authority. And they don't tell me more than they have to.' A thought struck her. 'Does your boss get many visitors?'

'A fair few, I suppose. He's in business.'

Lottie described the men who'd killed Ronnie Walker and Jos's baby. 'Have they ever been here?'

'The fat one, I remember him. He kept looking at me and licking his lips. It was horrible. I don't know about the other one.'

'Do you know the fat one's name?'

'I never asked. He was here to see Mr Donough, that's all. I kept out of the way as much as I could. Why?'

'He might be involved in something.'

'I wouldn't put that past him. He made my stomach all queasy.'

'Could you find out who he is? Just quietly.'

'I suppose so. I can try.'

'It would be a big help.'

'Is it something serious?' Andrea asked.

'Yes,' Lottie told her. 'Very serious.' She wasn't about to give more details.

'I'll ask. Someone's bound to know.'

'If you could leave a message for me at Millgarth police station, I'd appreciate it. You have a telephone here, don't you?'

'Of course.' She smiled. 'If it's new, we have it. Gadget mad, is Mr Donough. Vacuum cleaner, all sorts. I can't keep up with it.'

'How many cars does he own?'

'Only one,' Andrea answered. 'How many do you need?'

'I just wondered.'

'I know he has an interest in a garage, but the only motor car he has is the one that's out there now.'

They sat with a pot of tea and a plate of scones, the talk moving from the present to the past. People they'd both known at Barnbow, the strange twists life had taken.

'So you got married,' Andrea said, looking down at the ring.

'Yes. Do you remember Geoff Armstrong? The procurement officer who liaised at the factory?'

'I think so. Is he the one who was hurt at Gallipoli?'

'That's the one. He's a lovely man. What about you? Never wed?'

Andrea shook her head. 'Came close once. I was keen.' She gave a wry laugh. 'Turned out he wasn't.' A long, wistful pause. 'Do you remember Armistice Day?'

'Not much of it,' Lottie laughed. Groups of the Barnbow lasses had gone into town to celebrate the end of the war. Walking around and singing. Not having to pay for a drink anywhere. Late in the evening hundreds of them had gathered in City Square, belting out *Goodbyee* and *Tipperary*, kissing any serviceman they could find.

Five minutes more of conversation and she left. The woman would telephone, Lottie was certain; she'd left with the promise of it.

McMillan was waiting in the car, turning the pages of the *Daily Express*.

'Any luck?' he asked. From his face it was obvious that Donough have given him short shrift.

'More than you'd imagine,' Lottie told him.

'How long do you think it'll take her to find that name?' he asked as he drove.

'I've no idea.' He was eager, of course. But there was nothing she could do to speed things along. 'What happened with him?'

'He saw me, listened to the first question and told me to get out.'

'What about this garage he owns? The car could have come from there.'

'I'll check and send a pair of uniforms.' They went by Woodhouse Moor, the trees beginning to lose their leaves. Another week and it would be Woodhouse Feast, fairground rides and gramophone music. She and Cathy would be on a later shift, patrolling the area and keeping their eyes open for the young girls who'd be prowling around. With the night, the noise, and all the people it wasn't easy. But it was fun, too. Stallholders would slip them something to eat, people were friendly for the most part, eager to laugh and just have fun.

'You're smiling,' McMillan said.

'Just thinking.'

'I hear you and your oppo have a case, too.'

'Cathy's probably wrapped it all up by now. I'll see when we get back to the station.'

She found Cathy in the toilet. It had once been for civilian staff; all they'd done was change the sign. She was leaning over a washbasin, hands on the rim, head down.

'What is it?' Lottie put her arms around the woman's shoulders. 'What's happened?'

Cathy drew in a breath. 'He arrested her.'

'Who?'

Cathy turned her head. Her face was a mass of bruises, just beginning to flower. Her bottom lip had swollen, creased by a cut.

'My God. What...?'

'Mrs Manningham.' The words sounded thick in her mouth. 'I started to question her and she went for me. Someone saw it and ran off to find the copper on the beat. He pulled her off and put the handcuffs on her.' She stared at Lottie. 'Jimmy's going to be home in a few hours. What am I going to do? First he thinks I'm going with other men and now this.'

All the make-up in the world wouldn't hide the injuries. She'd wanted to look good for her husband's return and no wonder Cathy seemed so defeated. And after six months away...

'First of all we're going to get you cleaned up.' Lottie turned on the water and pushed up her sleeves. 'Then we'll decide.'

After a wash she looked a little better, but it was still bad. If she were to go home like that Geoff would go through the roof, and demand that she leave the force. What would Jimmy do? She couldn't even guess.

'You're going to have to tell him what happened today.'

'I know.' Cathy rubbed her cheek. 'God, I think the cow loosened a tooth.' She grimaced. 'You know the worst thing? That copper gets credit for the arrest and solving the Moorcroft case.'

'The credit for the case, too?' That was too much.

'Yes. I was there when she was booked in.'

'But you did all the work on that.'

'You don't have to tell me.'

It wasn't fair. Nothing was, though. They did the job, but there was always someone else ready to step in and grab the glory. All that, even a battering, to make half the money the men were paid. She could leave but what would she do? A housewife? She'd go mad at home all day. Work in a shop? A factory? Domestic service like Andrea? That was if she could even find a job. Millions were looking.

'You go,' Lottie said. 'I'll tell Mrs Maitland you're not feeling well.' It was close enough to the truth.

'Jimmy.' She sounded hopeless.

Lottie hugged her close. 'He'll see you like this and he'll just be happy to see you again. Trust me.'

'I wanted this to be special.'

'It will be.' She felt close to tears. Why today, of all days? 'Now go on. Get yourself ready for him.'

Mrs Maitland didn't press the point; she accepted everything with a simple curt nod.

'At least Sergeant McMillan seems willing to give credit where it's due,' she said as Lottie stood with her hand on the doorknob.

'That's very kind of him, ma'am.'

'No, Armstrong. That's simply how it ought to be.' She sighed. 'Still, it's better than it was during the war. That's something.'

'Ma'am?'

'The women were all volunteers then. Doing our bit.'

'You were one?'

Mrs Maitland nodded. 'Signed up in December '14 and stayed for the duration. We had to see to the moral welfare of girls. The authorities even ranked the special constables above us.' She exhaled. 'So there's been some improvement. Dismissed.'

CHAPTER FOURTEEN

'WHERE do you fancy going?' Geoff asked.

Where? Lottie had been thinking about it since she climbed out of bed and put the kettle on the gas. What would make for a memorable first trip on the motorcycle?

She gathered up the plates. The teapot sat under its cosy, another cup left if he wanted one.

'Skipton.' It was pure impulse. She'd never been there, didn't even know much about it. A castle, she remembered that much from school.

'All right,' he agreed with a smile. 'Get your skates on and we'll go.'

Cheek, she thought. He didn't have to do the washing up or clear the table. By the time she was ready, wrapped in a heavy coat, a headscarf tied firmly under her chin, he was sitting on the motorbike, turning the throttle gently. A long duster coat over a sports jacket and flannels, a wide grin on his face.

It was a thrilling ride, there and back. She was grateful for the goggles, and a few times her heart was in her mouth on the corners. But Geoff had been right. It was worth every penny.

Skipton itself was a disappointment. Pretty in parts, the castle hidden away at the top of the town, staring at the main street and the Saturday market. But the town felt smug, self-satisfied, as if it already had everything it wanted and looked down on the rest. She was glad when Geoff finally suggested they leave.

At home she suggested fish and chips to round off the day. For a few hours she had been able to escape her thoughts, to outrace them. Now, though, as they walked arm-in-arm down the street, life came rushing back. Jocelyn, probably back in Cross Green. Jane Walker, with her soul hopefully at peace somewhere. And Irene Walker, alive or dead.

She could smell the frying fish as they crossed Chapeltown Road at the parade.

'Can you get them?' Lottie asked. 'I just want to use the telephone box. Don't forget the scraps and lots of vinegar.'

She closed the door of the kiosk, feeling the small space around her. She knew the number by heart, dialling it and waiting with the penny in her hand, ready to push it in the box when someone answered.

'Sergeant,' she said, 'it's WPC Armstrong. Has anyone left a message for me?'

'How would I know?' The voice was gruff, weary. 'Let me have a look.' The man muttered, then he was back. 'Yes, there's something from an Andrea Baldwin. Is that what you want? There's just a man's name on it. Dennis Wilson.'

'That's the one. Has DS McMillan seen it?'

'Ee, I don't know. I only came on shift an hour ago. Your message came in this morning.'

'Could you make sure he sees a copy of it, please?'

'I'll put it out for him. That's all I can do.'

'Thanks.'

She replaced the receiver and pushed the door open. Geoff was waiting, the food wrapped in newspaper in his hand.

'Let's get home while it's still warm.'

'Yes,' she agreed. But she was distracted.

'You can't do anything about it,' Geoff told her when she explained. 'Do you even know how to get hold of this detective?'

'No.'

'Then it's out of your hands.' He smiled kindly. 'You've done your bit. He knows you were expecting the message, he can look for it.'

'Yes,' she said again, but she wasn't convinced.

The doubts remained all night. Lottie woke every few minutes, heart racing, anxious, lying there as Geoff slept calmly. She heard the dawn chorus, a symphony of birds, and finally slid quietly out of bed, unable to take it any longer.

The early morning felt chilly as she walked down the street, coat wrapped tight around her, not in uniform today, handbag swinging from her shoulder. All around the curtains were still closed, people enjoying their only full day of rest.

No trams or buses this early on a Sunday; if she wanted to get to Millgarth, Shank's Mare was her only option. Down Chapeltown Road and through the slums of Sheepscar and Regent Street. Some of the worst houses had been demolished, leaving small, empty streets of rubble, but far more remained.

All the walking she did on patrol served her well; by the time she reached the station she felt as if she'd taken nothing more than a stroll. The day was starting to brighten. Geoff would probably want to work in the garden later to finish all the tidying and harvest the last of the potatoes. And he'd mentioned something about adjusting the choke on the motorcycle. No doubt parts of it would be in pieces on the table when she arrived home. If not the wireless, then the bike…

She wondered about Cathy. With luck she'd have convinced Jimmy there was nothing to the rumours and they'd be back on the road to happiness. Her face would still be a mess, but surely he'd look past that.

Standing at the desk, she waited for someone to appear. It took the best part of three minutes before the desk sergeant ambled through, a mug of tea in one hand.

'Can I help you, luv?' he asked.

'I'm WPC Armstrong,' Lottie told him. 'You have a message for me.'

The man's face hardened. 'You're the one who got Tommy Berwick in trouble.'

All she'd wanted was to forget the matter.

'I think he managed that on his own when he decided to lie.'

'Bloody policewomen. You're neither use nor ornament.' He tossed the piece of paper down on the counter and strode away.

'You're good at making enemies.'

Lottie turned quickly, ready with a sharp remark. McMillan was leaning against the door, grinning.

'You're the reason I'm down here on a Sunday morning.' She held out the note.

'I'm flattered but I saw it yesterday. Spent the rest of the day looking for Dennis Wilson. He appears to have vanished. Did a flit from his lodgings the night after Ronnie Walker was killed.' He raised an eyebrow. 'No one in Leeds seems to have seen him since. His best mate skipped at the same time.'

'So you know the names of the killers.'

'For all the good it does us. We've put out a bulletin to all the forces around the country. And it doesn't help us find Irene Walker, either.' Before she could say anything, he added, 'Don't you worry, I hadn't forgotten about her.'

'How are Wilson and his friend connected to Donough?'

'Nothing directly. They don't work for any of his businesses. Thugs for hire, mostly. They'll turn up and we'll have them. Is that really why you came in, to see I got the information?'

'Why else?'

'I just wondered.' He jangled the key to the motor car in his fingers. 'I'll give you a lift home.'

'Are you any closer to finding Irene?' she asked as he accelerated away.

'I wish we were.' His voice was empty. 'Everywhere we turn is a dead end. If it was up to me we'd have been putting the screws on Walker long ago. But he's too well-connected.'

'It's his family, for God's sake.'

'You don't need to tell me. We keep going over the same ground with him but it's like talking to a wall.'

'Can't you drag Donough in and get something from him?'

'On what grounds? That remark your Jocelyn Hill thinks she heard is the only thing connecting him to Walker. It's so thin that any lawyer would make us a laughing stock. He'd have his brief down here and be walking out in a quarter of an hour.'

'And in the meantime there are two people dead and a girl missing.'

'I know,' McMillan said through gritted teeth. 'Why do you think I'm putting in fifteen-hour days?' He sighed. 'If I had anything concrete on Donough I'd have forced a confession out of him. As it is, I'm hunting around for anything at all that links him to Walker. That's what I'm doing with my weekend.'

'I'm sorry.'

'Don't be.' He parked by the parade. 'I wouldn't have got as far as I have without your help. This is your stop, isn't it?'

'I keep thinking about Irene Walker. Where she is, how terrified she must be.' If she was even still alive. But she was going to keep that pushed firmly to the back of her mind.

'I just hope she's still breathing,' he said.

The street was almost empty. A couple of families walking along to the Sunday morning service at St Martin's. A car passing. She left it all and walked home.

'Well?' Lottie asked.

They'd left Millgarth to patrol around the market and Commercial Street. Cathy had arrived just in time for morning report. The bruises had flowered, her face was still swollen, and worry clouded her eyes.

'Step by step.' She gave a sigh. 'He didn't want to believe me at first but I think I've convinced him.

'What did he say about your face?'

'Asked what had happened and that was it. But we talked a lot.'

'All weekend?'

'One or two other things.' A blush rose up her face. 'I just hope… I'm going to be the best wife he could imagine.'

'It'll be fine. Give it a little time. You still have to get used to each other.'

'He's going out job hunting today. Jimmy's got good qualifications, he should find something quickly.'

'I'm sure he will.' Lottie didn't say more. There were too many men looking for jobs that didn't exist. Men willing to work hard, men who were overqualified for positions but willing to take whatever they could find.

They cut through by the market clock and down past the fish stalls. Fresh from Grimsby, fresh from Whitby the signs said, even if some of the stock didn't smell that way. She held her breath until they'd gone by.

'Does Jimmy know people in Leeds?' It was often easier to find work if there was someone to put in a word for you. But he'd been off in the merchant marine for years.

'His dad and his brother. He popped over to see them yesterday. They're seeing what they can do. And he has plenty of money from being paid off. We won't starve.'

She needed someone to love, someone who was there, not away on an ocean. If they could give it a little time…

'Someone said they saw you in mufti in the station yesterday.'

'I popped in,' Lottie said. 'There was a message.'

'No CID work?'

She laughed. 'Hardly.'

'Look at us,' Cathy said. 'We each had a case and now we're back out here. It's not right.'

'It's the way of the world, isn't it?'

Albert's on Boar Lane for dinner, then more circuits. No complaints of any traders giving short weight. Not even a shoplifter at the market. As forgettable a day as any she'd had. But Lottie had only one thought as she paced around: where was Irene Walker?

'You're miles away,' Cathy told her. 'Off on that motorbike?'

'Chance would be a fine thing.' She snorted. 'I got home yesterday and Geoff had newspaper spread across the table and was taking the carburettor apart. When I asked where we were supposed to eat our Sunday dinner he just looked at me.'

'I warned you,' Cathy said. Her smile vanished. 'It's going to be all right, isn't it? Tell me it will.'

'You'll be fine. Just love him. You know you love him.'

'I won't tell you some of the ways…'

They giggled. Talk passed the time, especially on the slow days. But when their shift ended, Lottie felt as if the day had lasted forever. Two more days, then Thursday off before straight evenings all weekend during Woodhouse Feast.

Cathy dashed off as soon as Mrs Maitland dismissed them. Lottie took her time. No news on Irene Walker. Sergeant McMillan was out somewhere, and she wasn't about to disturb Inspector Carter.

In the toilet she buttoned up her mackintosh to hide the uniform collar, crushed her hat into her handbag, leaned close to the mirror and applied lipstick. Maybe there was something she could do to help.

CHAPTER FIFTEEN

THE Royal was much busier than she'd expected, many of the tables filled with people in earnest conversation. Women with women; the men had their own room on the other side. A few faces looked at her as she passed, but it was curiosity and hope, not mistrust. Auntie Betty stood behind the bar in her suit and tie, hair parted in the middle and brilliantined flat. She had her arms crossed and one eyebrow raised.

'At least you don't look like a copper now, I'll give you that,' she hissed. 'But I hope you've got a good reason for being here.'

'I need to talk to Alice Sutherland.'

'She went up to her room a little while ago. Alone,' she added pointedly. 'Slip on through. But when you leave, go the back way. I told you, I don't want police in my bar.'

'I know, Auntie. I'm sorry. It's important.'

The woman pursed her lips then gave a slow nod. 'Just this once. Now go.'

'Hello, Alice.' Lottie smiled. 'Do you remember me? WPC Armstrong.' She'd opened her raincoat and put her hat back on.

'Yes, of course.' The woman gave a vague smile. 'You've been here before.'

It was strange to be up here, just the two of them in the building, every other room empty and neglected. Alice could have sold the place for a tidy sum, enough to afford a large house. But something about the Royal kept her here.

The memories? The privacy? Who could tell?

'Last week. We talked about Irene Walker.'

'I remember.' She cocked her head. 'Would you like some tea?'

'That would be lovely. Thank you.' What she really wanted was to be on her way home, but tea was going to be the price for any information.

Alice Sutherland didn't have a kitchen, just a gas-fired hotplate by the window. She was quiet during the ritual of boiling water, filling the pot and letting it mash. Finally they were sitting across from each other. The woman looked sharper today, more alert.

'Have you seen Irene since I was here last?' Lottie asked. 'It's important.'

Sutherland shook her head. 'I wish I had.' She gave a wan smile. 'I liked her. But the people I like always go away, don't they?'

'Do they?'

'Yes.' There was a lifetime of sadness in her voice. And very likely a world of problems in her mind, Lottie thought. But she needed to stay on the subject.

'Did Irene talk to you a lot?'

'I don't know. What's a lot? We talked.'

'She's still missing, Alice.' Should she mention Jane Walker's suicide? Better not, she decided. Don't complicate things. Keep her focused. 'We're growing desperate.'

'That's terrible.'

'You know her well. Is there anywhere she might have gone? Somewhere she'd feel safe? Maybe she mentioned a place to you.'

The clock on the mantel ticked away long seconds before she answered.

'I don't think so. No, I'm sure she never said anything.'

It had never been more than a long shot. But if she'd never asked…

'Thank you.'

'I'd have looked after her, you know,' Sutherland said. 'If she'd asked me I'd have found her somewhere.' She raised her head and looked at the ceiling. 'There are dozens of rooms here. She could have stayed in one and nobody would have known.'

That was true, Lottie thought; an empty hotel would be the perfect place to hide.

'But she never asked you to help her?'

'No.'

'And she never said a word about where she might be going, the last time she visited?'

'Just that she needed to run. I gave her some money, all I had here.'

Lottie looked up sharply. The woman hadn't mentioned that before. 'How much?'

'About fifteen pounds. I didn't count it exactly.'

A fortune to most people. It could have taken Irene Walker a long way from Leeds. It could almost have bought her a new life. This was important.

'I see.'

Alice Sutherland stared at her. 'All I wanted to do was help her. She was scared that someone wanted to kill her, like they had with her brother. Wouldn't you have done the same?'

Lottie nodded. 'If you hear from Irene, can you ask her to telephone and leave a message for me at Millgarth? I'll come to her wherever she is.'

'All right,' Sutherland agreed after a moment.

'I'd appreciate it.' Lottie placed the cup and saucer back on the table. Expensive Derby china, delicate in her fingers. Things like that always made her uneasy, as if she was likely to break them. 'I'd better be going.'

'I'll tell her if she contacts me,' Alice said as Lottie walked towards the door. 'I promise.'

Mrs Maitland's expression was even more sour than usual as they reported for their shift.

'Taylor,' she said, 'I can tell you that Miss Manningham is going to be prosecuted for illegally performing abortions. The testimony Hannah Moorcroft gave you will be part of the trial, so you'll be required to give evidence.'

'Yes, ma'am.'

'However, they've decided not to charge her with the assault on you last Friday.'

'But—' Cathy started.

'I know.' Mrs Maitland raised her head. 'I'm not happy about it. If one of my officers is attacked, I expect the attacker to pay the price for it. I made that *very* clear. Unfortunately, I've been overruled. I'm sorry; I thought you ought to know.'

Lottie watched as Cathy took a deep breath and let it out slowly.

'Yes, ma'am. Thank you.'

'I don't need to tell you that the Feast is setting up at Woodhouse and you'll be on duty there for a few days. You've both done it before. But I want to remind you that it attracts some very bad types.' She looked at them, waiting for nods of acknowledgement. 'Some of them will be in the city centre during the day, and many of them will be pickpockets. Keep your eyes open for these people.'

'Yes, ma'am.'

'Sarge.' Lottie had dawdled in the station before they left on patrol, hoping to catch McMillan. Now, finally, he was there, dashing along the corridor for the stairs.

'Is it important?' He sounded annoyed. 'I'm in a rush.'

'Yes. It is.' Quickly she told him about her visit to Alice Sutherland and the money the woman given Irene Walker.

'We still have the coat we found down by the river,' McMillan pointed out.

'With that cash she could have replaced it and still be far away now.'

'So none of it helps, does it?'

'I just wanted you to know.'

'You did well,' he said. 'Certainly better than the rest of us. We're all chasing our tails.'

And he was gone.

Two quiet days. Cathy seethed, but it was hardly surprising. The bruises on her face were starting to fade, the beauty returning. But the sense that the beating meant nothing to the force, that pain wouldn't go easily. And not with all her other worries.

She didn't say much, but her silence spoke loudly. Lottie let her be.

Finally, as the strolled back to the station on Wednesday afternoon, Cathy said, 'Are you doing much with your day off tomorrow?'

'Not really. Cleaning, I suppose. The washing's been piling up. What about you? How's Jimmy?'

'He thinks we should go somewhere. Just for the day, since he doesn't have work yet.' She paused. 'Every day seems a little bit better. Sometimes it feels wonderful, sometimes we'll have a few words.'

'You're getting used to each other. It takes time.'

'I'm not sure he trusts me yet.'

'It'll happen,' Lottie told her. 'Give it a chance. Give *him* a chance. Are you thinking of going anywhere special?'

'I fancied Scarborough but he said he's seen enough of the sea. We're just going to see what we feel like in the morning.'

'The other thing, there's nothing we can do about it.'

'I know. It just makes me so angry. If Jimmy had a good job I'd have resigned.'

Lottie gave a gentle smile. 'Perhaps it's for the best he doesn't have one yet, then. I'm used to you, I don't want to have to break in someone new.'

They were close to the station when the door opened and McMillan came out, pushing his trilby down on to his head.

'Armstrong,' he called as he saw Lottie.

'Yes, Sarge?'

'With me, please. It's important.'

Lottie looked at Cathy and shrugged. What could she do? He was a sergeant and it was an order.

'What is it?' she asked as he started the Peugeot.

'Someone telephoned. One of Irene Walker's friends. Claims she saw her this afternoon.'

'What?' She felt her pulse quicken. 'Where?'

'We're going to find out all about it,' he told her as he drove up the Headrow and turned on to New Briggate, stopping outside the Grand Theatre.

'How long ago did she ring?'

'Just before I saw you.' McMillan was out of the car, pacing around, hands in the pockets of his overcoat. 'She was on the top deck of the tram and saw Irene walk by here about half an hour ago.'

'Is she certain?'

'She's positive. She's known Irene since they were five.'

So the girl was still alive, still in Leeds. More than that, she was free. But in a half hour she could have walked a fair distance.

'I'm going to have a couple of men go door-to-door.' He nodded at the dirty front door of the Central Hotel across the road. 'There's that place, for a start. The Wrens, over on the corner. Probably quite a few empty offices and rooms around.'

'My shift is over, Sarge. I'm not doing door-to-door now.'

He smiled. 'I wouldn't ask you to. I'd like you with me when I talk to the girl who saw her, that's all. Give me your opinion.'

'About what?' Lottie asked in surprise.

'If she's telling the truth.'

She was. At least, Gillian Bedrow was convinced that the person she'd glimpsed from upstairs on the tram was Irene.

'I'd know her anywhere,' she said. 'We've been friends for years. I can't believe everything that's happened.' She knotted a delicate handkerchief tight in one small first.

'How much of a glimpse did you have?' Lottie asked.

'It was just a moment while the bus passed, but I'm sure. I'd been fussing with the parcels I was carrying and looked out of the window. I couldn't believe it at first.'

She was small, barely scraping five feet tall in her stockinged feet. A capable manner and a direct stare. Fashionably dressed in a silk blouse and an expensive skirt of fine wool, the shopping bags from today's trip standing in the corner. She was sitting in the front parlour of her parents' house in Chapel Allerton, three tall storeys just off the Harrogate Road, separated from the traffic by a high wall.

'Does Irene know anyone near there? An actor at the Grand, maybe?'

'I don't know. I haven't seen much of her for months.' She lifted her left hand to show off an engagement ring. 'I've been busy.'

The girl wouldn't know about Jane Walker's suicide. No one did. The police had released information that Irene was missing. That had been on the wireless, her photograph in all the newspapers. But they'd deliberately kept the news of her suicide very quiet, and Lottie wasn't about to reveal it now.

'What was she wearing?' she asked the girl.

Gillian Bedrow squinted, as if she was trying to pick out the image in her mind.

'A coat. It looked like wool. Blue-grey. The same colour as those air force uniforms.' She looked up hopefully; Lottie nodded her encouragement. 'And her hat. Irene has a favourite hat. It's a cloche with a pattern of blue sequins where it turns up at the front. That's how I knew it was her, I recognised the hat.'

'Is there anything else?'

'That's it. Like I said, it was just seconds, then the bus was gone. But it was her,' she said in earnest. 'I know it was. I rang as soon as I got home.'

Lottie believed her. Bedrow knew Irene and she was certain. Even if it meant she was still alive, it raised more questions than it answered.

'What do you think?' she asked McMillan as he manoeuvred the car around.

'She saw Irene.' He seemed to have no doubts at all. 'It's the first good thing that's happened on this. We know she's alive and no one's got her. I'll take that and be very glad of it. A weight off my mind. You got everything she knew.'

'Thank you.'

'I owe your husband an apology, keeping you out so often.'

'He won't mind. He's probably tinkering with his new motorbike. What about your wife? You work long hours.'

He shrugged. 'She's used to it by now. And she knows it comes with the job. Her dad was on the force, she grew up with it.'

'What now?' Lottie asked.

'We ask around on New Briggate and hope her name or her face rings a bell. But at least we have something now. I feel like we've taken one step forward.'

CHAPTER SIXTEEN

BOILING the clothes, soap, dolly blue, rinsing, mangle. It was a morning of work, much harder than being out on patrol. By the time Lottie had everything pegged out on the lines that crossed the back garden she was sweating, ready for a cup of tea.

In the afternoon she took care of the shopping, walking away from the Co-op with one heavy bag. By the time she'd visited the greengrocer, the butcher, and the fishmonger, she had another to weigh her down.

A day off from the job but no time to herself. It always seemed to be that way. Part of her envied all the housewives who had all day, every day to do the things she had to cram into a few hours. The rest of her knew she'd loathe it.

Tomorrow she'd start late, but no chance to sleep in. Up at the usual time to cook Geoff's breakfast and see him off to work. Then more tasks until it was time for her shift.

No rest for the wicked. Or even those who stop people being wicked, she thought wryly.

'You both know the drill,' Mrs Maitland told them. 'You worked the Feast in April.'

'Yes, ma'am,' Lottie said.

'Make sure people know you're there, and keep your eyes on the girls. No drinking, no licentious behaviour, and no loitering to talk to men. There will be a pair of male officers circulating, too. I don't expect there will be much the two of you can't handle—' she gave them a pointed, knowing look '—but if there is, blow your whistles and they'll help.'

'Help or take over?' Cathy asked, a bitter edge in her tone.

'Help, Taylor, at least if I have anything to do with it. If any girl gives you a problem, escort her over to the Woodhouse station. It's close enough. Dismissed.'

'Did you go anywhere yesterday?' Lottie asked as they settled on the bus out to Hyde Park.

'In the end we popped over to Harrogate.' Cathy made a face. 'One of Jimmy's shipmates is from there and he'd promised to deliver a parcel to his parents.'

'You didn't like it?'

'Too snooty. We took a walk on the Stray and looked around the shops. The best part was going to a tea room. Betty's. Gorgeous cakes. But that was it. Still, it was a day out and we got along well.'

'More fun than my domestic drudgery.'

'I was hard at that this morning. It's going to be a long evening, isn't it?'

'I know.' She'd be exhausted by the time she reached home. But there was something exhilarating in all the music and the lights and the people. One or two bad lads and girls, but most of them were there to enjoy themselves, to let off steam. Both those who were working and the ones without a job; simply being at the fair, not spending a farthing, was entertainment.

'I'll bet you anything my stockings don't last, either,' Cathy said. 'I went through two pairs last time. This duty costs me a fortune.' She reached down, smoothing the black wool over her calf. 'Still, at least it's not raining.'

There was hardly anyone around yet. Most people were still at work, only a few schoolboys wandering from ride to attraction, egging each other to spend a halfpenny to see the three-headed man.

The cinders on the ground crunched under their shoes as they walked. Most of the rides hadn't even started operating yet; they'd wait until more people appeared. Once tea was done, the moor would be packed.

A pair of food vendors were already beginning to cook, preparing for those who were willing to spend a little. The smell of cooking meat filled the air.

'God,' Cathy said, 'I'm starving. I could eat a horse.'

'You probably will be if you buy anything here,' Lottie warned her. 'Take a look at those men. Would you trust any of them?'

'Not as far as I could throw them. But we have to eat sometime.'

Lottie patted the pocket of her uniform. 'I brought sandwiches. Meat paste. You can have one later, if you like.'

By eight they were tired. Their feet ached from treading over the rough ground and they felt bruised from pushing their way through the crowds. Music came from the gramophones on the rides, steam engines spluttered and whirred. The barkers competed to draw people to their tents, yelling through megaphones.

'My ears ache,' Lottie said. 'Too much noise.'

'We have tomorrow night, too.'

'Don't remind me. Still two more hours this evening, as well.'

By ten they'd taken two girls over to Woodhouse station. One couldn't have been older than thirteen, wearing a dress that was no more than rags and a pair of large, unlaced boots. She'd been propositioning men. Have her for tuppence.

It had taken the pair of them to drag her away. At least the noise of the Feast had hidden her screams. She'd tried to bite. Only a hard slap from Cathy had calmed her.

'Better check your uniform for lice in the morning,' she said as they walked back towards the lights and sound. 'She was filthy.'

The other girl had been drunk, passed out in the shadows. A dead weight as they dragged her away. At least she'd be safe in a cell, even if it meant being up before the magistrate tomorrow.

A final walk around after everything had closed for the night. The lines for the trams and buses were so long it was quicker to walk back to town. The pubs were closing, people spilling out on to the pavements. A few women, but mostly men, some happy, some angry, all of them quietening as they saw the uniforms.

Lottie stifled a yawn with her hand. 'I'm exhausted. I want to soak my feet but I'll probably fall asleep first.'

'I know. And another night of it tomorrow. Aren't we lucky girls?'

Saturday felt different. The Feast was full from the time it opened. The working week was over and people wanted to have fun. But there was something else in the air. An undercurrent, Lottie thought. She could sense it. An edge of danger. Anger. Once darkness fell it seemed to grow stronger.

'There's something,' Cathy agreed, looking around and trying to find an answer in the sea of faces.

The trouble came a little after nine. At first Lottie wasn't certain she'd heard anything, then the shouting became louder and clearer, drowning out the music and the noise of the rides.

'Come on,' she told Cathy, grabbing her by the wrist and starting to force a path through the crowds. The voices were on the far side of the fair. Angry, yelling, close to violence.

People were like sardines, squashed together between the rides and the tents, most of them oblivious to everything except the world in front of their noses. Lottie pushed ahead, squeezing, elbowing, until she was there, Cathy right behind her.

Two gangs. It had to be. They were facing off against each other, about ten on each side, some of them already bloody. One or two had chains wrapped around their fists. A hammer dangled from someone's hand. They were all young men, a few girls behind them, faces shining with excitement.

They were women police constables. They weren't supposed to get involved in this. There to deal with girls and women only: those were the standing orders.

But there were no other coppers around; if they didn't do something, innocent people could be hurt. People were pressing back, trying to get away.

Lottie tried to shout, but her voice was simply lost in the air. No one even heard it. Then she took out her police whistle. A long, shrill blast that cut through everything.

That worked.

The fighters turned to stare at her. No fear, just curiosity. One of them started to laugh, a harsh, barking sound.

Lottie took one pace forward, then another. She was close enough to smell them now. Sweat, drink, stale tobacco. Engine grease. Hate.

One of the gang leaders spoke. He was a tall, broad young man, handsome except for the two scars on his cheek. And too young to have got them in the trenches.

'Go away, luv, and you won't get hurt. We've got business here.'

'Not any more,' Lottie told him.

He smiled, showing broken brown teeth. 'You're not even a real rozzer. Bugger off.'

Idly, like she was nothing. Just a bluebottle that annoyed him. No, she thought. She wasn't standing for that.

'Come here,' she said.

He turned his head, grinning at his mates. He was going to have a laugh with her. Put her in her place.

So he thought.

Lottie's kick caught him square between the legs. She watched him crumple on the ground, folded, clutching himself.

Everything was silent around her. Then a yell as a lad from the other side charged towards her. Cathy appeared, her small fist swinging, catching him full in the chest. But he was too big, too strong, pushing her aside.

He raised his hand, ready to bring it down on Lottie's face. He was grinning, relishing this. But he waited too long. She jabbed her arm forward, fingers straight. It caught him hard in the pit of his stomach. Suddenly he couldn't breathe, gasping and falling down on to his knees.

The others started to move back. All except one. He stood his ground. Tall, older than the rest. So thin he was barely there, trousers too big, held up by an old pair of braces. But it was his eyes she noticed. Dead. Empty. Like the men who wandered around town, the ones who'd seen too much on the Western Front and could never escape it.

Slowly, lovingly, he pulled a knife. Lottie felt a trickle of fear run down her back. Light caught the blade. It was clean, shining.

'Put it down,' she said gently. He didn't notice, didn't hear. He was in a world of his own. It was as if she'd never spoken.

She was the enemy. 'Weapons down.' She tried to shout it out like a sergeant, but it had no effect.

Lottie breathed deeply, watching the man as he came towards her. She was terrified, the sweat clammy on her skin. All it would need was one cut…

Before he could strike he was falling, the knife arcing out of his grip and flying through the air to land on the cinders. Cathy struggled from under him and to her feet.

'I told you I'd ruin a pair of stockings,' she said. Her knees were bloody, dirt all over her uniform.

Lottie felt herself start to tremble inside. She knelt and picked up the blade, hand shaking so much she could hardly grab it.

'I'll buy you new ones,' she said. 'Silk, if you want. What did you do to him?'

'Rugby tackle.' Cathy laughed. 'My brothers used to practice them on me when I was little. I never thought it'd come in useful.'

The man lay there, not moving a muscle, eyes open, his mouth no more than a straight line.

'Can you blow your whistle?' Lottie asked. 'I don't think I've got the puff right now.'

Five minutes passed before the constables arrived, eyebrows raised in disbelief. She gave them the knife, watching as they dragged the man away. Lottie was a little calmer, not shaking every second now.

'I need a cup of tea,' she said. 'Let's find a stall.'

'All that you did with those two,' Cathy said. 'Where did you learn it?' She was hobbling slightly as she walked. A wound in the course of duty.

'When I joined the force, Geoff said I ought to know unarmed combat. Just in case. He insisted, drilled me like a soldier.' She shook her head in disbelief. 'I just did what he taught me. I didn't think about it.'

'You should get a medal, facing them down that way.'

'And you might have saved my life.'

'Do you think the brass will praise us for stopping that fight?' Cathy asked wryly.

'Probably haul us over the coals for doing men's work.' She drained the last of the tea from the mug. 'Come on, once more round the Feast before they close for the night.'

'Really?' Geoff asked in amazement as they ate Sunday dinner. 'You did all that?'

'You're the one who showed me.'

'I know,' he said, 'but I never thought you'd need it.'

'Neither did I, but I'm glad you made me learn.'

'So am I,' he agreed with relief.

'Armstrong. Taylor.' Monday morning report and Mrs Maitland looked up, holding two sheets of paper. 'This is from the constables who arrested a man with a knife at Woodhouse Feast on Saturday night.'

'Yes, ma'am,' Lottie said.

'It says the two of you disarmed and disabled the man before they arrived on the scene. Is that correct?'

'It was Taylor. She tackled him.'

Mrs Maitland turned her head. 'Is that so?'

'I did, ma'am,' Cathy said. 'But Armstrong was willing to take him on.'

'I heard. One of the men from my church saw some of it happen.'

Now it was going to start, Lottie thought. 'I can explain, ma'am—'

'There's no need.' Mrs Maitland smiled. 'He isn't given to exaggeration and he was full of praise for your courage.'

'Thank you.' She felt herself redden.

'You took on two of them before the man with the knife?'

'I don't know. I wasn't counting, ma'am.' It was the only reply she could give that didn't sound boastful.

'And you stopped what could have been serious violence. Innocent people might have been hurt if it had gone ahead. I intend to put you up for a commendation. Both of you. Bravery over and above the call of duty.'

Lottie straightened her back. She'd been expecting the worst, not this. From the corner of her eye she could see the astonishment on Cathy's face.

'Thank you, ma'am.'

'That's all. Dismissed. And well done.'

'I'm not sure I believe that,' Cathy began as they walked down the corridor.

'You go on, I'll just be a minute,' Lottie told her. She'd spotted McMillan walking out to the yard. 'See you outside.'

'Sarge,' she called and he turned, the key to the Peugeot in his hand.

'Well, well. Your name's getting around, you know,' he said with a smile. 'I've heard three people mention you this morning.'

She blushed again. 'I was just wondering, has there been any word on Irene Walker? Or those men who killed her brother.' Until she'd seen McMillan, she guiltily realised she hadn't given them a thought; her head had been brimming with Saturday night.

'Nothing,' he told her with a shake of his head. 'I've had men asking all around, into the Leylands and up towards Woodhouse Lane. Nobody's seen her. I'm beginning to think that friend of hers was wrong.'

'No.' Lottie thought back to the Gillian Bedrow's face as she told them. 'She saw Irene, I'm sure of it.'

He sighed and shrugged. 'She's vanished into thin air, that's all I know. The inspector's still getting nowhere with the father. But we're certain the murderers have left Leeds. Scotland Yard think they're in London. They're searching.'

'Maybe today will bring something.'

McMillan gave a wan smile. 'From your lips to God's ears.' He hesitated for a fraction of a second. 'Did you really beat up Tim Molloy?'

'Who?'

'The leader of the Fraser Boys. It was his gang at the Feast on Saturday. They were going to have a ruck with the Quarry Hill lot.'

'I don't know who it was,' Lottie admitted.

He started to laugh. 'Most of the constables here would be too scared to go up against him and you put him on the floor. You're quite a girl, you know that?'

'Thanks, Sarge.' She didn't want to hear any more about it. 'I'm sorry, I need to go.'

'Wait here,' she said to Cathy as they passed Bridges the milliner on Lands Lane. 'I'll only be a moment.' In less than two minutes she returned with a brown paper bag. 'Put that in your pocket.'

'What is it?'

'One pair of Clevernit black stockings. I owed you those for Saturday.'

'Don't be daft,' Cathy told her, but she still folded the package away in the pocket of her uniform jacket. 'Do you think the sergeant was pulling your leg about them being two gangs?'

'He was serious. Maybe it's as well we didn't know.'

'You had that look in your eyes. You'd have piled in anyway.'

Would she, Lottie wondered? Or would knowing have immobilised her into just standing by? Sometimes knowledge could be a dangerous thing; it was safer to learn after the fact.

'Too late now. It happened.' She glanced at her wristwatch. 'It's almost twelve, we should find something to eat. Lyons today?'

The place was full, but the nippies gave good service, taking their orders and bringing the food inside five minutes.

'Do you think old Maitland meant it?' Cathy asked. 'About the commendation?'

'I suppose so. She wouldn't have said it otherwise.'

'Jimmy would be so proud.'

Geoff was too, Lottie recalled. He'd shown it quietly, but it was there. She was doing her duty, at least the way she saw it; nothing more than that.

'I'm sure he's proud of you, anyway. Things on an even keel?'

'Getting that way. I like having him around, someone at home every night. And he has an interview this afternoon down at Hunslet Engine Company. A mate of his works there, says he can get him on regular. It'd be a weight off his mind if it happens.'

The rest of the shift took them to Quarry Hill and out to Marsh Lane, almost within shouting distance of Millgarth. The soot and smoke from the factories seemed to collect there, leaving the air thick and dirty and on the tongue. Street after bleak, cobbled street, all the hope sucked out of them.

They'd gone along two roads of the back-to-backs when Lottie heard the sound: the fast slap of feet on pavement. She turned, seeing a little girl dashing headlong towards them.

No shoes, no socks, a dress that was rags, and her face contorted with pain.

Lottie crouched and held out her arms, letting the girl run into them.

'Shhh,' she said, pulling her close. The lass couldn't be more than four or five, so skinny that it was like holding a bag of bones. 'I'm Lottie. Why don't you tell me what's wrong?'

'It's my nan, miss.' The girl gulped in breaths between her tears, tracks of them running down her grimy face. Lottie wiped them away with her thumb. She knew what was coming but she had to ask anyway. 'What about your nan?'

'She won't wake up.'

'Come on,' she said gently. 'Show me where you live and we'll take a look.'

The girl took her hand, led them around the corner, pushed open the door of a house and walked into the parlour.

It was filthy. Piles of paper on the floor, the smell of excrement and urine everywhere. Dirty clothes. She tried not to breathe, but it was impossible to ignore the stink. It seemed to cling to her skin as soon as she entered.

'Where's your nan?'

She was sitting in a chair in the kitchen, her face peaceful and very dead. Dirty pans were piled on the table, rubbish on the stone floor. Lottie spotted movement, a rat's tail vanishing as it burrowed into a pile of something in the corner. She forced herself to stay calm.

'What's your name?' she asked.

'Annie,' the lass answered. She was staring at her grandmother. 'Is my nan going to be all right?'

Lottie nodded at Cathy, sending her back to Millgarth to ring for the coroner. Nothing suspicious about this death.

'Where are your parents?' she asked.

It came out in bits and pieces. Annie was four. Her mother was dead. She'd seen her dad a year ago but didn't know where he was now. She lived here with her nan, the only home she could remember.

'Is there anyone else around? An aunt?'

'No, miss. I've never seen one, anyway.'

Lottie sighed. Another girl for the orphanage. But maybe she'd be better off there. At least it would be clean and she'd have enough to eat. No lice in her clothes or nits in her hair. And no rats sharing the kitchen.

'I tell you what, why don't you and I go and have something to drink and a piece of cake? What do you think about that?'

Annie looked worriedly at her grandmother. 'But what about my nan? What's going to happen to her?'

'Someone will be here in a minute to take care of her.'

Still, they waited outside until Cathy returned. Lottie talked to a couple of the neighbours, giving them the news in whispers.

'Poor little mite,' one of them said. 'Still, it might be for the best. There were nowt for her behind them four walls.'

The canteen at Millgarth was warm and steamy. She sat Annie down, returning with a glass of milk and a bun for the girl who stared at it wide-eyed and fearful.

'I don't have no money, miss.'

'My treat,' Lottie told her. God knew, she deserved something. 'There are a few things I need to tell you…'

She found an empty office and sat Annie down with a pencil and a piece of paper, waiting with her until the man from the children's home arrived. Mr Blaine; she'd met him before. He was balding, officious, the type who looked down his nose at the world.

'I'd have thought you might have put some decent clothes on her, Constable. At least a pair of shoes.'

'As you might have noticed, sir, we're a police station, not a clothes warehouse.' Lottie stared at him. 'I'm sure you'll have things to fit her at the home.' She handed him a folder. 'Those are her particulars. As far as I've been able to gather from her.'

He nodded. 'Come along, girl,' Blaine said. 'No shilly-shallying. We don't have all day.'

The room felt empty without Annie. Lottie picked up the drawing, stick figures of an old woman and a little girl in a house. There were smiles on their faces. Through the window a bright sun was shining. She folded it and tucked the paper away in her pocket.

Cathy was standing outside the house, talking with several of the neighbours and scribbling in her notebook.

'The coroner's inside. I've found out all I can. The dead woman was called Gertie Gardener. Been here as long as anyone can remember. Husband died years back. Had six children, but only one lived more than three years.'

'That's Annie's mother.'

'Yes. She died two years ago. Consumption, not surprising in that place. No other relatives that people know about. The girl's father took off before she was born. Arthur Leech. In and out of jail. He'd slip by and see the lass every once in a while. Violent when he's drunk. Sounds like she's better off without him.'

'She's on her way to the home now,' Lottie said. They'd done all they could. All that remained was locking up when the body had been removed and filling out the report. Not the first time they'd done this. But she'd never been in a house as dirty as that before.

Dismissed, raincoats covering their uniforms, they came chattering out of the station. Cathy stopped short, mouth wide open. A few yards away, holding a bunch of flowers, stood a man in a suit, a cigarette dangling from his grinning mouth.

It had to be Jimmy.

'You got it?'

He nodded and Cathy flew to hug him, not even caring that people stopped to stare.

'Start tomorrow.'

'That's wonderful. I'm so pleased. Jimmy, this is Lottie, I've told you all about her. Lottie, this is my husband.'

She said it so proudly, her arm through his. He was good-looking in a slick way, his skin tanned and weatherbeaten from those years on the water.

Lottie said hello and left them to it. They were jabbering away nineteen to the dozen. With regular work everything would settle down. They wouldn't even notice she'd gone. And there was something Lottie wanted to do before she went home…

CHAPTER SEVENTEEN

THE side door of the Royal Hotel gave with a little pressure. Inside, Lottie stood for a moment, listening for footsteps and taking in the gloom. Very carefully she climbed the stairs, ready to work her way through the place.

The idea had come to her in the scullery of the dead woman's house, when she'd seen the rat hiding itself away. If Irene Walker was in Leeds, she needed somewhere to stay. There were plenty of places in the hotel, and Alice Sutherland would have keys to them all. The woman had even mentioned it herself.

In a place like this the girl could burrow, hard to find.

She wasn't even sure how to search. All she could do was walk along the corridors, looking for marks in the dust on the carpet and testing doorknobs. Nothing on that floor. Two more to go.

More steps, and the door opened with a slow creak. She froze, waiting, ready to scurry away at the slightest sound. But there was nothing ahead of her except an empty silence. Cautiously she paced along, alert for everything.

At the far end, close to another set of stairs, a short passageway led towards the back of the building. It was dark, almost black. Lottie put one hand against the wall to steady herself, the other out in front.

Five paces and her fingertips touched a wooden door. She felt for the handle and slowly closed her hand around it, holding her breath.

Now or never, Lottie thought.

After the shadows in the hall, the light in the room seemed unnaturally bright. She needed to blink before she looked around. Someone was living here. The furniture had been dusted. There was make-up on the dressing table, nail varnish, a jar of Pond's cold cream. A pair of stockings hung over the back of a chair. Sheets, blankets, an eiderdown and candlewick covered the bed, a blue cloche hat with a pattern in sequins lying on top. Hanging from a hook behind the door was an overcoat in RAF blue.

Now she knew where Irene Walker was hiding.

Carefully, Lottie left, closing the door quietly behind her. She wanted to run but forced herself to go slowly downstairs and out into the fresh air. She pulled the wood against the jamb, breathing as hard as if she'd run a race and standing for a minute until her heartbeat slowed to normal.

She marched to Millgarth, jaw set, wanting to sprint and knowing she couldn't. It was part of her training: a police officer never runs, unless responding to an emergency or stopping a crime. And this would wait another minute or two.

McMillan's car was still in the yard. Lottie clattered up the steps and into the CID room. Two men were hunched over a desk, examining a document: the sergeant, along with Inspector Carter.

'What do you need, Constable?' Carter asked. 'The usually etiquette is to knock before barging in.'

'Beg pardon, sir, but I have some important information.'

'Go on.'

'I know where Irene Walker's staying, sir.'

Carter had nothing to say, his face like stone. McMillan's eyes shone with glee. His mouth twitched, and in a moment he was moving.

'That's excellent work, Constable,' he said, taking her by the elbow and ushering her out of the room. 'You'd better show me the place.'

'Where?' he asked as he nosed the Peugeot out on to George Street. 'And how?'

'The Royal Hotel,' Lottie told him. 'It was just something that came to me earlier.'

She told him what she'd found. 'I'll park on Duncan Street,' McMillan said. 'We can walk down.'

He followed her, treading carefully up the stairs and along the corridor, letting her open the door to the room and enter first. Everything was still there, in exactly the same places. McMillan started to move forward, but Lottie held up a hand.

'Can't you smell it?'

'What?' he asked.

'The perfume.' It was faint, no more than a hint, but it hadn't been there before; she'd have noticed. Tabac Blond. She'd smelt it in Alice Sutherland's room. It was a popular scent, though. Irene Walker might have worn it, too. 'Someone's been in here in the last few minutes.'

'Miss Walker?'

'Maybe.' Lottie made a decision. 'Come with me.'

Up a flight of steps to the top floor of the hotel.

'Wait here,' she whispered, a few yards from Sutherland's room. 'I'll shout if I need you.' McMillan nodded.

She knocked and waited until the door cracked open.

'Hello, Alice.' She smiled. 'Do you mind if I come in for a minute?'

She had no idea what she was going to say, what questions she could ask. All she could do was hope something would come to her as Alice Sutherland stood aside to let her enter.

A gramophone was playing softly, Paul Whiteman's Orchestra and *Felix The Cat*. The air was heavy with a familiar scent. A shaft of late sun came through the window, lighting up the Oriental pattern on the rug.

No Irene Walker.

Alice gave Lottie a quizzical look.

'Have you found her?'

'Not yet. I wanted to see if she'd been in touch with you since I was here last. Everyone's starting to fear the worst.'

'No.' Her face showed nothing but concern. She ought to be on the stage or in pictures, Lottie thought. So believable.

'And you'll let us know if you hear anything?'

'Of course.' Just the slightest trace of annoyance. 'I said I would. If you'll excuse me, I was about to get ready to go out.'

'Of course. Sorry to take your time.' She paused. 'What's that perfume? It's lovely.'

'Oh.' She brightened. 'Tabac Blond. It's very evocative, isn't it? I started using it when it came out. Irene loves it, too. I bought her a bottle for her birthday.'

'Thank you.'

In the hall, hearing the door close and the key turn in the lock, she put a finger to her lips and hurried outside, McMillan behind her.

'Well? You weren't in there long.'

'Alice definitely wears that scent. She must have bought some for Irene.'

'So Miss Walker could have been back in her room?'

'She probably was.' Lottie took off her hat and handed it to him. 'Hold that, will you? I'm just going to poke my head into the women's bar in case Irene's there.'

But she wasn't. The place was almost deserted, not even a glimpse of Auntie Betty. She was in and out in seconds, shaking her head.

'I'll have someone keep watch on this place,' Sergeant McMillan told her. 'Irene will be back if she wants a bed for the night.' He shook his head. 'You're quite a girl, you know. I can't think of a detective who could do what you've done. And it was worth it just to see the look on the inspector's face.'

Lottie gave him a nervous smile. She didn't know how to reply; she couldn't think of the words to respond to praise like that. All she'd done was put two and two together and hope it made four.

'Let me ring in and get someone here then I'd better run you home,' he continued with a wry grin. 'I'm starting to feel like your personal taxi service.'

'I can take the tram,' she offered.

'Don't you dare. You've earned a lift.'

Who was she to refuse?

Geoff was at the kitchen sink, scrubbing motorcycle grease off his hands with heavy carbolic soap.

'I was just making a few adjustments,' he explained. 'The carburettor. I wanted to make sure it didn't stick.' It sat on the corner of the table, on top of a copy of the *Daily Express*. 'I'll put it back on the bike after tea.'

She stood and watched him, fascinated by the deft movements. He seemed to understand exactly where everything should go. With it all connected, he started the engine, letting it idle as he brought out a screwdriver, making tiny changes until he smiled with satisfaction.

'Just right.'

'If you say so.' She couldn't hear any difference. As he worked Lottie had told him about her day, the death, the discovery. She wasn't even certain he'd been listening.

'You've been through it today,' Geoff said tenderly. 'Do you fancy popping out for a drink?'

She thought of the washing up she'd just finished, the small chores she could probably do and the pile of darning waiting by her chair.

'Very much,' she replied.

The Skyrack in Headingley was almost empty. The ride had been exhilarating, up and down hills, Geoff grinning wide as he opened up the throttle. Lottie sat with a gin and tonic, still catching her breath.

'It sounds like the force is beginning to realise what a treasure you are,' he said with approval. 'Up for a commendation, and you're doing that sergeant's work for him.'

'Get away with you.' She watched as he lit a cigarette. 'It's my job, that's all. I just try to do it well.'

'Sounds like you succeed.'

'I enjoy it.' She sipped the drink. 'I'd go barmy if I was at home all the time.'

'I know that.' He chuckled. 'You were never the type to do that. It's one of the things I always loved about you.'

He'd said it before. But it always gave her a warm feeling. Geoff appreciated her for who she was, not who he could turn her into. She was lucky; most men wouldn't accept their wives working. It was the last resort to feeding a family.

'You'll have to put up with it for a while yet,' Lottie warned him. 'Unless they sack me for doing too much.'

'Not a chance,' he told her. 'Not a chance.'

She didn't see anyone from CID in the station next morning. There was no word passing around about Irene Walker. When she asked, people shook their heads. All she could do was go on patrol with curiosity buzzing in her head. She'd find out sooner or later, Lottie told herself. Patience.

On Commercial Street, by the entrance to the private Leeds Library, young John perched on his cart, a sign in front of him: *Gave my legs for England. Please be generous.*

They saw him often on patrol. He'd been blown up on the Somme, surviving for almost two days in a shell hole before he'd been rescued. He'd lived, but his legs had been amputated.

The pension he'd been promised never arrived. Now he propelled himself around Leeds on a small wheeled cart, spending his days begging. Lottie and Cathy always gave a penny. He was a constant reminder of the war, part of the city's conscience. Others still carried their wounds. The men without an arm or a leg. The ones whose minds would never return from the trenches. And then there were the ones who'd lost their faces only to have them built up again by the surgeons. Lottie knew they were good, brave souls who'd done their duty and suffered. But it was still hard to bring herself to look at them.

'Did Jimmy get off to work on time this morning?' she asked Cathy as they moved on. He'd been taken on in Hunslet, a good job and a decent wage.

'He's not going to be late the first day. I had his snap packed and waiting for him.' She smiled. 'He was over the moon last night. Made me a happy girl in every way.'

'Now, now,' Lottie told her with a chuckle. 'Less of that, young lady. We're a clean patrol, no matter what anyone else thinks.'

'I'm just pleased. It's all going to be fine, I can feel it.'

Cathy was still on top of the world when they stopped for their dinner at a sandwich stall on City Square. She rushed through the food then bought a packet of potato crisps, opening the blue twist of salt and emptying it over the potatoes.

'You know,' she said, 'after the last few days, probably nothing exciting will ever happen to us again.'

'It will,' Lottie told her. At least she hoped it would.

McMillan wasn't at the station when they reported back to Millgarth in the late afternoon. The CID room was empty. Lottie could see the shadow of Inspector Carter behind his glass door, but she'd have no thanks if she knocked.

Instead she took the long way to the tram stop, along the Calls and slowly up Lower Briggate. If she spotted someone from CID watching the Royal Hotel then Irene Walker was still out there somewhere. If not… well, she didn't know.

Lottie wasn't afraid of being recognised. With a raincoat over her uniform she was in mufti. And she was a woman; she was invisible in the crowds on the street.

She passed within three yards of him and he never even noticed. A detective constable she'd seen around Millgarth. He was pretending to read a newspaper, the brim of his trilby pulled down low to try and hide his eyes.

No Irene, she thought as she climbed on the tram and stared out of the window as they went along North Street. What did that mean?

She still didn't know the next morning as she entered Mrs Maitland's office. Cathy was late again, running headlong down the corridor and straightening her uniform.

'Your skirt isn't straight and your cap's not on properly. Smarten up, girl. You're representing Leeds City Police out there.'

'Yes, ma'am,' Cathy answered softly.

'Armstrong, Sergeant McMillan wants you this morning.'

'Yes, ma'am,' Lottie said in surprise.

'Now, if you don't mind.'

'Yes, ma'am.' She raised her eyebrows at Cathy and left.

CHAPTER EIGHTEEN

HE was leaning against the post at the bottom of the stairs, smoking a cigarette, his face grave.

'It's not good, is it?' she asked.

McMillan shook his head. 'Not at all.'

The Royal Hotel was full of noise and activity. Policemen in uniform on every floor, examining all the rooms. In the room where Irene Walker had been staying a photographer and a fingerprint man were working busily. The coat had gone from behind the door and the girl's favourite hat was missing from the bed.

'She's vanished again,' Lottie said.

'I've had someone watching the place. When there hadn't been any sign by first thing this morning I came in for a look. You can see for yourself. I've taken that other woman in for questioning.'

'Alice Sutherland, you mean?'

'That's her.'

'Don't believe a word she says. She's a very good liar.'

'I don't intend to.' He grimaced. 'It doesn't help us find Irene, though. She must have seen we were watching this place.'

If she'd been at all careful she couldn't have missed it, Lottie thought. But she kept quiet.

'I don't understand why you want me here.' A flashbulb popped loudly and she jumped.

'You've been through the room. You can tell me what's missing.'

'I only had a quick look. Her hat and coat have gone. Apart from that, I don't know.' She glanced around. 'The bed looks exactly the same as when I was here. Did you open the curtains?'

'They were that way when I came in earlier.'

'Then she probably ducked in, grabbed a few things and left again.'

The cosmetics were still on the dressing table, the stockings over the back of the chair. Beyond that, Lottie didn't know. She'd never checked the wardrobe.

'What has Alice said?'

'She admitted Irene was staying here but said she hadn't seen her since yesterday morning when she gave her five pounds.'

It was more than she'd told Lottie. But Sutherland was clever, doling out information piece by tiny piece. And she was wealthy; she would be able to afford a good solicitor to protect herself.

'Have you talked to Mr Walker again?' she asked.

'For what it's worth. Sits there with his lawyer like we don't exist.'

'And this mysterious Mr Donough?'

McMillan sighed with frustration. 'If we can ever come up with a proper connection. We talked to Scotland Yard. They said they might have a lead on Ronnie's killer down in London but they haven't found him yet. I feel like I'm playing blind man's bluff in a minefield, to tell you the truth.'

'There's nothing more I can tell you here,' Lottie said.

'If she's anywhere around the hotel we'll find her.'

'She won't be. Irene's too clever for that.'

'That's what worries me. She's too clever by half.'

As they came out into the grey daylight, someone was waiting by the door. Auntie Betty, dressed in a man's Harris tweed suit and mustard yellow waistcoat, checked shirt and wool tie.

'You've just ruined my business,' she told Lottie.

'I haven't, Auntie. Alice did that when she let her friend stay.' She paused a second. 'I'm sorry, I really am, but we were bound to find out she was here.'

'Except she's not, is she?' There was a tease under the words. A taunt.

'Do you know where she's gone?' Lottie asked urgently.

'Not a clue,' the woman said with a smug smile. 'Not that I'd tell you if I did.'

'You will,' McMillan said. 'If you know something, you'd better spit it out.'

Betty stared at him with contempt. 'What makes you think I'd do something for a man?'

'You'll—' He took a step forward. Lottie held out an arm to hold him back. Anger wasn't going to help. Betty would dig in her heels, just to be bloody-minded. If she had any information they needed it now.

'Betty, please,' Lottie said. 'We need to know. Someone murdered her brother and they're after her. Why do you think she was hiding here? Come on, please.'

Auntie Betty's shoulders slumped inside her jacket. 'I don't know anything.' She held her hands up, palms out. 'Honestly, I don't.' Betty turned to McMillan. 'I don't think Alice knows too much, either. She's besotted, she was happy to let that girl get away with a lot. Gave her money, presents, and Irene was happy to take them.'

Lottie saw the distaste on McMillan's face. That didn't matter now. They wanted information. They wanted the truth.

'Go on. We need to know. Anything might help.'

'Irene liked Alice well enough, but that's as far as it went. She was someone to turn to when she was in trouble. But she didn't give away her secrets. I *know* that. Alice told me.'

'Was there anyone else Irene talked to? Anyone who might help her?'

'Not really.' She stopped herself. 'There's a woman called Agnes. I've seen her and Irene talking once or twice.'

'Agnes who?'

'Don't know,' Betty replied. 'By the look of her, she has money. Cultured voice. And a wedding ring,' she added. 'In her early forties, always well turned-out. And she has a little scar here.' With a finger she traced a line from the left corner of her mouth down towards her jaw.

Lottie heard McMillan draw in his breath. Please don't let him say a word, she thought.

'We'll see if we can find her.'

'Just get your coppers out of here as soon as you can before all my trade goes to the King Edward or the Mitre and doesn't come back.' She turned and strode away, leaving McMillan to glare at her back. Lottie dragged him to the car.

'I can't stand that… thing,' he said, lighting a cigarette.

'Who's Agnes? You knew her from the description.'

He hesitated for a long time before answering.

'It's going to be messy.'

'Who's Agnes?' Lottie repeated.

'Her surname's Rogers. Her husband's Councillor Rogers.' He paused for a second to let the name sink in. 'He's head of the watch committee.'

At first she didn't know what to say. The watch committee was in charge of the police: the budget, everything to do with it. If his wife was helping someone the police were seeking, even someone innocent… the sergeant was right; it was going to be very messy.

'I need to telephone Inspector Carter,' he said, looking around for a kiosk.

'There's one up Briggate,' Lottie told him.

'Do you mind waiting in the car?' He tossed her the keys. 'I'm not about to see Mrs Rogers without approval.'

She was sitting primly when he returned.

'We're on our way to Alwoodley.'

They drove in silence. McMillan kept slowing to check the addresses along King Lane. There were fields around, cattle grazing; Leeds seemed far behind them.

'This is it,' he said finally and turned along a rutted drive. The house had probably been a farm once, when this was all countryside. It was stone, sturdy, built to outlast generations of owners. A maid in her black dress and white apron ushered them to a parlour, a fire burning in the grate. The shutters were pulled back on the windows, offering a view of acres of grass and woods. Rogers probably owned it all, Lottie thought. Hunting scenes on the walls. Every inch the residence of a country squire.

Agnes Rogers was every inch the city girl, though. She bustled in, her dress rustling as she moved. The garment hadn't come from a market stall. Not even from Marshall and Snelgrove. It was probably bought in some tiny shop in London, Lottie decided, and there'd be a French label inside. The chic bobbed hair wasn't from Leeds, either; no one in the city could manage a cut as angular and sharp as that. Yet for all the surface, there were lines around her eyes and mouth that even good make-up couldn't hide. She'd covered the scar well, though; in the light of the room it was hardly noticeable. The woman was in her late thirties, Lottie guessed.

The maid followed her into the room, carrying a tea tray.

'I'll be mother, shall I?' Mrs Rogers said with a crisp smile. 'Now, what brings the police here to see me? Usually the officers want to talk to my husband.' Her eyes widened. 'It's terribly exciting.'

'Irene Walker,' McMillan began as he sipped from a small cup.

The woman's mouth closed sharply.

'You know her,' he said.

'I've talked to her once or twice,' Agnes Rogers admitted cautiously.

'At the Royal.'

She nodded.

'You know what's happened with her family.' He made it sound like an accusation.

'My husband told me.' Her voice was calm.

'Then you understand she's in danger.'

'I haven't seen her for a little while.' She looked at him from under her eyelids. 'Honestly.'

'Mrs Rogers,' Lottie said, 'did you know she was staying upstairs at the Royal?'

'She was?' Her surprise seemed genuine. 'I thought it was empty.'

'The problem is, she's vanished again. Do you know where she might have gone? Somewhere she might feel safe.'

'Not really.' Mrs Rogers shook her head. 'I only knew her to chat.'

'Did you ever give her anything? Presents? Money?'

'I lent her a few pounds here and there.' She offered a small smile. 'My husband knows her father, of course.'

Of course, the families would move in the same circles.

'Does your husband know about your friendship with Irene?' McMillan asked.

The pleasure vanished from her face immediately. 'It's hardly worth mentioning.'

'Are you a regular at the Royal, Mrs Rogers?'

'I've only been a few times, slumming.'

'The place has quite the reputation.' It was his turn to smile.

'That's why I wanted to go. To see what the fuss was all about.'

Slumming was one giggling visit as part of a crowd, Lottie thought. Several times, on her own, was something altogether different. No wonder her husband didn't know.

'Please,' Lottie said, 'if you have any idea at all where Irene could be, we need to know. She's in danger.' Maybe a woman-to-woman appeal would help. She glanced at the sergeant from the corner of her eye. 'And anything you tell us will be in absolute confidence.'

'If I knew, I'd tell you. Everything that's happened, it's terrible. I'm sorry. I wish I could do more.'

She was lying. It was there on her face. But they couldn't push a woman like Agnes Rogers. The only choice was to nod and accept it.

McMillan tried a few more questions. They were powerless, though, and she knew it. They dared not accuse a woman whose husband effectively ran the police.

At the bottom of the drive McMillan stopped the car and lit a cigarette, waiting before he turned on to the road.

'Councillor Rogers chases everything in skirts. She goes to a bar like that. What kind of marriage can they have?'

There were all sorts. She knew that very well indeed. But no point in starting that discussion; he'd never understand. Instead Lottie said, 'She was lying.'

'Of course she was. She's untouchable, though.' He ran his hands wearily down her cheeks. 'I can't drag her down to Millgarth and bring out the cosh. That's the problem with this case. All the people who have the answers also have influence.'

'What now?'

He started to drive. 'We go back, start looking again, and hope we have a stroke of luck.'

'What about me?'

'Back on patrol. I'd keep you if I could, believe me. But the inspector would never allow it. He probably thinks the earth would stop turning if we had a female detective.'

He dropped her on Vicar Lane, by the entrance to the market. Another ten minutes and Cathy should be along. There was a hint of rain in the air, enough to make her wish she'd worn her cape; if it started to bucket down she'd be soaked.

Millgarth was close enough, though. If she hurried she could be back in time for Cathy. Lottie trotted down George Street, through the back door of the station and to her locker. Slip the cape over the uniform, button it at the neck. A quick check in the mirror and she was on her way.

'Lottie! Come here.' The voice was loud enough for a foghorn. She stopped and turned, seeing the woman standing in the doorway of the Market Tavern and waving her over. The landlady. Nancy.

With her hard face and clothes cut tight over her ample figure, the dress stopping just below the knee, she looked blowsy.

A glass of gin stood on the bar. Nancy swallowed it in one and grinned.

'Always a good pick-me-up before opening time. That lad you were in here asking about…'

'Ronnie Walker.' It seemed long ago now, almost ancient history.

'Did you find whoever killed him?' She brought a small clutch purse from under the bar, took out a silver cigarette case and lit one.

'Not yet,' Lottie said. 'Why?'

'There was someone in last night mentioning his name.'

'Last night?' She felt a prickle down her spine. 'Who?'

'A girl. She was only here a couple of minutes.'

'Blue-grey coat, blue hat with sequins?'

'That's her.' Nancy raised an eyebrow, impressed. 'How did you know? Who is she?'

'Ronnie's sister. What did she want?'

'That makes sense, I suppose. She was looking for some man who'd known him. But she didn't know his name. All she had was a rough description.'

'Can you tell me?' Lottie asked.

'About six foot tall, black hair, widow's peak. I told her it sounded like Gerry White, but he hasn't been around here in weeks. When I turned round she was gone.'

'How did she seem?'

'Scared. Looking around all the time. Jumpy. Someone bumped into her and I thought I was going to have to scrape her off the ceiling.' She shrugged. 'I just thought I'd tell you.'

'I'm glad you did.' She put her hand over Nancy's for a second. 'You might have helped.'

'Don't let it get round I'm helping the coppers or my reputation's shot. Off you go, back to work.'

CHAPTER NINETEEN

SHE caught up with Cathy at the back of the Corn Exchange, talking to a pair of boys not old enough to have left school yet.

'You and whose army's going to make me go?' one of them said to her. He didn't hear Lottie come up behind. But he felt the clout she gave him.

'We are,' she told him. 'And you'd better say sorry for your cheek.'

'Sorry, miss.' Looking down, red-faced, he rubbed the spot.

'I've got their names and addresses. They go to York Road School.'

'We'll be having a word with your headmaster,' Lottie warned them. 'He'll be seeing you after. If you know what's good for you, you'll be back in class this afternoon.'

The pair didn't need another hint. They took off running, not even looking back to shout an insult.

'Lucky it was us and not the truant officer,' Cathy said. She finished writing it up in her notebook. 'I'll send the school a letter this afternoon.' She packed everything away, looking expectantly. 'Well? Aren't you going to tell me what it was all about this morning?'

'While we walk. I need to see Sergeant McMillan.'

He was standing outside the hotel, nodding absently as he listened to a constable with a heavy moustache. He saw Lottie, held up a finger and heard the man out before dismissing him.

'Have you found her?' McMillan asked.

'No. But there's something you need to know.'

'Gerry White,' he said thoughtfully when she'd finished. 'I know him well enough. Time to pay him a visit, I think.' He noticed the look on her face. 'Alone. Sorry.'

By Friday afternoon she'd heard nothing more. Rumours usually flashed around the station like a wildfire. But this time people had nothing to say. Doors were carefully closed. Lottie hadn't even seen McMillan to try and discover the truth.

She reported for the end of her shift then slipped on her mackintosh. Cathy had left quickly, going to meet Jimmy down on Hunslet Lane when he finished work. At the doorway of the station she raised her collar against the rain and began to walk down the street.

Lottie felt frustrated, not knowing what was happening. She'd done a lot on the Walker case and now she felt locked out of it. And patrol had been quiet. A pair of drunken women, a gaggle of prostitutes down in the Dark Arches. Everything routine. The excitement seemed to be receding to a distant horizon and it left her feeling flat.

She kept hoping that McMillan would pull alongside in his Peugeot, tapping the horn impatiently, apologising and needing her help. But he hadn't appeared by the time she stepped on the tram.

If the weather remained there wouldn't even be an outing on the motorbike tomorrow afternoon. Geoff had a heavy tarpaulin tied over the machine and sidecar; a puddle of water had gathered in one of the dips. Never mind.

She'd almost cooked the tea when she heard a knock on the door. Lottie turned off the gas under the food, untied her apron and pulled it over her head. Not the muffin man; she'd have heard the bell streets away. And a neighbour would come to the back door.

It was the detective sergeant who stood in front of her.

'I'm sorry,' McMillan said. 'You must think I'd abandoned you.'

Lottie felt flustered. Strange, she thought, careening around Leeds in his car, seeing a dead body with him, those things hardly worried her. So why did having him on her doorstep send the butterflies fluttering around her stomach?

'You'd better come in.' The curtains would be waving all along the street.

He shook his head. 'I can't stop. I just wanted to say I'm sorry. It's been too busy and we're keeping everything hush-hush.'

'That man, Gerry White. Did you find him?'

'Oh yes.' A dark smile crossed McMillan's face. 'But I probably shouldn't even tell you that. He's in custody now, but it's nothing to do with this case.'

'Still no word about Irene Walker?'

'Nothing at all.' He clicked his tongue against the roof of his mouth.

She saw Geoff turn the corner, marching at his usual brisk pace, briefcase weighing down his arm, bowler hat perched neatly on his head, umbrella unfurled. The two of them were just going to have to meet.

It was simple; she barely had time to make the introductions before the men shook hands, said 'How do you do,' and Geoff vanished through to the kitchen.

'I probably came at a bad time,' McMillan apologised again.

'It's fine,' Lottie told him. 'I appreciate it. But it sounds as if you won't need me.'

'Not until we find Irene. Or something else comes up. That's not a hint,' he added, then jangled the car keys. 'I'd better get back. No early knocking-off for me.'

'Thank you,' she said, and meant it.

'That's the sergeant, is it?' Geoff seemed unconcerned, trying to tune in 2LS and the BBC.

Lottie struck a match and relit the gas under the pans. 'He felt guilty for not keeping me up to speed.'

'Looks like an efficient chap.'

'He is. At least he doesn't mind a woman doing something.'

'Why would he?' Geoff grinned. A small flourish of his wrist and the music started, the sound of an orchestra emerging from the crackles. 'I was thinking: if it clears up tomorrow, why don't we go to Chesterfield?'

'Chesterfield?' He'd never mentioned the place before. 'What for?'

'The train went through there when I was being shipped out. There's a huge leaning spire on the church.' His eyes seemed to turn towards memories. 'I've always had a hankering to see it properly.'

'Of course. Why not?' How could she refuse a wish like that?

'My Jimmy's taking me to a matinee,' Cathy said as they left Millgarth. The week was over. For all Saturday morning had brought, they might as well have stayed in bed.

'Anything good?'

'*Beau Brummel*.' She winked. 'It's got John Barrymore, that's enough for me.'

Down the street a motorcycle engine roared into life.

'We're going out on the bike.'

'So I see. You're in the sidecar?' Cathy stared at it doubtfully. 'It doesn't look very safe.'

'It's fine.' Lottie brought a pair of goggles from her pocket. 'Put these on, a scarf around my hair and it's all the joy of the open road.'

'If you say so. I'll stick to a film and canoodling on the back row of the Plaza.' She waved at Geoff then left.

'Ready?' He asked. The grin on his face was as broad as a boy's.

'Ready,' Lottie told him.

'How was the bike trip?'

'Fun.' Chesterfield had proved to be a sweet little market town, full of history and hidden streets. 'How was the cinema?'

'Didn't go in the end.' The corners of Cathy's mouth turned down. 'Jimmy was asked to work overtime. I ended up standing around waiting for him and looking like a good time girl.'

Lottie kept the comment on the tip of her tongue.

Kirkgate Market was quiet, just a few early Monday shoppers. She nodded to the faces she knew, the butchers and the bakers and the flower sellers.

The whole area seemed hushed. Not many people around, nothing at all that needed a pair of policewomen. By noon Lottie felt as if she was wasting her time out on the streets.

'We're close to Millgarth. We could eat in the canteen,' she said.

'You know what that place is like.' There was a reason they avoided it. The men staring and whispering to each other. Leering grins. A few catcalls. Sometime a man trying to grope. They were on display. And Lottie knew her run-in with Berwick had left policewomen even more unpopular with the male constables. The only advantage was that the food was cheap and filling.

'I'll brave it if you will. We can't let them think they've won and scared us off.'

Cathy sighed. 'All right. I had my heart set on Wray's, though.'

'Another time,' Lottie promised.

The meat in the stew was tough and chewy, but the jam roly-poly with custard was hot and sweet, the tea dark and strong. They sat by themselves, backs against the wall. Lottie knew men were watching them, and tried to ignore it.

They were passing the front desk, ready for the long afternoon, when the sergeant called, 'Armstrong!' He had a face like thunder, mouth a thin line under the moustache, thick hair slicked down with pomade.

'Sarge?'

'Message for you.' He pushed a piece of paper across to her. 'Don't make a habit of it. I'm not your secretary.'

She read it quickly.

'How long ago did this come in, Sarge?' she asked.

'I don't know.' He glanced at the clock on the wall. 'Two hours or so.'

She turned to Cathy. 'I'll catch up with you.'

The soles of her shoes clattered as she dashed up the stairs and threw open the door of the CID room. Empty. A cough from next door: Inspector Carter was in his office. She didn't have any choice. Taking a deep breath, she knocked on his door.

There was no kindness in his gaze.

'Well?' he asked as he looked up from the stack of papers in front of him.

'I'm sorry to disturb, sir, but I got a message that CID ought to know about.'

He steepled his fingers under a thick, fleshy chin. 'Well?'

'It's from Mr Donough's housekeeper, sir. I knew her during the war. She took a telephone call this morning. Someone wanting to talk to him.'

'Go on. Or is this a guessing game?'

'It was Mr Walker, sir. She heard part of the conversation. They've arranged to meet tonight.'

'Where?' He'd picked up a pen and was scribbling notes.

'She doesn't know, sir. Donough didn't mention a place. Walker must have suggested somewhere. But it's at eight o'clock.'

'I see. Good job,' he said reluctantly. 'I'll pass the information to Sergeant McMillan.'

'If you follow Walker you'll find where they're getting together.'

'Thank you for that insight, Constable.' He kept his voice even, staring at her. 'I'd never have come up with it myself.'

Lottie felt the heat on her face. Put in her place. Humiliated.

'Sorry, sir.' Stupid, she thought. She should know when to keep her mouth shut.

'I'll pass the word and see you receive the credit,' Carter told her. 'Now you can go back to work.'

She felt deflated as she descended the steps. Outside, a wind had started to blow. She needed to keep a hand on her skirt to stop it blowing up.

Cathy was at the top end of Kirkgate, taking the details from a dazed woman who'd had her handbag snatched.

'He was just a lad. Ran off up Briggate. I shouted, but no one paid attention. The world's coming to a right pass when no one wants to help an old woman who's been robbed.'

There was little the police could do. No real description of the thief. The woman wasn't even sure what she'd had in her bag. All she could say with certainty was what it looked like: black leather with an old gilt clasp. That didn't help much.

'We'll keep our eyes open,' Cathy assured her, taking a few pennies from her uniform pocket. 'That should take care of your bus fare home. If we find it we'll bring it to you, all right?'

They set off along Briggate, poking into all the alleys and lanes that led off the street. He might have taken the cash and thrown the bag away, out of sight. As soon as they turned away from the bustle, the world seemed like a distant place.

They worked their way up the street: nothing.

'Let's try the far side,' Lottie suggested. They had nothing better to fill the time.

They searched along New Briggate as far as Merrion Street before turning back. No luck. Slowly, they turned, ready to return to patrol.

'There,' Lottie said. She pointed: a woman in a blue-grey coat and cloche hat. 'Look.'

'Who?'

The figure was on the other side of the road, her back to them, passing the entrance to St John's churchyard.

'Irene Walker,' Lottie called over her shoulder. 'Come on.'

She started to dodge through traffic, trying to keep her eye on Irene. A lorry sounded its horn as it screeched to a halt, the driver yelling. She moved behind a bus, in front of a tram. Then, breathless, she reached the pavement and began to run.

Cathy was ahead of her; God knew how she'd managed it. But there was no sign or Irene Walker. No coat in RAF blue, no dark hat.

'She could have gone up Mark Street or through the churchyard,' Cathy said as she caught her breath. 'We're never going to find her. Too many places she could be now.'

Lottie nodded sadly. It was true. There was a maze of streets less than a hundred yards away. But they'd definitely seen Irene;

she'd bet her badge on it. And it was the second time she'd been spotted on New Briggate. There had to be *something* that kept bringing her back here.

'What do you want to do now?' Cathy asked.

'Wait here a moment.' There was a telephone kiosk by the Grand Theatre. 'I want to ring in with the sighting.'

Grudgingly, the desk sergeant agreed to pass the message on to McMillan. Lottie stared up at the buildings. So many windows, so many rooms. So many people. Almost a hopeless task, she thought. But one of them knew Irene Walker.

The constables had already gone round and asked questions. But half the men on the force were as useful as teats on a bull. Barely a brain between them. This needed a woman's touch.

'How do you fancy a little door-to-door?' she said.

Each of the buildings along New Briggate was a warren of small businesses and offices. Photographers, insurance agents, accountants who didn't look as if they could add a column of figures. Manufacturers' agents.

But none of them knew anything about a girl named Irene in a grey coat the colour of an RAF uniform.

After thirty offices Lottie was hoarse, sick of repeating the same questions. Cathy had started from the other end of the block. They'd meet somewhere in the middle, at the Central Hotel.

This was a good idea, she *knew* it was. But after so many people shaking their heads and saying no, it felt frustrating.

She walked down the steps and out into the daylight. The building had smelt of overboiled cabbage and old urine. Lottie breathed deep. The Leeds air was hardly pure, but it was cleaner than that.

The Peugeot was parked outside the Grand. She could see Cathy standing by the driver's window, chattering merrily. McMillan had obviously received the message.

'You're absolutely certain it was her?' He kept his eyes on Lottie as she joined them.

'Positive. The clothes, something in the way she walked. It was her.'

He smacked the palm of his hand against the steering wheel. 'Nothing yet?'

'Only blank looks. You got the message about Donough and Walker earlier?'

'The inspector told me. We'll be keeping an eye on them. Let them have their meeting and we'll pull them both in.'

'Don't tell Donough where you got the information, please.'

'Not a word,' he promised with a smile, opened the door and surveyed the street. 'We'd better get to work. There's still plenty left to cover.'

The office was on the top floor, a window gazing down at the road. A name was painted on the glass door: Maurice Hartley, Theatrical Agent. Lottie turned the knob and entered.

The man was younger than she'd expected. In his middle twenties, at a guess, and so slick she felt her words would slide right off him. A little too handsome, with a cheap, easy smile, a thin moustache, and carefully arranged hair. But his suit was good quality and he appraised her with intelligent eyes.

'Can I help you?' A lazy drawl. 'Thinking of a career change, are you? You don't have the look for music hall and you're definitely not film star material.'

She knew. She could feel it inside. He'd given nothing away, no flicker of his eyes, no sign of nerves. But she *knew* this was the man Irene Walker had visited. Lottie just had to make sure she didn't give the game away just yet. Think fast. Fast.

'I'm sorry to bother you, sir.' She put on her brightest smile. 'We're chasing a lad who snatched a woman's purse. He was seen heading along the street. You haven't noticed anything, have you?'

He gave her a condescending smile. 'In case you hadn't noticed, I'm on the top floor.'

'Of course. But you didn't hear anything at all?'

'Nothing.' His attention was back on the papers in front of him. 'Was there anything else?'

'No. Thank you for your help.'

Lottie took her time going down the stairs, keeping her eyes open for back exits and letting her heart slow down. She believed she'd played it well. He didn't look as if he suspected anything.

Crowds were passing on the pavement, queueing for trams and buses, talking away or reading their newspapers as if nothing had happened. She spotted Cathy and waved her over. Now they needed McMillan.

'What's his name?' the sergeant asked once she'd explained. His head was tilted back, glancing up at the building.

'Maurice Hartley,' Lottie said. 'That was the name on the door.'

'Young, good-looking?'

'Yes. Do you know him?'

McMillan snorted his disgust. 'I've arrested him twice. He's an invert. Notorious for it. Still, if Irene Walker's going down to the Royal, it makes sense she'd know him. It's probably home away from home for the likes of him. Top floor, you said?'

'Yes. No back way out.'

'Leave him to me. Thank you, girls.' He tipped his hat. 'You've done better than the men.' And he was gone.

'Is that it, then?' Cathy asked as they strolled back to Millgarth. 'Well done and goodbye?'

'Looks like it.'

'Makes you wonder why we bother,' she said.

'It's our duty. At least he said thank you. And it's more fun than patrol, you have to admit that.'

'Well, yes.'

'Armstrong, I need to speak to you for a moment,' Mrs Maitland said as she dismissed them.

'Ma'am?'

The woman waited until Cathy had gone and the door was firmly closed.

'Inspector Carter came to see me this afternoon. He had a complaint about you.'

'Me?' She couldn't believe it.

'He said your attitude left a great deal to be desired.' She raised an eyebrow. 'You were telling CID how to do their job, apparently?'

'I got a little carried away, ma'am.'

'I asked him for the details. You gave them some information that could help solve the Walker murder?'

'I don't know if it will or not—' she began.

Mrs Maitland cut over the top. 'I pointed out to him, very gently, that he ought to be grateful to the WPCs here, rather than finding some minor fault.'

'Thank you, ma'am.'

'Still you might want to keep out of his way for a few days. That's all.'

CHAPTER TWENTY

AS soon as Lottie walked through the door at Millgarth the next morning she could sense the mood. Jumping, electric. The constables were striding as if they had a real purpose. Voices were hushed and focused.

'McMillan brought in Hartley,' Cathy said as she hung her coat in the locker. 'And there was someone else last night, too.'

'Donough?'

'That's it. They're still questioning them both. Everyone seems to think they'll wrap up the Ronnie Walker killing today.'

Maybe they would. It would be good news and a little justice. But the pair who'd murdered him were still running free somewhere. It couldn't be fully over until they were behind bars. Only then would there be something for Jocelyn Hill.

It was the kind of day when Lottie wondered why she'd taken the job. The rain was coming down, just heavy enough to be annoying. Huddled in their capes, vainly trying to keep dry, they walked. The streets were almost empty. The only people who had to be out dashed from cover to cover or hid under wide umbrellas. There'd be next to no crime with weather like this.

They were grateful for the steamy warmth of the Exchange Restaurant, shaking out the rain. Through the morning they'd barely spoken, too miserable and damp for idle chatter. With the first sip of tea Cathy leaned back and sighed.

'I was ready for that,' she said. 'We could cover the indoor market this afternoon. Or go down to the Dark Arches. At least we'd be dry.'

Lottie shook her head. This was the kind of day Mrs Maitland would come out and check they were working. It would be better to return to the station looking like a drowned rat.

'You won't melt.'

'No, but I'll be in a mood.' She laughed. 'Still, someone has to keep Leeds safe. But I'm going to make sure I have something hot inside me first.' She drank a little more tea. 'Do you think they've solved it all yet?'

'I don't know.' It had been on her mind all morning. CID should be able to get the information they needed. They'd been forced to hold back with Walker; they wouldn't have the same constraints with the other two men.

Lottie had heard what happened during interviews. She didn't doubt it was true. But if that was what they needed... fine.

And meanwhile Irene Walker was out there somewhere.

'I have an idea,' Lottie said suddenly.

'What?'

'As soon as we've eaten I want to go somewhere.' She saw Cathy's suspicious look. 'Don't worry, it's inside.'

No policemen at the side entrance to the Royal Hotel. They'd finished searching and moved on. The lock gave easily enough and they were inside.

'Do you think Irene might have come back?' Cathy whispered.

'She needs somewhere to sleep. It's probably the last place anyone would expect.'

Lottie started with Irene's old room, but there was no sign anyone had been there in the last few hours. The same with

Alice Sutherland's. Clothes, cosmetics, magazines were all strewn across the floor, bedclothes thrown around. It seemed a shame. Alice had looked so secure here; could she ever feel that way again?

Doors were flung wide everywhere, an indication that the place had been inspected. They worked their way down from the top floor. Nothing to indicate anyone had spent the night.

'Oh well, it was just a hunch.' She shrugged as they finished and emerged into the rain. Time to return to the rainy patrol.

'A good idea, though.'

No shortage of those, Lottie thought wryly. Just not always good enough.

Hope Brothers stood on Briggate, just up from Marks and Spencer. A paper sign in the window announced a stocktaking sale. Inside, Miss Barker the manageress paced around the floor as she explained about the shoplifter.

'She was so nicely dressed that I never gave her a thought.'

'What did she take?' Lottie asked. Her notebook was ready, but so far the woman hadn't said anything useful.

'Three pairs of silk stockings.' Her fingers pulled at a lace handkerchief. 'I didn't even realise until she'd gone. They'd been out on the counter. At first I thought one of the girls must have put them away.' She nodded at the two assistants; both were talking to Cathy. 'When they said they hadn't, I put two and two together.'

'What did she look like?' Lottie asked.

'Very well presented. An emerald green hat with a feather, fox stole, a pale grey dress.'

'I mean her height, eyes, hair.' Clothes could be changed in a minute. Other things were harder to disguise.

'Well,' Miss Barker began slowly, 'she was about normal height, I suppose. On the slim side, but not a rail like these girls nowadays. She was definitely in her thirties but she looked after herself, you could tell.'

It wasn't much. 'Did she give you a name?'

The woman shook her head. 'I never ask until I'm filling out the receipt.'

'Well, that was a waste of time,' Lottie grumbled. They stood outside, under the awning.

'Not completely.'

'Oh?'

'One of the girls said the shoplifter let her cut-glass accent slip for a moment and it came out pure Leeds.' A smile twitched across her lips. 'Ten to one it's Pam Leech.'

'Isn't she still in jail?' Lottie asked. 'And three pairs of silk stockings? She usually does better than that.'

'We can go to her house and find out.'

Lottie looked up at the sky. 'All right, but we're taking the tram.'

Pam Leech lived in a house on Brudenell Road, a minute or two from Woodhouse Moor. No one knew why she liked to steal. She had money. Not a fortune, but ample for her needs. By all accounts, her parents had provided well in the will, leaving her the house and an income. She simply seemed to enjoy the challenge of taking things. It was a compulsion. She never tried to deny it when she was caught, just giving her disarming smile.

As they opened the gate into the tiny front garden and sidestepped a puddle, Lottie said, 'She's all yours.'

Cathy beamed.

Leech hadn't even changed clothes from the shoplifting expedition. The stockings were draped over the back of a chair, along with a scarf and some filmy underwear, and a hat that looked as if it had come from Bridges shop on Lands Lane.

'What are we going to do with you, Pam?' Cathy asked, shaking her head. 'How long have you been out, anyway?'

'Last Friday,' the woman answered quietly. 'Today was my first day shopping.'

'It'll be your last for a while, too.' She gave a sigh. 'It's probably just as well you didn't decide to go into Ramsden's. Even you might have had a problem pinching a piano. I'm going to have to take you in. You know the routine.'

They wrapped the goods in brown paper, made sure the gas was off and the door locked. Another few minutes and they'd booked Miss Leech in at the tiny police station next to the library.

'What do you want me to do with her?' the constable asked. 'I've only got room for one in the cell.'

'That's fine; there's only one of her,' Cathy pointed out. 'If you ring HQ they'll send a wagon out.'

'I don't know,' he muttered as he rolled his eyes. 'Women.'

'Honestly, you'd think he'd be grateful we put someone in his pathetic little cell,' Cathy said as they marched along Woodhouse Lane, through the rain and back into town.

'He's a man,' Lottie told her. 'You really shouldn't expect too much.'

Her cape was sodden, her skirt was soaked and her shoes seemed to squelch as she walked down the corridor to the lockers. The only consolation was that the beat bobbies looked no better as they returned to end their shift.

Lottie saw McMillan leaning against the wall, smirking.

'Don't you dare,' she warned.

'I had years in uniform myself, remember? And trust me, it's nothing compared to the trenches.'

'Sorry.'

'People forget. I wanted to tell you, Maurice Hartley's in the infirmary.'

'What happened?'

'He had an accident.' McMillan's gaze slid away and she knew exactly what he meant. 'Broken leg, a couple of teeth knocked out.'

'Before or after he talked?' That was the way it worked. And they'd be especially hard on anyone like him.

'Swears he doesn't know where Irene is. They became friends at the Royal. She stopped in and he lent her two pounds; it was all he had on him. That's it.'

'Do you believe him?'

'He was telling the truth. No doubt about that,' McMillan said darkly.

'What about Donough?'

'We'd barely started talking to him then his solicitor arrived. God only knows how he found out.'

'Not much help?'

He shook his head, took out a Black Cat and lit it. 'He admits Walker telephoned him and they arranged to meet. But he insists it was strictly business. That's all he'll say.'

'No nearer the truth, then.'

'No. We had to let Donough go, not a thing on him.'

'What now?'

'I wish I knew. Trying to get anywhere in this case is like wading through bloody treacle. Pardon my French.'

'I've heard worse,' Lottie said with a smile.

'I feel as if we're never going to get anywhere. We'll end up with it never closed and Irene Walker off somewhere until Doomsday.'

'We'll find her.' But even as she spoke she didn't believe the words. The girl could easily disappear if she chose. She'd done a good job of it so far. Now you see her, now you don't. She probably didn't even know her mother was dead.

'The servant at the Walker house,' Lottie said suddenly.

'What about her?'

'Have you talked to her again? Irene might have telephoned.'

'I never even thought about it,' he admitted. 'I don't suppose…'

'Not until I'm dry.' She caught sight of herself in the mirror. 'I look a fright.'

'I'll do it myself, then.'

'It'll be good for your soul.'

For a second she believed she'd been too cheeky. Then he winked and walked away.

At home, Lottie hung her uniform from the wooden airing rack in the kitchen and pulled it up to the ceiling. As she cooked, the smell of wet wool filled the air. Not pleasant, but no worse than the cabbage boiling on the cooker. With luck it would be dry by morning. It had better be; she didn't own a spare.

Mostly dry. Still a little damp on the shoulders and around the collar, but not too bad. She went over the uniform with a stiff brush before putting it on and looking in the mirror. Mrs Maitland wouldn't find fault with that.

At least the rain had stopped. A faint, half-hearted sun tried to peer through the clouds as she walked to the tram stop. A much better day to be out on patrol.

Almost October. A few more weeks and the fogs would begin. Thick as soup, people coughing with bronchitis.

She wondered if McMillan had learned anything from Walker's servant. She'd seemed a fearsome, cold creature, yet perhaps Irene had found a little warmth there. But McMillan just shook his head when he saw her in the corridor at Millgarth. No need for words; that said it all.

Back to square one.

The Dark Arches were damp and cold; thin rivulets of water ran down the brickwork, the River Aire roaring close by. No women loitering or soliciting. Lottie and Cathy walked through to Holbeck, stopping at the canal. Men were busy unloading barges; still plenty of activity on the waterways, and smoke billowed from a hundred chimneys as factories produced their goods.

Back over the Victoria Bridge and along Neville Street. It was going to be one of those days when nothing happened, she could tell, and the shift went by with the grinding speed of a glacier.

By dinnertime all they'd done was talk to a couple of beggars and given directions to a lady and her daughter visiting from Ripon. Sometimes it was like this, she knew very well. But that didn't make it easier to take.

'You've been in a mood all morning,' Cathy said.

'Have I?' She hadn't even realised. 'Sorry.'

The waitress at the Kardomah was showing them to a table when they heard the sound. Unmistakeable, the piercing blare of a police whistle. They froze, mid-step.

Lottie said, 'I'm sorry, we have to go. Emergency,' and they dashed down the stairs, dodging between customers as they squeezed out on to Briggate.

They peered round, waiting for another blast to tell them which way to run. As soon as it came, Cathy was ready.

'Lower Headrow,' she called, pushing her way through the lunchtime crowds.

Lottie followed. She wasn't as slim or as quick, and she moved more slowly, following the sound of the whistle as it called again.

It was still going on as she arrived. Two beat bobbies going up against four men outside the Three Legs public house. The coppers had their truncheons out, but the men had broken beer glasses and a poker dragged from the fireplace inside as weapons.

Cathy was standing back, out of range. The WPCs only had a pair of handcuffs; they hadn't been given anything to defend themselves. It was unfeminine. Never mind that they needed it at least once a week.

A crowd had gathered in a ring. Some of them yelled encouragement to the men. Others watched quietly, a fire in their eyes.

It was a stand-off. Lottie knew the coppers; both of them close to retirement, not seeking danger or a fight. And the men facing them had slightly stunned looks on their faces, aware they'd taken things too far, but not willing to back down and walk away.

Men, Lottie thought. No better than boys, the lot of them.

'You.' He wasn't much more than a lad, not even old enough to shave properly, bum fluff on his upper lip. He turned at the shout, eyes nervous. 'What do you think your mother would say if she saw you now? She'd give you a clout and be sending you off to bed without your supper.' One of the men laughed. He had to be in his fifties, leather skin, half his teeth missing, the rest stained brown. 'And what about you?' she continued.

'Don't you think you're a bit old for this? Maybe you need to grow up a bit.'

More laughter, a few shouts of derision.

'Happen you should get back home and look after your husband,' someone cried, others yelling their agreement.

'Is that what you've come to? You think you're big men because you can insult a woman? Is that all the Western Front was for? You, where did you serve?' She pointed at the man holding the poker by his side.

'Too young,' he said. 'But me dad did, and he died.'

'And my husband was wounded at Gallipoli,' Lottie said. She could feel the blood pounding in her neck. Her temper was up and she wasn't going to let this drop until she'd shamed them. 'Well, are you big enough men to do time in Armley for assault? Keep this up and that's where you're headed. What are your wives going to say when there's no money coming in? Think they'll be proud of you then?'

She let the question hang. The men were looking at each other. This was the moment; they'd either charge or walk away. It was the lad who gave up first. She hadn't expected that. He'd seemed like the one with something to prove. Maybe there was hope for him after all.

As soon as he turned away, it was like a house of cards. The men seemed to melt back into the pub. She stared at the two constables then walked off, almost at the corner of Vicar Lane before Cathy caught up.

'Blimey,' she said in surprise. 'I didn't know you had that in you.'

'Makes two of us,' Lottie confessed as the tension seemed to drain out of her. 'Honestly, I was so furious I could have wrung all their necks. Call themselves grown men…'

'You know you've probably put the cat among the pigeons now.'

'How?' She strode angrily down Briggate then up Thornton's Arcade towards Lands Lane. It was quieter in here, away from the bustle of the street.

'They blew their whistles,' Cathy told her. 'It'll be in their notebooks, they'll have to report it. Word's going to get around.'

'Let it.'

'The brass will want arrests. They need to make an example of people.'

She knew. Arrest a few, punishments harsh enough to discourage the others. That was how the law operated. But WPCs saw the other side of it, the wife and children living off charity, sometimes evicted, while their husbands were in jail. No one thought about that as they were putting up their fists or storming into a fight.

'I've done what I can.' For what it was worth, anyway. 'I don't know about you, but I'm absolutely famished now.'

The station was quiet when they walked in to report for the end of shift. Cathy looked at her and raised her eyebrows. It wasn't going to be good.

'You seem to have a knack for getting yourself noticed, Armstrong,' Mrs Maitland said. She read out the report the beat officers had submitted. Her barracking had given the suspects the chance to elude the constables outside the pub. Arrests had been imminent until she'd taken it on herself to speak up. As it was, no one had been taken into custody.

'Beg pardon, ma'am—'

'I'm not asking you, Taylor. How much truth is there in this, Armstrong?'

'Hardly a word, ma'am.' Almost every day of her life a man had tried to do her down. She'd had enough. 'I stopped a fight;

that's true. It was the choice of the constables not to make any arrests. It was probably the wisest thing to do.'

'I received a telephone call this afternoon from Miss Silkston. Do you know who she is?'

'No, ma'am.'

'She happens to be a friend of the chief constable's wife. She was passing on the other side of the Headrow when the incident occurred.'

That was it, Lottie thought. She was for the high jump.

'According to her,' Maitland continued, 'you prevented a brawl in which two officers could have been severely injured. She said it was very brave and quite foolhardy.'

Her brain felt empty. All she could do was try to keep a foolish smile off her face.

'The problem is that you're gaining a reputation,' Mrs Maitland went on. 'I don't know what's happened; you used to behave according to the rules and regulations. All of a sudden you've become very independent-minded. It's not good. It places a spotlight on us, and not in a flattering way. Do I make myself clear?'

'Yes, ma'am.'

'Your job is not to involve yourself in violence. I've always been very clear about that. You overstepped your bounds. I have no option but to suspend you for two days without pay. Dismissed.'

She was numb. Cathy was talking to her but she didn't hear a word as she put on her raincoat and walked out of the station. She'd expected a dressing down, but not that. From being put forward for a citation to suspension in a matter of days. From the sublime to the ridiculous. It hardly seemed believable. It was humiliating.

Lottie barely noticed as someone took hold of her arm. Someone was speaking to her. It took a moment before she realised it was Sergeant McMillan.

'I said I'll give you a lift home,' he repeated.

'No.' Her voice seemed to be coming from the other side of a fog. 'Honestly, I'd rather…'

'You're in no fit state to be wandering round town. Come on.'

He didn't seem to give her a choice, ushering her to the Peugeot and pressing a small silver flask into her hand once she was seated.

'Take a sip. You'll feel better.'

The brandy burned in her throat. But he was right. It brought her bumping out of her daze and back to reality. She handed it back to him.

'I know all about it,' McMillan said. 'It was Carter's doing. The beat men complained to him and he went to the superintendent. You never had a chance of a fair deal.'

The knowledge was cold comfort. She still had the suspension, two empty days ahead when she could have been working. The next step after suspension was dismissal and it would be hanging over her if she didn't toe the line.

'What about Irene Walker?' Lottie asked. She didn't want to think about her own future. Better that something else filled her mind.

'No further along.' He pulled out a cigarette and lit it while he negotiated the traffic through Sheepscar. 'I have the men on the beat out asking questions. She vanished into that area past St John's; they're trying back there.'

'Can you drop me at the parade. I don't have anything in for tea. Again.'

'Do you want my opinion?' McMillan asked as he parked. 'You're too good at this job for them to dismiss you. That matron of yours would kick up an almighty stink. I heard her going hammer and tongs with the super this afternoon.'

'Mrs Maitland?' After everything the woman had said it didn't seem possible.

'Yes. She's on your side. And she's canny, take it from me. She might lose a battle or two but she'll make sure she wins the war.'

'Suspended for two days?' Geoff asked. He put down his knife and fork and rested his elbows on the table. 'But *why*?'

'For stopping a fight,' Lottie replied. 'That's the short answer, anyway.' She gave a wry, sad smile. 'Probably more for being a bit Bolshie and not knowing my place.'

'Ah.' He said it as if he understood. But, kind as he was, he could never comprehend. Not properly.

She fretted herself to sleep and was still worrying when she woke. Without the routine of preparing for work the morning seemed empty. Once Geoff left she sat in the kitchen cradling a cup of tea.

There was no shortage of things to do. The house needed a good clean from top to bottom. Washing to be done. A mountain of darning and mending. But she couldn't bring herself to face it.

Instead she took her time at the dressing table, carefully applying her make-up, brushing her hair until it was just so, then selecting her best dress, rayon in a pattern of burgundy and pale blue. Buckle shoes with a low, comfortable heel. Her good coat over the top, hat adjusted until it showed off her face perfectly and she was ready to go.

It felt strange to be wandering around town without purpose. She went from shop to shop, Schofield's to Matthias Robinson to the Pygmalion. Glancing in Greenwood the jeweller at the rings and baubles. Lovely, but nothing she coveted. Maybe her taste was too ordinary, she thought with a smile.

She did buy a few small things. More black stockings for work; wishful thinking, perhaps. A bottle of Cutex nail polish in dark red because she couldn't resist the colour; God only knew where she'd wear it, though. Not for work, not on the motorcycle. She'd have to persuade Geoff to take her out to a restaurant.

At the top of Briggate, waiting to cross the Headrow, a hand tapped her on the shoulder. She turned, expecting it would be Cathy or someone she knew. Instead it was a man, unshaved, in his forties and looking apologetic.

'I'm sorry, luv, I didn't mean to scare you.' He held up a small packet in his large hand. 'They're getting us to give these out, free, like. Samples. You have it for your breakfast with milk.'

She didn't understand. 'What? Like porridge, you mean?'

'Cold milk. Cereal, they call it. It's by this American company. They've hired a few of us to give these out.' He shrugged. 'It's a job and there's not too many of those about.'

She took the packet cautiously, inspecting it. Corn Flakes. Still, it was free; why not? When she looked up to thank him, the man had moved on, already talking to another woman.

A gap in the traffic and she darted across the street. Another few yards and she was by the yard in front of St John's Church. This was the last place she'd seen Irene Walker. On a whim she walked past the gravestones, following the path around the building and eventually out.

Irene might be somewhere on these streets. She didn't know the area, but she could tell exactly what it would be like. There were so many exactly the same in Leeds. Run-down houses and run-down lives. Children with rickets and diphtheria and whooping cough. Men with tuberculosis, too ill to work and too poor to afford a doctor.

Without thinking she began to walk. The same even, steady pace of patrol, gazing around, taking it all in.

Then she was at a crossroads, staring across at something that seemed out of place in the middle of so much desperation. Queen Square, the sign read. Three sides of a square, anyway, facing on to the road, the buildings genteel and decaying, huddled around a patch of scrubby grass.

It was curiously beautiful, all the houses with their faded elegance. They were still occupied. There were businesses and offices, movement behind the grubby windows. Lottie stood and stared. It seemed like a dream she'd had once when she was a little girl. The square of her imagination had been magical, lively, and this made her remember it vividly, along with her mother's words: 'It sounds lovely, pet, but you know we'll never afford a place like that.'

The grass was fenced like a garden, with a path and benches. Tentatively she opened the gate and entered, half-expecting someone to appear and threaten her for trespassing. But nothing happened. She took a seat, drinking in everything around her, revelling in her new discovery.

She wasn't sure how long she stayed; it could have been five minutes or an hour. For a while the suspension and the possibility of losing her job were forgotten. Her thoughts drifted and she could enjoy the peace of a place that seemed out of Leeds and out of time.

Finally she stirred. She was hungry, ready for some dinner, feeling peaceful and oddly happy. As she left the square Lottie looked back over her shoulder. And stopped.

It was no more than a flash, then gone behind glass. But she was certain. That had been Irene Walker.

CHAPTER TWENTY-ONE

SHE knew it, she felt it in her bones. But there was nothing she could do. Suspended for two days. She daren't show her face at Millgarth until that was over. And since the incident with Sergeant Berwick the men on the desk didn't like her; if she rang in and gave her name they'd probably end the call. But she had to let McMillan know.

The idea came as she opened the door to the telephone kiosk. Lottie sorted through the change in her purse, taking out pennies and a threepenny bit then dialling the number of the station.

'Is Sergeant McMillan there, please?' She tried to make her voice sound husky.

'I'll take a look. Can I tell him who wants him?'

'It's his wife.' Had he ever mentioned her name? Lottie didn't think so. 'Can you tell him it's important.'

'Just a minute and I'll see if he's around.'

A long pause and then: 'Sarah? What is it? What's wrong?'

'It's Lottie. Lottie Armstrong.' She hissed the words, a loud whisper even though no one could hear her. 'I had to pretend so they'd put me through. I've just seen Irene Walker.'

'Where?'

'Queen Square.'

'Stay right there,' he told her. 'I'll be over as soon as I can.'

He was as good as his word. Not even ten minutes later he parked the Peugeot on the other side of Clay Pit Lane.

'Which house?' he asked. No hellos, just straight to business.

'Above the chemist, over in the corner. I only had a quick glimpse through the window, but I'm certain it was her.'

'I believe you.' He looked at the building thoughtfully. 'There's bound to be a back door. If we go marching in she could slip out that way. We're going to need a plan.'

They didn't have many options. Lottie would go into the shop and McMillan would wait at the back. Now she only had to hope she'd been correct and that Irene was really there.

Inside, the place could have stepped from the pages of an old book. A heady mix of smells she couldn't identify, items in tall jars on shelves. A polished wood counter and display cases. It was impossible not to stare, to reach out and touch things.

'Can I help you, madam?'

She hadn't noticed him at first, in the shadows, almost hidden. He had a thin, feral face, dark smudges under piercing eyes.

'Yes,' Lottie said. They'd gone through it outside. Being blunt was the best way. 'You have a young woman upstairs. Miss Walker. I'd like to speak to her, please.'

For a moment his expression showed nothing. Then a mix of confusion and panic for a moment.

'I'm sorry, madam. I'm afraid I don't know what you're talking about. This is a chemist, not a hotel.'

She smiled. 'I saw her through the window, I know she's up there. It's vital that I speak to her.'

'Madam, I can assure you there's no one upstairs.' He tried to sound insistent but there was no conviction in his voice.

'Please,' Lottie said. 'I know there is. It's very important.'

'I've told you, there's no one else here.' She could see him clenching his fists, his face reddening. 'If you don't leave I'll have no option but to call the police.'

She produced her identification. If it ever came out she'd used this…

'No need, sir; we're already here.' She waited breathlessly as he read it. 'Now, sir, I think we need to take a look upstairs, don't you?'

It was wrong, it was daring. The whole thing was a gamble. If the chemist complained to anyone she was sunk. Immediate dismissal from the force. But she was here and she was positive that Irene Walker was upstairs. In for a penny, in for a pound.

'If I might just come through, sir, and see for myself.' Lottie took a step forwards but the man was surprisingly fast. He opened the door behind him and shouted,

'Irene, run, the police are here.'

Then he stood firm by the counter.

'I need you to move out of the way,' Lottie said, but it was pointless. He wasn't going to shift an inch yet. Footsteps running down the stairs. The sound of a key turning in the lock and then a door slammed. He smiled and stood aside.

'As you wish.'

She pulled the door open, going into a small hallway, the back entrance right there. Lottie yanked it open. Ten yards away McMillan was trying to keep hold of Irene Walker, who squirmed in his grip. He had one hand tight around her wrist, the other grasping the collar of her coat.

'Do you think you could you give me a hand?' he asked. 'The handcuffs are in my jacket.'

The girl struggled and fought, cursing and spitting, but soon enough they were on, with the harsh rasp of metal. She stood there, defeated but with her eyes still flashing hatred.

'You've been leading us a merry dance,' McMillan told her. 'We need to have a talk down at the station.'

His hand on her arm, the sergeant escorted her to the car, settling her in the back seat.

'Could you come down with us?' he asked Lottie. 'I want to make sure she doesn't try to get away.'

'Yes,' she answered, surprised by the question. 'But just to the door. Not inside. You…'

'I know.' He smiled at her as he started the vehicle. 'You're good at this lark, you know. If you get any better you'll be putting me out of a job.'

'If.' She didn't need to say more. McMillan held up his hands.

'Don't blame me. I didn't make the rules.'

Irene Walker sat with her head turned away, staring out at the traffic, a sullen air about her.

'Could you pull over somewhere before we get to the station?'

'Why?' He glanced at Lottie. 'Is something wrong?'

But he parked on Vicar Lane, leaving the engine running.

'Irene,' Lottie said. 'I need you to listen to me.' Slowly, the girl turned her head. Nothing showed on her face. 'I don't think anyone's told you. I'm so sorry, but your mother's dead.'

There was never going to be a good time to tell her, but even here, with shoppers flowing by on the pavement, was better than a room in Millgarth.

'No. You're lying.'

'I wish I was.' Her voice was quiet, trying to soothe. 'She did it herself. At Eccup Reservoir.'

Irene nodded, blinking hard, trying to hold back the tears that were always going to fall. Lottie put her arms around the girl, pulling her close, whispering words that were just soothing sounds.

Finally the crying softened to sniffles and hiccoughs, and Irene pulled away, rubbing at her eyes with her hands in the cuffs. McMillan threw the rest of his cigarette out of the window and put the Peugeot into gear.

He left the car round the corner from the station, far from prying eyes. Gently, they brought Irene Walker out. She seemed dazed, hardly able to stand; no surprise, Lottie thought.

'Come on,' McMillan said to the girl. 'As soon as we're inside I'll see you get a cup of tea.' He glanced back over his shoulder at Lottie with a smile and a nod of thanks.

She stood and watched them go. Irene was so close she was almost leaning against him. He was speaking gently to her, his mouth close to her ear; from the back they looked like a pair of lovers.

Lottie stood until they vanished round the corner, then set off at a brisk trot. Wednesday, half-day closing at the market. But nothing to catch her eye; she simply wanted to be away from Millgarth in case anyone saw her.

She pottered, trying to fill time, but the spell had stopped working. She kept thinking about Irene. The girl was safe now, but that was only the start of the story. The loss, the future of all the days and years beyond.

And the explanation. Lottie wouldn't hear that. Irene could help the police close the case quickly. She knew something; she wouldn't have run otherwise.

The whole thing could be finished before Lottie returned from suspension. McMillan would take the credit. That was fair, she thought; he'd put many of the pieces together. But she'd done her bit, too, and the brass would sweep that under the carpet. It was convenient and it avoided any embarrassment.

A good tea. At least she could salvage something from the day. A pair of lamb chops from the butcher, not too much fat, carrots from the greengrocer. She had potatoes in the larder and there were still a few sprigs of mint on the plant in the back garden; enough to make a sauce, anyway.

But as she worked in the steam of the kitchen, Lottie knew she was simply trying to find some consolation. This was no substitute for sitting with Irene Walker and discovering the truth of everything. She loved Geoff, but work gave her that real sense of purpose, of achieving something. She'd had that at Barnbow. They all had back then, the sense of going all out to win the war, to help the boys defeat the Kaiser.

That spirit had evaporated after the men came home and found life as it had been before. Often it was worse. The politicians' promises were hot air. Jobs vanished, factories closed. The dole helped, but it was never enough.

Serving as a policewoman made her feel like someone. Mrs Maitland was right: for a long time she'd been happy to obey all the regulations, not to do more than the rules permitted. But this investigation had opened a gate and now she couldn't close it again. She could do the job as well as any man. Better than most, really. Just try, though. Sometimes they'd commend you, then other times they'd slap you down if you happened to embarrass a man.

Life wasn't fair. Lately, though, she felt as if she'd had enough.

Silly, Lottie told herself as the front door closed and she heard Geoff's greeting.

'Almost ready,' she said as she mashed the potatoes. The mint sauce was on the table, meat and vegetables arranged on the plate. Everything as it should be. Just like a good housewife.

The next day she worked. Scrubbing the kitchen, doing the washing, running it through the mangle then pegging it out in the weak autumn sun. Sweeping the parlour, the hall and the stairs. Polishing the wood until the place smelt of beeswax.

She cut some stems of lavender, long past their best but still with a good scent, and brought them in the house. By three she was exhausted. Sitting with a cup of tea and a biscuit, she felt pride when she looked around. Everything sparkled; her mother would approve.

Tomorrow, at least, she'd be back on patrol. Part of her had hoped that McMillan would visit, eager to tell her everything. But no one came, not even any of the neighbours, curious as to why she was at home.

A little before five, as she put the finishing touches to a cottage pie before popping it in the oven, the knock finally came.

It was him, looking sheepish and a little ashamed.

'I know,' McMillan began. 'I'd have been here first thing if I could.' Across the street, a curtain moved. A motor car, a strange man. The least Lottie could do was fuel their gossip and invite him in. It didn't seem as strange as the first time he'd appeared on her doorstep.

'Well?' she asked when he was seated at the table. 'What did Irene have to say?'

'Not as much as I'd hoped,' he admitted with a long sigh. He lit a cigarette and blew out the smoke. 'And there's absolutely nothing in the way of proof. She claims her father owes Donough thousands. The way I understand it, Walker got Donough to invest in the factory a year or so ago. Showed him books that made it look as if the place was in the black and he'd get a good return on his money.'

'Jane Walker told me the business was going under,' Lottie said.

'It's sinking at a rate of knots. According to Irene, the money that Donough put in went straight to her father, not a penny to the factory. He was going to let it fail and skip out with Donough's cash.'

'But what about his family?' She put a mug of tea in front of him, strong, dark brown. 'What was going to happen to them?'

'They weren't part of his plans. Irene said he has a mistress in London. He was going to take her and the money and go overseas. What he didn't bargain on was the way Donough would take his revenge once he found out the truth.'

'How does Irene know all this?'

'Listening at doors, standing where she could overhear telephone calls, looking through letters in her father's desk.'

'Why didn't she come forward and tell us? And what about her mother? After Ronnie was killed...'

'At first she thought Ronnie might have been involved in something crooked himself. He had that wild side and liked to spend time with criminals. Then her father received another telephone call from Donough and she put two and two together.'

'That's when she ran?'

He nodded. 'Not a word to anyone. She thought she was next. And now she thinks it's all her fault that her mother committed suicide.'

'Poor girl.' What a weight to carry. Irene had lost everything. Her brother, her mother, a father ready to abandon his whole family. Nothing left. 'But at least you'll be able to charge Donough and arrest Walker now.'

'No,' he told her. 'Walker destroyed anything that was in writing and he won't say a word. Donough denies everything. I don't have a scrap of real evidence.'

'But Irene—'

'Irene is under twenty-one; she's still a minor. It's her word against theirs. You know who a judge would believe.'

'Not a girl.'

'Not a girl,' McMillan agreed. 'I'm sure she's telling the truth.

I daren't even let her go in case something happens. She's petrified. Your matron's been looking after her.'

'Mrs Maitland?'

'She's been very good, shown a gentle side. It surprised me.'

It barely sounded believable. But so much about all this was strange.

'What are you going to do now?' Lottie asked.

'I don't know. I really don't know.' He gave her a weak smile. 'You don't have any bright ideas, do you?'

Cathy was waiting in the corridor, beaming as soon as she saw Lottie.

'Thank God you're back. Patrol's been awful on my own. I've had no one to moan at.'

'I'm glad to be here.' She was. Millgarth seemed comfortable and natural. The sounds and smells of the place were so familiar. 'Why do you need to complain, anyway? Jimmy?'

'Not really.' She shrugged. 'We had words but we made up after. The after almost makes it worthwhile. Oh, did you hear what happened?'

'About Irene Walker?'

Cathy's face fell. 'What happened, did Sergeant Dreamboat stop by to tell you?'

'Something like that.' She winked. 'Come on, we'd better go in or she'll tell us we're late.'

Even the patrol along Vicar Lane and down by the side of the market seemed like a joy. An old woman who was confused, not sure where she lived or what she was doing, took half an hour of their time, delivering her gently back to her frantic daughter in Cross Green.

'I only popped out for a moment to get some sugar,' the daughter told them. 'There wasn't sight nor smell of her by the time I got back.' She looked at the old woman, love in her eyes. 'What am I going to do with you, mam?'

At least they'd done some good, Lottie thought as they started back to the city centre. A little thing like that made the job worthwhile. For a moment she stood by St Hilda's church, looking down the hill into Hunslet, everything below covered by smoke from the factory chimneys.

She only turned her head when Cathy nudged her. That was when she heard the shout. Jocelyn Hill was walking slowly towards her; she'd forgotten the girl lived round here. She was still pale and thin as a stick; it might be a long time before she fully recovered. The lass with her hung back, as if she didn't want to be seen too close to the police.

'You're looking a little better,' Lottie said.

Jos only shrugged. 'I wish I felt it, then.' Her face was harder, the lines set. Hardly astonishing, after everything, but it made her appear old before her time.

'Give it a few weeks and you'll be good as new.' Her body would recover but would her mind ever be quite the same? Both the lad she loved and her unborn baby murdered. Almost dead herself. How could anything in life seem normal after that?

'Have you found them yet?' The ones who'd committed the murders.

'No. We know they left Leeds. One of them might be in London. Scotland Yard's looking for him,' she added, hoping the name might impress.

'I'll believe it when I see them in the dock. I've been thinking about something Ronnie said when we were together. You know, before…'

Lottie nodded. Before the knives. Before the deaths. 'What was it?'

'That his father was in trouble. He thought it was a bit of a hoot.'

'Did he say what kind of trouble?'

'I don't know, I didn't really understand it all. Seems he'd been thieving from his business or something like that.' She cocked her head. 'If it's his business how can it be stealing? That doesn't make sense.'

'I'm not sure,' Lottie admitted. 'What else did Ronnie say about it?'

'This and that. Grumbling that his dad wouldn't give him more, I remember that.'

It wasn't just Irene who knew what was happening. That was interesting, but it didn't change anything. Ronnie was dead; there was nothing he could tell them.

'Nothing more?'

'Not that I recall. Like I said, it didn't make that much sense so I didn't pay it any mind.'

'What are you going to do?'

'Me mam says I need to find a job and start earning my keep. I keep telling her I'm still poorly but she thinks I'm just swinging the lead.'

'You look after yourself.' But Lottie felt as if she could see the future. Jos would be bullied by her mother. It would be off to the mills before she was well and a short life with her health broken. 'What about that lad who's sweet on you?'

'Ray?' For the first time the girl's face brightened. 'He's been coming round. Maybe you're right about him.'

'Give him a chance.'

'Maybe. I'm…'

Not ready yet. Everything was still too raw, in her body and in her mind.

'Of course.'

They were down by East Street Mills when Cathy spoke.

'What she told you, does it help at all?'

'Not really. Ronnie's dead. It's hearsay. And too vague.'

'All adds up though, doesn't it?'

The problem was that it added up to zero, she thought. They knew but they couldn't prove who was responsible. Maybe they'd never be able to convict anyone. All those lives ruined for one man's greed. And many more she didn't know: the people in his factory who'd lose their jobs.

'Penny for them,' Cathy said.

'Nothing really.' She sighed. 'Come on, we'd better get back. If Mrs Maitland's out looking she'll think we're skiving somewhere.'

Quiet for the rest of the day. A heavy crush of people on the tram as it crept along Chapeltown Road, so full that the conductor couldn't even move between them. Standing on the pavement, she felt relieved, able to breathe again.

Another week nearly over, just Saturday morning duty. The weekend looked fair. Geoff had suggested taking the bike out on Sunday, packing a picnic and making a day of it in the Dales. Why not? Winter would be here soon enough, bringing bronchitis and chilblains. Something to look forward to when she was marching around the market looking for shoplifters and pickpockets.

CHAPTER TWENTY-TWO

MORNING report was short, in and out of the office in two minutes. But as Lottie had her hand on the doorknob, Mrs Maitland called her back.

'I didn't agree with your suspension, Armstrong. I argued against it. I wanted you to know that.'

'Yes, ma'am. Thank you.' What more could she say?

'You should be aware that Miss Walker is leaving today.'

'Ma'am?' At first Lottie wasn't sure she'd heard correctly. Irene was safe here. She had to know that.

'Miss Walker telephoned a cousin who has agreed to take her in.' The woman sighed with frustration. 'I've talked to her, Sergeant McMillan's talked to her, but she's determined to go. She's gone from being terrified to insisting she'll be safe now. We could charge her with obstructing justice, but no jury's going to convict under the circumstances. Not when she's a minor.'

'Do you think she'll last long at the cousin's?'

'No,' Mrs Maitland said as she shook her head. 'She'll be out of there like greased lightning. You've met her. But there's nothing we can do if the cousin is willing to take responsibility for her.'

'Yes, ma'am.'

'One more thing.' The matron raised an eyebrow. 'The sergeant told me you were the one who spotted her in Queen Square and helped him bring her in.' Lottie felt her throat go dry. Duty she'd done while suspended. 'It won't go any further. Sharp work. Well done.'

'Thank you, ma'am.' Lottie felt relief flood through her.

'I know you've put a great deal into finding Miss Walker. It seemed only fair to tell you what was happening.'

'Thank you.'

And dismissed.

'You've got to be kidding,' Cathy said in disbelief. 'She'll be out of there before bedtime.'

'There's not much we can do about it.'

'They can't stop her? Hold her or something?'

'They're not willing to. It sounds like the brass have decided to give up on the whole thing and hope the story goes away and dies a quiet death.'

'It won't if someone kills Irene, too.'

Lottie looked at her. 'I know. Believe me, I know.' She'd been thinking of nothing else since they left the station. But there was nothing she could do about it. The decisions to let Irene go to her cousin had been made by the brass. She was a mere WPC, and hanging on to that job by the skin of her teeth.

Time to change the subject. 'What are you and Jimmy doing with the weekend?'

'Nothing.' A flat answer, but Cathy's eyes flashed. 'He said that after working he wants to rest. Maybe the pub tonight, but that's it. I told him he'd better not be like this all the time. He just grinned and winked, cheeky beggar.'

'You'll have to train him.'

'Don't you worry about that,' Cathy told her. 'Once everything's really settled I'll get him doing things my way.'

'It's going to be fine.'

'Yes. I really think it is.'

Off in the distance Lottie could hear a gramophone. *Kitten On The Keys*. It had been popular a few years before, one of those melodies that burrowed into the brain. She'd be humming it for days now.

As they returned to Millgarth for the end of shift, she saw a slim figure in a blue-grey coat and dark blue hat climb into a taxi.

'That's it,' Cathy said. 'She's gone.'

'Let's hope that's not as true as it sounds.'

She was up early on Sunday to make sandwiches. Meat paste, salmon paste, and plenty of them. The country air and walking would give them both an appetite. A couple of jam tarts she'd picked up at the baker on her way home yesterday and a bottle of beer each. Just right for a picnic in the Dales.

Lottie could hear Geoff upstairs, the sluice of water as he washed and shaved in the bathroom. She sang as she worked, *It Had To Be You*. She couldn't carry a tune in a bucket, but with no one listening, who cared? Today she was going to enjoy herself, forget the week that had just passed.

In the hills above Grassington they leaned against a drystone wall, looking down at the valley and the river that ran along the bottom. They'd marched a good five miles across the hills, relishing the clean beauty of the countryside.

The clouds hadn't parted all day but it didn't matter. A light breeze had blown away the cobwebs from her mind. She was smiling and happy as she drained the last of the beer and placed the empty bottle in the basket.

'Sometimes I think it would be perfect to live in a place like this,' Geoff said.

'Only for a little while,' Lottie said. In his heart she was sure he knew that, too, but for a few minutes it didn't hurt to let the imagination wander. A stone cottage, a simple life. A lovely dream, but within a month they'd be packing up and going back to Leeds. Like this, close enough to visit, was just right. The bike was a good idea, she had to admit it. A couple of cushions in the sidecar so she didn't feel every dip and bump in the road and the trip was a joy.

She put her hand over his. 'Maybe one day,' she told him. They both knew it was a beautiful lie.

Millgarth was busy as she walked in to report for duty. She spotted Sergeant McMillan, but he was deep in conversation with Inspector Carter.

'What's going on?' she asked Cathy.

'From what I overheard, Mr Walker and that other man in the case—'

'Donough?'

'That's him. They've both vanished and everyone's panicking.'

'What about Irene?'

'No idea.' Cathy shrugged. 'No one's said a word.' She looked at her watch. 'Come on, we don't want to be late.'

Leaving for patrol she saw McMillan again, striding away towards his car. He stopped when she called out.

'You heard?' he asked and she nodded.

'The basics. What about Irene?'

'Still at her cousin's.' He gave a quick grin. 'I've had a man watching the house; I'm not about to let her slip away again. I have to dash.'

'Of course.' And he was gone.

The hunt for Walker and Donough was nothing to involve her. The policewomen had patrol, a day of walking, watching, and helping people. For the first hour Lottie seethed with frustration, knowing that the men would be finishing something she'd helped to start.

Finally she settled back into the routine. They gave directions, waited with an old woman who'd fallen and hurt her hip until the ambulance arrived to take her to the infirmary, and moved on a pair of girls who were loitering neat the bottom of Kirkgate. An ordinary morning.

'Do you mind if we go to the canteen at Millgarth for dinner?'

'You want to know what's going on, don't you?' Cathy grinned.

'Don't you?' Lottie asked.

'Go on, then, I can see you're dying to find out.'

The station was strangely quiet, only a few men still there. The rest were out searching, Cathy learned from a large records sergeant as he ate his suet pudding.

'Keeping a lid on everything,' he said. 'The way I hear it, they've been dragging men off the beat to help, too.'

'Have they had any luck?'

The man shrugged. 'With Carter in charge they'll probably do as well as the captain of the *Titanic*.' He put his head down and started to eat again.

Cathy raised her eyebrows at Lottie and they took seats in the corner. 'He's a little ray of sunshine, isn't he?'

'Still, it means no one knows anything.'

'They haven't found them yet,' Cathy said. 'The word would be all over otherwise.'

That was true. The men would be trooping back, full of themselves and feeling victorious. Whatever was happening, it wasn't bringing in the results. She thought about Sergeant

McMillan. When she'd seen him that morning he'd looked haggard, strained. By now he was probably ready to crack. At least those years in the trenches would have helped him stay steady.

Back out on Kirkgate they had to attend to the injured after a bus crashed into a tram. No one badly hurt, but it was a chance to put their first aid training to use. Cuts and bruises for the most part. By the time they were done and all the walking wounded were on their way, an hour had passed.

'Let's finish this circuit back at the station,' Lottie said. 'I need to swab the blood off my uniform, anyway.' She showed the dark stain on her sleeve.

Cathy winked. 'It's as good an excuse as any, eh?'

'Well, I do!'

This time a few more men were milling around. As Lottie scrubbed at the blood over the sink she heard Cathy asking questions before rushing back in.

'They've found Walker.'

'In Leeds?' She dabbed at the wool with a towel to dry it.

'London. Scotland Yard picked him up. They're questioning him and sending him back.'

'What about Donough?'

'Nothing yet, they said. They're still out beating the bushes.'

'Do they believe he's still in town?' A thought came to her.

'I suppose so.'

'Was McMillan out there?'

'I caught a glimpse of him. Why?'

'I just need a word, that's all.'

She found him outside the back door of the station, leaning against the wall with his eyes closed as he smoked a Black Cat cigarette.

'Penny for them,' she said.

'They'd be overpriced at a farthing.' He sounded dead on his feet.

'How many men are keeping an eye on Irene?' Lottie asked.

'Just one, I told you. The last I heard, she hadn't stirred out of her cousin's house.'

'What if Donough's looking for her? Have you thought of that?'

He smiled but his eyes didn't open.

'Of course I have. But I can't see him doing it. He's going to be more concerned with saving his own skin. The Yard rang a few minutes ago. I don't know what they've done, but Walker's telling them everything. And they've arrested the man who killed Ronnie.'

'That's wonderful news.' She saw him frown. 'Isn't it?'

'Yes and no. The Yard gets the credit.' He sighed. 'I don't know, maybe they deserve it. We couldn't get anything from Walker. But we had orders from upstairs to treat him with kid gloves. They don't have that.'

'And what about Donough?'

'I don't have a clue. Any suggestions greatly appreciated.'

'I told you: Irene. I think he'll go after her to finish things off.'

McMillan turned his head and opened his eyes to stare at her. 'I know you've been right before, but not this time. He wouldn't even know where her cousin lives. She's safe enough, believe me. The only person she needs protecting from is herself.'

'Have you told Irene that Scotland Yard has her father?'

'I haven't had time.'

'I'll go there if you want. After my shift ends.'

'No. But thank you.'

'Why? Do you want to push me out of this?'

'It's not like that,' he began, then tossed the cigarette end away and lit another. 'There's nothing to be gained from you talking to Irene. We already have everything from her. And there's no other way they'll let you help. I'm sorry.'

'I see.' Her voice was cold. 'I'd better get back on patrol.'

She left him standing there, smoke pluming from his mouth.

'Well?' Cathy asked.

'Come on, we've an hour left yet.' She set off through the empty open market area at a quick march.

'What's wrong? Don't take it out on me.'

'I got the brush-off. He was keen as mustard to have me around when they were looking for Irene. Now they can't let me help. How would you feel?'

'Angry,' Cathy admitted.

'There you are, then.' She felt humiliated, on the edge of tears. They'd made use of her and as soon as that was done, sent her back where she belonged. Even McMillan. It had all been a con. What was worse, she'd believed it. She'd believed *him* when he said he was grateful.

'Let's go down by the river,' Cathy suggested, and Lottie smiled. There wouldn't be too many people past Crown Point Bridge. No one to see her face and wonder.

'Good idea.'

She was halfway up George Street, on her way to the tram stop after her shift, when she felt the hand on her arm. Lottie turned, angry at being touched. The fury stayed in her eyes when she saw him.

'I've chased you all the way from the station,' McMillan said. 'I'm sorry. What I said earlier, it came out wrong.'

She shook herself free of his grip. 'Thank you. If you'll excuse me, I need to get home.' She knew people were staring. Let them; he deserved it.

'Do you still want to go and see Irene?'

She stopped. 'Why? What made you change your mind? Desperation?'

He pushed his hands into his trouser pockets. 'It's a simple question: yes or no?'

'I thought you said you already had all the information she could give. Besides, she doesn't know Donough.' He'd turned down her help once. She wasn't going to make it easy for him.

'Maybe there's something. A scrap. Anything.'

'Why me? Mrs Maitland talked to her at the station.'

'I owe it to you.'

'Maybe you should have thought of that a couple of hours ago.'

'For God's sake, I said I'm sorry.' He sounded on the verge of exasperation. 'Now, are you coming?'

Was she? Lottie saw the pleading in his eyes. It was honest, it was a man at the end of his tether and with nowhere else to turn.

'All right,' she told him after a moment.

CHAPTER TWENTY-THREE

MEANWOOD. Past the factories and the municipal swimming pool that lined the road, and beyond the cheap houses that clung to the hillside as it climbed from the valley. All the way out, almost to the park. Where the homes stood tall and clean.

McMillan parked on a quiet street. A few other vehicles, one twenty yards away with a man at the wheel. He gave a quick look as McMillan emerged, then a small shake of his head.

'That's Logan. He's good. Anything suspicious and he'll be on it.' He pointed. 'This one.' It was the middle of an Edwardian terrace. Villas, really. Three storeys tall and probably a cellar under it all. Fresh paint on the woodwork. The small front garden was well-tended, roses all deadheaded, ready to be pruned towards the end of the winter. It was a place the owner cared about.

'What's the cousin's name?' Lottie asked.

'Mrs Winter. Lost her husband and her son in the war.' He glanced up at the house. 'Comfortably off, though.'

A harried maid of all work showed them through to a parlour. Mrs Winter sat in an easy chair, lowering her book as they entered. She was probably only in her early fifties, but there was nothing modern about her. Grey hair gathered in a tight bun. A black dress to her ankles, as if she'd never left mourning, and a harsh, disapproving expression on a pinched face.

'Sergeant,' she said. 'I hadn't expected to see you again.'

'I'm sorry to disturb you,' he said, twisting his hat in his hands. 'But we just need a few words with Miss Walker if we might. This is Woman Police Constable Armstrong.'

The girl had her back to them, staring out of the window over the garden. Her fingertips rested on the sill, body tense, as if she was a prisoner here, not a guest.

'I told you everything I know,' the girl said. She didn't turn around.

'Irene,' Lottie began. 'The police in London have your father.' No movement, although Mrs Winter's head snapped up. 'He's given them everything.'

'I see.' Her voice was dull. Maybe she'd stopped caring in order to protect herself. The last couple of weeks had thrown more at her than most people endured in a lifetime. Perhaps the miracle was that she was still standing. 'What's going to happen to him?'

'We'll need to speak to him,' McMillan told her. 'I have to inform you, he'll almost certainly be in court. He might possibly go to jail.'

'Sergeant,' Mrs Winter said, 'my cousin has had a terrible time. She needs peace and calm to recover herself.'

'I'm sorry. But she also deserves the truth so she can make her plans.'

'She can remain here as long as she chooses. Blood is thicker than water.'

If only that were true, Lottie thought. Ronnie Walker and his mother would still be alive and Irene wouldn't be standing here.

'We don't have Donough yet,' she said. 'He's vanished.' But Irene didn't move a muscle. 'Do you have any idea where he could be?'

'I've never even met him,' the girl answered. 'How would I know what he'd do?'

'You've been hiding from him.'

Irene turned, a fast, fluid movement. Her face looked sharp, mouth pursed, voice cold and exact.

'I was keeping myself alive. He killed Ronnie. He told my father he'd kill me. What would you have done?'

'Exactly what you did,' Lottie said softly. 'But you were lucky. You have people who'd look after you.'

'The inverts and the mannish, you mean?' A vicious smile crossed her mouth.

'Friends.'

'Maybe they are.' She shrugged.

Irene Walker seemed like someone who'd detached herself from life, who wouldn't let herself grow too close to anyone. Maybe that was her armour. But Lottie knew she'd gain nothing by asking more about it.

'Donough,' she said. 'Is there anything about him that you can think of? Anything at all?'

'No.' She didn't even hesitate, didn't even think.

Lottie glanced at the sergeant. He was staring out of the window.

'Down!' he ordered.

The shot came before anyone could move. Glass shattered. Irene Walker began to scream, slumping to the ground, blood seeping from her side. McMillan was already on the floor, crawling over to the girl.

'Get the woman out of here,' he hissed. 'Now. Keep low.'

For a second Lottie couldn't move. She was too terrified, the sound of the gun echoing round her brain. Then her senses kicked in and she dropped to the carpet, taking hold of Mrs Winter and gently urging her along on hands and knees until they were safely in the hall, where the maid was cowering.

She didn't know how badly Irene was hurt. They needed an ambulance and a doctor.

'Do you have a telephone?' Lottie asked urgently. Mrs Winter just looked at her, dumb with shock. Lottie slapped her lightly on the face until she blinked. 'Telephone?' she asked again, but the woman shook her head.

There was the detective in the car across the street. Logan. Lottie wrenched the front door open and ran outside, waving her arms. But he was already in the garden.

'A shot,' she explained, surprised to find herself breathless. 'Back garden. Irene's hurt. We need an ambulance.' She saw him hesitate and glance towards the house. 'Now. And get some constables here as soon as possible.' After a second he nodded and began to run. As he reached the corner she heard the shrill note of his police whistle.

Back in the hall she could hear crying and moaning and McMillan's low, soothing voice. Crawling into the parlour she saw him cradling Irene's head in his lap, stroking her hair as if she was a little girl. His jacket was off, and he pressed it against the wound in her side. The blood had spread across the rug.

'Logan's gone to call an ambulance,' Lottie said. At first she couldn't take her eyes off Irene. So pale, her breath shallow, just quiet sounds coming from her mouth. Then she looked at him. The tiniest shake of his head.

Another shot, more glass breaking. He must be trying to keep them pinned down. Irene whimpered, hardly stirring. Without thinking Lottie was on her feet. Back outside, moving cautiously along the side of the house, feeling the stone rough against her uniform. Holding her breath and turning her head just enough to peek around into the back garden.

Donough. Was he still here?

No sign. She waited, listening for anything at all. The shuffle of feet, the breaking of twigs. Nothing. If she showed herself and he was there, he'd shoot her. But if she stayed here and he'd already gone…

Seconds passed. Ten, twenty: Lottie counted them off in her head. She had to do *something*. Crouching, not even daring to think, not breathing, she scuttled to the cover of a bush, half its leaves gone. She waited for the worst. Her hands were shaking. She pressed them hard against her skirt. Fear was buzzing through her veins. The thick smell of cordite still hung in the air.

Stay here, she thought. Safe. Please God, safe.

But staying here wouldn't catch Donough.

She listened. Only silence. At the end of the garden a magpie swooped from a branch, down into the long grass. The thought flashed through her mind: it wouldn't be doing that if someone was there.

One cautious step, trying not to make a noise, then another. Her heart was hammering so hard she thought all Leeds must be able to hear it.

A third step. Still no voice. No shot. Donough had gone. He wasn't stupid. He'd know the police were bound to come out in force.

Lottie ran to the back wall and pulled the gate open. A long, open slope of grass. Beyond it, the woods and the beck. And, in the distance, a man disappearing between the trees.

No choice. She had to go after him. Who else was there? It was her duty.

Lottie ran.

It felt as if it took forever. She wished she was a sprinter like Cathy. Halfway there and she was already puffing. Exposed. An easy target.

But Donough hadn't looked like a man about to make a stand. He was rushing to escape, to save his own skin.

She slowed as she reached the woods. The trail was easy to follow. Long grass trodden down. Lottie followed cautiously. Steadily. Alert, eyes watching for movement. Burrs tugged at her skirt. Twigs tore her stockings.

Down between the bushes and the trees, something dashed through the undergrowth, making her gasp. Just a startled animal.

Where was he?

The arm tightened around her throat, shutting off the scream before it could begin. Her fingers tried to pull it away. But he was too strong. The grip was too firm.

The smell of gunpowder. Something cold against her temple. Metal. A click right by her ear. Cocking the hammer on the gun. He was going to kill her here. In cold blood.

She had one chance. Just one chance. Do it the way Geoff had taught her.

Lottie brought her foot up sharply. Her heel caught him on the shin, then she stamped down hard on his foot. Donough grunted and she rammed her elbow back into his gut.

She twisted away, turning to face him. He was bent over, clutching his stomach and trying to breathe. But the revolver was still in his hand. And it was still pointing at her, the muzzle black and big as the world.

She'd tried. Done everything the way she'd been taught. It's for your own protection, he said, taking her through every move until it was second nature. She hadn't even needed to think, just let her body work.

But she'd lost.

He must have been waiting behind a tree. She'd walked right into it.

Donough was staring at her, eyes full of hate. He was a big man, maybe fifty-five, fleshy, his face red and puffy under thick eyebrows, veins broken across his nose.

'Walk,' he ordered. 'And don't try anything like that again unless you like the idea of dying.'

Lottie began to move. He stayed two paces behind. Close enough to shoot, far enough to be safe. Her mind was racing.

He could have killed her. There was no one around. Simple enough to pull the trigger. He wanted her for something else. A hostage. A guarantee he'd get away.

Good.

She was alive, she wasn't hurt. And now she had a little time.

'Where are we going?' The voice surprised her; she sounded so calm, so steady. In control. Lottie gulped down air.

'Never you mind. Keep walking where I tell you.'

They were following a dirt path. Nettles brushed against her legs, stinging hard. At a fork she asked, 'Where?'

'To the left.'

Somewhere in the distance she could hear a child crying, a full-throat wail that would stop as suddenly as it began. Signs of life. The grinding of a bus changing gears for a corner. There had to be a road close by. He wouldn't dare gun her down in front of witnesses, would he?

Her mouth was dry. Her muscles ached. She was tense, so scared that every part of her seemed to be trembling, on the edge of tears. If she'd stuck to her proper duties, if she hadn't wanted more… But if wishes were horses…

'To the right.'

The words pulled her out of her thoughts.

The path took them to a bridge. It was nothing more than a thick, heavy plank over a stream. The wood was greenish where patches of moss were growing.

Lottie eased her way across, arms extended to keep her balance. It was treacherous. Slick. One foot started to slide and she gasped before righting herself. Her heart was thumping as she took another step, then another. She kept her eyes down, watching where she placed her feet.

The bridge was no more than nine feet long, but by the time she stepped on to the dirt path again, she felt she'd covered a mile. And Donough still needed to cross.

She glanced back. He was on the plank, concentrating. Another glance, ahead. The track twisted between the trees, a sharp turn after a few yards.

A few more seconds and he'd be over. Lottie lifted the hem of her skirt and started to run.

The shot rang wide. She crouched and kept going. No more came. She was out of sight. Dodging between the trees. Moving faster. Not daring to look over her shoulder. She dragged a wooden gate open and dashed out into a street. One car parked, no one in sight.

A single, deep breath and Lottie ran again, pushing her soles down on the cobbles, willing herself to go faster. Fear coursed through her. He could be coming now, raising the gun…

She turned the corner, holding on to the rails to stop herself falling. Two bobbies were there, walking towards her. Their eyes widened.

'In the woods.' She could barely speak, gasping for air. The sudden realisation she was safe now. 'He has a gun.'

'We heard it,' the older constable told her.

He looked her up and down. She looked a wreck, Lottie knew that: uniform and stockings torn, face flushed and red.

'Are you all right, luv?'

She nodded. 'Aren't you going to go after him?'

'Our sergeant told us to stop here for now.'

Lottie stared at him until he turned away.

'He's shooting people, for God's sake.' It exploded out of her: all the fear and the anger. 'There's a girl up the hill who might be dead. He tried to kill me. And you're hiding out of sight?'

'Sergeant's orders,' he insisted. 'We're here if he comes out this way. There are others gone in after him. Don't you worry, we'll get him.'

'And you're going to do that skulking around here?'

'Miss—'

'It's WPC,' she told them. 'Not Miss. I have a rank, same as you. Have you got that?' They said nothing, faces impassive in the way only coppers could manage. 'Well, don't you have anything else to say for yourselves?'

She knew full well they wouldn't. They were time servers, almost like prisoners waiting out a sentence and doing as little as possible. They'd never take a single risk they could avoid.

She was seething. But helpless. She couldn't order them. They didn't even take her seriously. Finally she turned her back on them.

At the corner she gazed towards the woods. Someone shouted, too far off to make out the words. A gun sounded, the crack echoing through the valley. And she knew she had no choice. It was her job.

CHAPTER TWENTY-FOUR

LOTTIE halted at the entrance to the woods. Her hand gripped the gate so hard that her knuckles were white, fingers aching. She knew what she had to do. But standing here she wasn't sure she could make herself go any further. To take that step…

She'd done her bit. She'd had a gun to her head, for God's sake. She'd done her best to stop him. She'd tried. But she'd failed. She hadn't been good enough.

The hinges creaked as she pushed the gate open and for a moment she paused, feeling panic flood through her mind.

'Wait a minute.'

The voice was low, quite calm. She turned, lifting her hand off the wood, feeling as if she was coming out of a trance.

'I think he's still in there.'

McMillan stood beside her, watching the woods.

'What happened to you? You look like you've been through the wars.'

Lottie shook her head. 'I'll be fine. What about Irene?'

'On her way to hospital. It's up to the doctors now.' He paused. 'I've got four men coming in from the top.'

'And two around the corner back there.'

He gave her a quizzical look but said nothing.

'I need to go and find him.' Before she could speak he shook his head. 'Just me. I'm sorry.' He reached into his jacket and drew out a revolver, the twin of Donough's. 'The chief constable authorised it.'

'And it's not a job for a woman?' she asked.

'Not this one, no.'

'I've already escaped from him in there.' She nodded towards the trees. 'When he had a gun to my head.'

His jaw moved. For a moment he looked at her and didn't say anything.

'No,' he said again.

'I can help, John.'

'It's Sergeant to you, WPC Armstrong. I've given you an order.' He pushed the gate open and began to walk, not looking back.

He meant well, she thought. He believed he was doing the right thing. Keeping her safe. Chivalrous. But it was too late for that. She could still feel the gun barrel on her skin and Donough's breath on her neck. For a second she shivered. Then she put her hand on the gate and opened it. It didn't matter what McMillan said. She had to do it. Duty.

She couldn't see the sergeant. Men's voices echoed from the far side of the woods. They might as well have been wearing electric lights.

Lottie trod carefully, skin prickling with goose pimples. No more than ten yards from the gate and the terror was roaring through her. Maybe McMillan was right; maybe she didn't belong here. She could hardly put one foot in front of the other, like trying to stride through glue. But she wasn't going to back away. She couldn't. She wasn't going to run.

Donough could have gone. God knew how many ways there were out of these woods.

She knelt and selected a sharp stone. It fitted in her palm. At least she'd have a weapon. Not much, but it was better than nothing.

Walking was overwhelming. Each step was an effort, forcing herself on.

She wanted to find Donough.

She was petrified that she'd find him.

The shadows were beginning to lengthen. Another hour or so and dusk would begin. If he could stay hidden until dark they'd never find him.

Lottie reached out, stroking the coarse bark of a tree. If she tucked herself in here she could keep watch. And she'd be ready if Donough came. But she knew the truth.

She was too terrified to go any further.

Half an hour? More? Things seemed to settle all around her. The tramping of boots off in the distance, an occasional shout. Closer, though, Lottie could hear the birds, the rustle of leaves. A conker dropped, landing softly in the dirt. Almost peaceful.

A sound. Something moving awkwardly through the undergrowth. Too large to be an animal. She crouched, out of sight, the stone tight in her hand. Probably only one of the coppers crashing around, but just in case…

The seconds stretched and dragged.

Then she could see him. Stumbling, dragging his right leg. Face twisted in pain. He still had the gun in his hand but it seemed more like a weight than a weapon. Another few moments and he'd be close enough to touch.

He must have caught the movement from the corner of his eye. Lottie raised her arm, ready to bring the stone down on his wrist. But he fell away from her, landing in the bracken. Her blow slipped through empty air. Donough was lying on his back, the revolver raised, pointing straight at her. A rictus grin on his mouth. Satisfaction in his eyes.

She couldn't run this time. No escape.

His finger was tightening on the trigger. It seemed to be taking all his strength.

The shot took off half his face. Lottie began to scream as she sank to her knees.

'You're fine,' McMillan told her. He'd wiped her face cheeks with his handkerchief but she could still taste the blood, still smell it as she breathed. 'You're safe now.'

She glanced back at the body. It was surrounded by uniforms now, almost hidden. The scene replayed in her head again. The awful smile, the gun, the finger on the trigger.

'Come on, we'll get you out of here. A cup of tea, that'll help.'

Her body was numb. She was walking but she couldn't feel a thing. Tears were pouring down her cheeks and she couldn't stop them.

'Stay here,' he said, leaving her to lean against a garden wall. Lottie could hear his voice, but it was a hum, a background; the words wouldn't stick and form in her mind. She began to shake. Hands first, then her arms and her legs. And nothing she could do to stop it.

Then he was there, holding a mug against her lips, tipping it gently. She swallowed. Tea. Warm, sweet. But the shaking wouldn't stop. Her whole body now.

He held her. Gently, like a child. Shuddering, shivering. Her body was beyond her control. Slowly, very slowly, it passed, smaller and smaller spasms until it was gone completely. McMillan picked up the mug from the wall and put it in her hands.

'Drink up,' he ordered. 'Then we'll get you home.'

'But—' she began. She knew the procedure. A statement at the station. Questions and more questions.

'It can wait until the morning. I don't think you could do it now anyway, even if you wanted to.'

He was right. The whole thing was a jumble in her head. Like a film, a small clip that played over and over, one she couldn't turn off.

In the car she gazed at the roads without really seeing them. She wanted to cry again, to let all the feelings come out and never return. She wanted a long, hot bath to wash the day away. Most of all she wanted to be with Geoff.

McMillan only said one thing as he drove: 'I wish you'd listened to orders.'

At the house he helped her inside. She felt as if she was in a daze that she couldn't shake off. Geoff took one look and folded her tight in her arms. Finally she felt safe. She felt secure. The world couldn't hurt her here.

McMillan was speaking, his voice low and urgent, but she paid no attention to the words. She knew what had happened. She knew it all too well. It was still going on behind her eyelids.

CHAPTER TWENTY-FIVE

LOTTIE sat on the hard chair, back straight, hands clasped together in her lap, uniform neat and clean. Facing her, on the other side of the long table, sat Mrs Maitland, Inspector Carter, and the Assistant Chief Constable in his dress uniform, all the scrambled egg of rank on his collar.

An official disciplinary hearing, with a secretary sitting off to the side taking every word down in shorthand. They'd already heard testimony from the two constables she'd seen after escaping from Donough. McMillan had also been in front of them. He couldn't lie; he'd told her that beforehand and she didn't want him to. There was nothing shameful in the truth. She'd disobeyed his direct order. She was willing to admit it.

At least Irene Walker would survive. For the first few hours in hospital no one could predict either way. Somehow she'd managed to stay alive. She'd lost plenty of blood and she'd still need more operations but eventually she'd return to something approaching normal life.

That was the only good thing to come out of this.

Calm, in control of her voice, Lottie recounted everything that happened after the sergeant found her at the bus stop. Going to Meanwood, the house, the shot, following Donough, the way he'd caught her, how she'd manage to break free. All the details she could recall.

'To be absolutely clear,' Carter began. He was smiling, trying to look solicitous, but he was relishing every second. 'You were aware that Sergeant McMillan had given you an express order not to go back into the woods.'

'Yes, sir.' She fixed her stare on him. 'There was no mistaking it.'

'But you ignored it,' he continued.

'I did, sir. I thought it was my duty.'

'You don't believe it was your duty to obey orders?' Carter's voice was rising. A gesture from the ACC silenced him.

Mrs Maitland gave a small cough. 'Wait outside while we discuss everything, Armstrong. We'll send for you when we're ready.'

The hardest part was sitting alone in an empty room, the only company the ticking of the clock. She knew what the decision would be. So did they. It was simply a matter of form, letting a few minutes pass before they announced it.

That was fine. It felt strangely like a play, all of them acting out their roles.

She'd given her statement the day before. Reported for duty on time, then spent most of the shift in an interview room going over every tiny thing again and again. She'd expected it. That was the routine. Geoff had urged her to take a day to recover, but there was no point; it was simply postponing the inevitable.

He'd been wonderful. As soon as McMillan left he'd been attentive, taking off her uniform, heating water and washing her from head to toe. By the time he finished drying her like a baby, all the energy had drained out of her body. He helped her up to bed, kissing her softly.

'I love you.' He stroked her cheek tenderly. 'You've no idea how proud I am of you,' he said as he turned out the light.

In the morning her uniform was hanging up, cleaned and smoothed. Whatever he'd done, it had worked like magic;

the material looked like new. Maybe it was something he'd learned in the war.

She put it on, standing proudly in front of the mirror. Right, she thought. Right.

The door opened and Mrs Maitland stood in the opening.

'Come in, Armstrong,' she said.

Standing at attention for the verdict, she looked from one face to the other. They were giving nothing away. Finally the Assistant Chief Constable gave a small sigh.

'We've had a chance to deliberate. No one's going to deny you're a very brave young lady,' he acknowledged with a dip of his head. 'However, you're well aware of the parameters of duty for a woman police constable. They exist for your own safety. You've exceeded those on numerous occasions lately. This time, though, you defied a very specific command from Sergeant McMillan. Your put your own life in danger. If he hadn't been such a good shot you might have been killed. That's very grave.'

She stayed silent; the last thing he wanted was an answer.

'In the light of that,' he went on, 'and on top of everything else, I'm sad to say we have no choice in the matter. It's been decided to dismiss you from the Leeds City Police force.'

Lottie raised her chin. 'Yes, sir.'

She turned and marched out of the room.

It was what she expected. Cathy had warned her. McMillan had warned her. She knew it would come. But that didn't make hearing the words any easier. Something else burned into her brain.

Standing in the toilet she removed the insignia and badges from her uniform, weighing them lightly in her hand. She'd leave them on Mrs Maitland's desk.

Not a copper any more. Lottie smiled wanly. She'd done what she felt was right. She'd done her duty. She'd done her job. Carefully, she applied lipstick. When she walked out of here she was going to look her best.

She was dabbing her lips when Cathy came in.

'I heard. It's all over the station.'

'Everyone loves juicy gossip.' She tried to smile.

Standing next to her, crowding her aside, Cathy began to remove her own badges.

'What are you doing?'

'Resigning. What do you think?'

'Why?' Lottie stared, uncomprehending. 'You weren't the one on the carpet.'

'You did what the men they employ here should have done if they'd had the guts. In return they dismiss you.' She shook her head. 'That's not right. And my Jimmy's been after me to turn in my notice. Now he's earning he says he wants a wife at home, the way it should be. After the way they've treated you…' She shrugged, took off the cap badge and grinned. 'Come on, let's go out in style.'

They walked down the corridor arm in arm. McMillan was waiting, looking as if he wanted to say something. Lottie smiled at him as she strode past. Outside, the light seemed very bright.

***

Next in the series

(Due Autumn 2017)

THE YEAR OF THE GUN

CHAPTER ONE

Leeds, February 1944

'WHY are there suddenly so many Americans around?' Lottie asked as she parked the car on Albion Street. 'You can hardly turn a corner without running into one.'

'Are you sure that's not just your driving?' McMillan said.

She glanced in the mirror, seeing him sitting comfortably in the middle of the back seat, grinning.

'You could always walk, sir.' She kept her voice perfectly polite, a calm, sweet smile on her face. 'It might shift a few of those inches around your waist.'

He closed the buff folder on his lap and sighed. 'What did I do to deserve this?'

'As I recall, you came and requested that I join up and become your driver.'

'A moment of madness.' Detective Chief Superintendent McMillan grunted as he slid across the seat of the Humber and opened the door. 'I shan't be long.'

She turned off the engine, glanced at her reflection and smiled, straightening the dark blue cap on her head.

Three months back in uniform and it still felt strange to be a policewoman again after twenty years away from it. It was just the Women's Auxiliary Police Corps, not a proper copper, but still… after they'd pitched her out on her ear it tasted delicious. Every morning when she put on her jacket she had to touch the WAPC shoulder flash to assure herself it wasn't all a dream.

And it was perfectly true that McMillan had asked her. He'd turned up on her doorstep at the beginning of November, looking meek.

'I need a driver, Lottie. Someone with a brain.'

'That's why they got rid of me before,' she reminded him. 'Too independent, you remember?' McMillan had been a detective sergeant then: disobeying his order had put her before the disciplinary board, and she'd been dismissed from Leeds City Police. 'Anyway, I'm past conscription age. Not by much,' she added carefully, 'but even so…'

'Volunteer. I'll arrange everything,' he promised.

Hands on hips, she cocked her head and eyed him carefully. 'Why?' she asked suspiciously. 'And why now?'

She'd never really blamed him for what happened before. Both of them had been in impossible positions. They'd stayed in touch after she was bounced off the force – Christmas cards, an occasional luncheon in town – and he'd been thoughtful after her husband, Geoff, died. But none of that explained this request.

'Why now?' he repeated. 'Because I've just lost another driver. Pregnant. That's the second one in two years.'

Lottie raised an eyebrow.

'Oh, don't be daft,' he told her. He was in his middle fifties, mostly bald, growing fat, the dashing dark moustache now white and his cheeks turning to jowls. By rights he should have retired, but with so many away fighting for King and Country he'd agreed to stay on for the duration.

He was a senior officer, effectively running CID in Leeds, answerable to the assistant chief constable. Most of the detectives under him were older or medically unfit for service. Only two had invoked reserved occupation and stayed on the Home Front rather than put on a uniform.

But wartime hadn't slowed down crime. Far from it. The black market had become worse in the last few months, gangs, deserters, prostitution. More of it than ever. Robberies were becoming violent, rackets more deadly. Criminals had guns and they were using them.

And now Leeds had American troops all over the place.

ABOUT THE AUTHOR

Chris Nickson is the author of the Richard Nottingham and Tom Harper series (Severn House). He has also written *The Crooked Spire* and *The Saltergate Psalter*, set in fourteenth-century Chesterfield, and the Dan Markham Mysteries, all for The History Press. He lives in Leeds.

www. chrisnickson.co.uk

PRAISE FOR CHRIS NICKSON

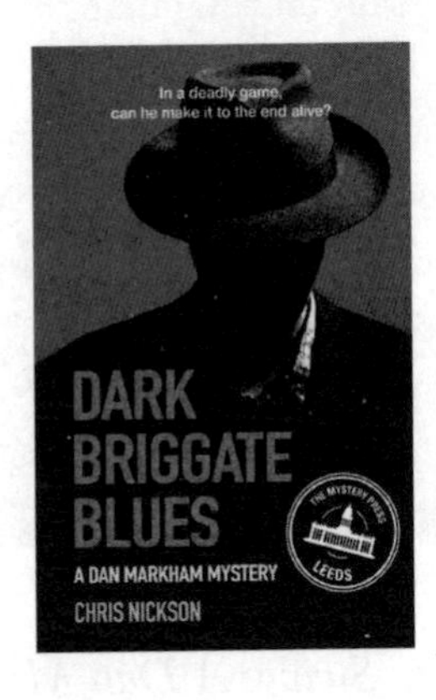

Dark Briggate Blues: A Dan Markham Mystery

'The book is a pacy, atmospheric and entertaining page-turner with a whole host of well-rounded characters'

Yorkshire Post

'[*Dark Briggate Blues* is] written with an obvious affection for the private investigator genre, this is a skilful take in an unusual setting. It has real depth which will keep you turning the pages'

Hull Daily Mail

'This is a tense thriller, all the more disturbing for the ordinariness of its setting among the smoky, rain-slicked streets of a northern industrial city. Nickson has captured the minutiae of the mid-twentieth century perfectly'

Historical Novel Society

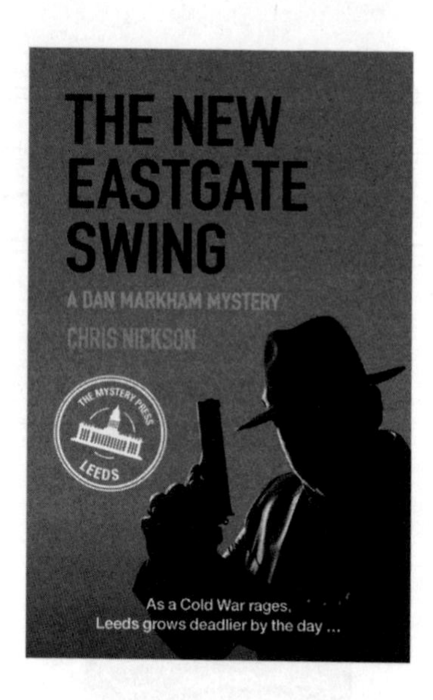

The New Eastgare Swing: A Dan Markham Mystery

'[The New Eastgate Swing] provides a fast-paced and unpredictable insight into the dark underbelly of 1950s Leeds'
Leeds City Magazine

'Chris's enormous affection for his home city shines through the books'
Mystery People

'Chris writes with such gusto, pouring his immense knowledge and passion for Leeds into every story he brings to life and I love his clever fusion of history with fiction'
theculturevulture.co.uk